THE
Wrong
WIFE

THE *Wrong* WIFE

MAYA ALDEN

Also By Maya Alden

I have spread my dreams under your feet;
Tread softly because you tread on my dreams.
William Butler Yeats, "Aedh Wishes for the Cloths
of Heaven"

Love looks not with the eyes, but with the mind;
And therefore is wing'd Cupid painted blind.
William Shakespeare, "A Midsummer Night's
Dream"

Chapter 1

DECLAN

I was marrying the wrong woman; I thought as I slid the wedding band on the ring finger of Esme Hartley in my cousin's chambers in the Beverly Hills Courthouse. She probably wanted a proper wedding, but I was too heartbroken to go through that.

She was shorter than Viv, about five-two to Viv's five-eight and my six-two. She was curvier than Viv. Her hair wasn't blond and straight; it was black and wavy, a little out of control and messy. Her eyes were dark, not blue. She wore little makeup, and I knew she wore glasses, which her mother had yanked off her nose as she entered the chambers.

Judge Forest Knight was supposed to officiate mine and Viv's wedding, but he was marrying me to my fiancée...no, ex-fiancée's half-sister. Viv was now someone else's wife. And *I was someone else's husband*; I reminded myself when Forest said we were husband and wife, and I could kiss the bride. She looked up and smiled as if trying to comfort me for being second best. I gave her a perfunctory kiss—a brush of my lips against hers.

I had married a woman eleven years my junior—she was *fucking* twenty-three years old. Viv was a grown-up compared to Esme. She was twenty-nine and a high-powered lawyer at one of the most prestigious law firms in Los Angeles. Had Esme even graduated from university? What was she studying? I wasn't sure. I didn't know Esme. I knew she went to the University of Washington in Seattle. Viv had gone to Harvard, as had I. We were an Ivy League family, and here I was with someone who couldn't get into an Ivy despite her father's wealth and position. Not the sharpest pencil in the box, Viv had said about Esme. I shrugged it off. Now, she was a noose around my neck.

My mother was stiff; her parents were solicitous. My father was in Asia and sent me a thumbs-up emoji when I told him I was getting married to the wrong Hartley.

No one was happy about this.

I had no choice. The Hartley family business bylaws set up a couple of generations ago were clear. Mergers require marriage to keep the business in the family. Who the fuck still did such archaic shit? I hadn't had a problem with it because I'd been in love with Viv—and she'd been in love with me. We had been friends for five years and dated for one. We had been engaged for six months, and the day before we were to be married, everything changed. Viv announced she'd fallen in love with some tech bro in San Francisco and had married him. She was sorry, but there was nothing she could do about how she felt. She broke up with me through the Hartley family lawyer.

We were going to have two weddings; one in private, with Forest officiating to ensure that the merger was not delayed and one six months later, a public one with all the pomp and show a Knight wedding demanded and deserved.

Julien and Monica Hartley suggested I marry Esme to keep the merger going. I had said sure, why the hell not? So, on the day when I should have been marrying Viv, I was marrying Esme.

I looked at the diminutive woman standing next to me with a champagne glass in her hand. Forest had opened several bottles of Dom Pérignon to celebrate the occasion. She looked happy. Well, why the fuck wouldn't she be? She was married to someone with whom she would never have a chance with. Her father's money would get her a decent match, but not a Knight. She was a wallflower, far removed from the vibrant woman Viv was.

"Welcome to the family, Dec." Julien hugged me. He wasn't happy about this either—but guess what, he wasn't marrying a twit, which made him better off than me.

"Yes, Dec, welcome," Monica added. And I thought maybe Julien was not doing all that much better. Because speaking of twits, Monica Hartley had the not-so-rare distinction of being a trophy wife. Esme had not got her mother's looks—just her personality. *Christ, talk about the wrong wife!*

"Take care of my little girl," she whispered. Her eyes were filled with tears.

"Of course," I said, my smile tight.

When we exited the courthouse, I was angrier than before the wedding ceremony. I was tired, and *this* woman was now my wife. A woman I had no interest in.

We got into the back of the Escalade, and I immediately pushed the button to pull down the privacy screen. My driver knew where we were going.

"I'm going to drop you off," I told Esme. "I have to go into the office."

She nodded and took her glasses off. She'd gotten them back from her mother right after the ceremony. I was confident the glasses did not have a designer label. Just essential *and* unflattering.

I watched her as she leaned back, eyes closed. She had opted for simplicity and worn a sleeveless cream-colored dress with nude heels. Her hair was a dark cloud around her shoulders. Not a statuesque Scandinavian beauty like Viv. She wore minimal makeup. Her lips were painted pink. She was, I thought as I observed her, not unpresentable. With some money thrown at her, and with the help of salons and boutiques, she could look like someone I might be interested in being with for the following year.

She didn't have a purse with her. Viv always wore an expensive handbag that matched her outfit. I had bought her a few in orange boxes with the Hermes logo on them. Viv loved presents. I wonder how Esme would react if I bought her a designer bag. But why would I?

She sighed and opened her eyes. She flashed a smile at me.

"I'm sorry. I've had some long days lately," she told me. "I finished my thesis defense yesterday and then got on a flight early this morning, so my brain is cotton."

"What are you studying?" I undid my tie. I felt like it was choking me.

"I just finished my Master's in Social Work," she said excitedly.

"Social work?" I asked.

"Yes. I already have interviews lined up here in LA. If I'm lucky, I should have a job soon."

"Job?"

She tilted her head and grinned. "Even though we had to have an arranged marriage, I'm hoping you're not too archaic to say something like, 'My *wife doesn't work*.'" She said that last part by changing her voice to sound masculine.

I couldn't help it. I smiled. "No. I'd never say that. Where would you work?"

"We'll see," she sighed. "I'm hoping for a health center like UCLA or Keck. I specialized in pediatrics, and LA county has a child maternal program that I'm hoping I can...why are you looking at me like that?"

I shook my head. "I'm sorry. I don't know anyone who...well...."

"Has a government job?"

"Forest is a judge, as was my mother."

"True," she yawned. "I'm not *that* lofty. I'm just a licensed clinical social worker."

Her eyes closed again. Her breathing slowed as the car drove through the Los Angeles traffic.

I had not expected this to be our first conversation. I had thought she'd talk about the marriage or...well, anything but that she had finished her Master's program and was exhausted.

I got a text from Forest and smiled when I read it: *She seems like a nice girl. Maybe it won't be a horrible year for you.*

I texted back: *Yeah. She has a Master's in social work.*

Forest responded immediately: *No kidding. From U Dub? That's a damn good school for social.*

Me: *She wants to work with some child maternal program.*

Forest: *Nice. Only a few people in our circles want to do social work unless they're elected for something and have a PR team to put it on social media.*

Before I could respond to his last message, she woke up with a start and looked at me with blank eyes that turned sheepish. "Did I fall asleep mid sentence?"

"No. You completed your sentence."

"Whew! I sometimes do that. God, I'm sorry. You said something about dropping me off at my parents' place?"

"No, at *my* place," I corrected her. The place where Viv and I had lived for the past three months. That home.

"But all my things are at my parent's place."

"They've been moved," I informed her. She behaved like she didn't come from money, like she was expected to pack her stuff.

"Really?" she frowned. "Who'd do that?"

"I asked my assistant to take care of it."

Her eyebrows rose. "Your assistant takes care of things like that?"

I sighed. "Esme, you're a fucking Hartley. Your father and mother have assistants. Viv had a personal assistant and two of them at the law firm."

Something shifted in her eyes when I mentioned her sister. But it was fleeting, and I didn't know her well enough to deduce what that meant.

"Oh, I've never had...I mean...look at me," she said, rolling her eyes. "I do little on the...ah...social front. And so, I've never needed assistants, personal shoppers, or whatever else everyone around me seems to have. Now that we're married, am I expected to attend charity blah blah and all that stuff?"

"Sometimes. If you're into social work, charity galas should be up your alley."

She shrugged. "It's all theater. If you want to do social work, then show up. This going to a fancy party and buying a table is for show. Most of the money goes to the people arranging the gala, not the porpoise, hungry kid, or whatever the event purports to save."

"You being my wife, there will be an expectation for you to come, but I will make sure it's minimal." I'll keep it to the minimum.

"Thanks. My mother warned me I'd have to do lots of stuff I didn't like." She yawned again. Her eyes were half closed as she mumbled, "I'm pretty annoyed with Viv. I mean...come on, she does this a week before the merger? Right before the wedding?"

I couldn't stand that she was bad-mouthing Viv.

"Please stop talking," I snapped.

"I'm sorry." Her eyes opened wide, and I could see she was sincerely apologetic. I ignored her and looked away.

The car stopped, and I looked out of the tinted windows. We were at my high rise.

"I'm on the 53rd floor."

"Nice."

I pulled out the extra key fob I had gotten that morning from Baker, my assistant, and handed it to her. "My housekeeper, Calliope, has set up your bedroom. If you need anything, she can take care of it for you."

She took the fob from me. "Okay." She put her glasses back on.

"Well... that's it," I said because she seemed to be waiting for something more.

She smiled again. "Thank you."

She stepped out, and I saw her put the key fob in her dress pocket. She seemed to look around for a moment, unsure, and I almost rolled down the window to ask if she wanted me to take her upstairs, but I didn't. I was being unfair. This wasn't her fault. But I was angry with her. Angry because she was now my wife. Angry that she wasn't Viv.

I looked away from her and tapped the privacy screen, telling the driver to take me to my office in Bunker Hill. Esme was my wife for at least one year. That was what the bylaws said—one year. And then I could get rid of her.

Chapter 2

ESME

As the elevator took me to my new home, I saw the simple wedding band on my ring finger. I was married.

My father had to buy the rings quickly because Declan refused to use the rings made for his wedding with Viv. It surprised me that Declan wore the ring I put on his finger. I thought he'd take it off as soon as the ceremony was over. I wondered if I should take mine off. But I liked the simple gold band and decided to wear it unless Declan had a problem.

I was married to the man I had had a crush on since Viv had become friends with him five years ago. I was disappointed, not despondent, when they began dating a few years after they met and got engaged. She moved in with him three months ago, but *not really* because she had an apartment in San Francisco, where she had been working on a case. Now, she was living in that apartment with her new husband.

I was married to the man who was in love with my sister. I didn't know him well, but I watched from afar when I could and maybe had built a fantasy or two. But it was only in my mind. I knew that there was no way a man like Declan Knight would look at someone like me.

When my mother called me last night to tell me I had to marry Declan because, without that, the merger would fall through, and if it fell through, Hartley Industries would not survive—I'd first refused and then agreed.

The arrogant Julien Hartley could not hold his head high. *So, couldn't I marry my sister's fiancé as a favor to the family?*

"It's just for a year, Es," my mother had pleaded. "Daddy cannot lose everything."

Why can't he? I wanted to ask.

When Viv started dating Declan, it was just what my father needed and wanted. He could hand over the company to his son-in-law and retire as a wealthy man. He'd be a Knight Technologies board member as part of the deal. With the merger, two tech cyber securities companies would come together to become one of the biggest in the world.

So, Viv married a man she fell in love with.

Declan was going to be the CEO of a banging tech company.

Daddy would be wealthy and retired, able to do magical things to his golf handicap.

My mother could buy the trinkets she was so in love with.

And me? Well, here I was, stepping into my new home, a home my husband had not bothered to take me to. He'd just dropped me off outside. *And* he'd clarified that I'd have *my* room—we wouldn't even pretend in the house. We wouldn't share a room or a bed. Why did he even want me to live with him? I wondered as I stepped out of the elevator into an expansive living room.

An elegant woman in her mid-fifties awaited me with a big smile and a bouquet of white roses. She wore jeans, comfortable-looking brown leather shoes, and a white dress shirt. She looked both casual and professional.

"Welcome," she said brightly and handed me the flowers. "And congratulations."

She didn't even look behind me to see if my new husband had walked me in. No, she knew. Everyone knew I had married my sister's leftovers. A man she'd cheated on and then dumped. If I cared about society, this would be a death knell for me. Good thing I didn't. And let's face it; society thought I was a complete loser even before this debacle. I was the *ugly* Hartley—the *lesser* sister. I'd heard various versions of that my whole life.

"Thank you." I smelled the roses, and their perfume filled my senses. When the world around you was falling apart, you had to find joy in the small things...like flowers.

"I put all your things in the bedroom with a great view," she declared.

The master suite, which was Declan's, probably had the *best* view, I thought. The room I would not be allowed into. The room he and Viv had shared. Were her things still in the room? None of my business, I concluded.

"That's so nice of you. Can you show me where you have vases? I can put the roses in. Maybe I can have them in my room?"

Calliope looked at me as if surprised. "I can do that for you."

"But they're my flowers now," I told her. "And I want to care for them."

Calliope took me to the kitchen and gave me a quick tour as she showed me where she kept the vases and other glassware to set the table.

I didn't grow up with servants or assistants. Declan thought I had because I was a Hartley. But my grandmother hadn't been. And it was my *abuela* who had raised me, while my father's wealth and status had dazzled my mother, who had forgotten I existed. My father doted on Viv, and he'd never had much time for me—so, from the start, I'd been the unwanted child, an accident that no one cared for except my grandmother.

When she passed, I had started university. I occasionally returned to my parent's home when my presence was requested for occasions such as Viv's engagement party, her graduation party, her promotion to partner celebration, my parents' wedding anniversaries, my father's sixtieth birthday.... My parents had a marriage that was based on convenience. My father got a beautiful woman on his arm, and she got financial security.

I had promised myself that when I married, I'd marry someone who loved me, for whom I was their world, and build my family. I could still do that. After a year, I could satisfy the bylaw's demands and move on to find love. And I would. I promised myself as Calliope led me to my new bedroom, the flowers in a vase in hand.

It was a large room with floor-to-ceiling windows with a beautiful view of downtown Los Angeles. In the distance was the Hollywood sign, and it made me smile to see it.

"You have a lot of books," Calliope commented and waved to the filled bookshelves. "But not much else."

I had shipped all my stuff to my parents' house from my apartment in Seattle to store until I found a place to live. I had expected to find a modest apartment near my place of employment, wherever that would be. I had not imagined moving from my grad student studio apartment to this penthouse with six bedrooms, seven bathrooms, three balconies, a swimming pool, a sauna, a gym, and a view to die for. My mother had told me about Declan's townhouse as if it were a perk for marrying my sister's fiancé.

I had momentarily felt excitement, just for one nanosecond, when my mother said I'd marry Declan. He was a handsome man. Tall. Well built. His blue eyes were bright and intelligent. He looked like a young Paul Newman, and I, for one, was susceptible to his good looks. Not that he'd paid me any attention the few times we'd been in each other's company. He'd had eyes for Viv only, and why shouldn't he? She was his equal in looks. Everyone noticed her tall and slender figure. I had never competed with Viv. When I was younger, I looked up to her. By the time I was older, I knew I didn't want what she wanted—and there had been no need to compete. I never envied her...well, not until she brought home Declan. But it was not *actual* envy—just a longing. Between me and Viv, a man would always pick her. She was beautiful, charming, powerful, and elegant. I was short. Not stick thin. My hair didn't listen to me. I wore glasses because contact lenses irritated my eyes. I didn't dress well, partly because I didn't care and partly because I couldn't afford it. My father had money. My mother had his money. Viv had a high-paying job. I had a small inheritance from my grandmother that I'd used to pay for school, and I still needed two jobs to stay afloat. I'd always known I would never have what Viv did, and I didn't dare to aspire for it either.

Now, I was married to Declan, and I still couldn't compete with her. He was heartbroken. I could see it in his eyes, and that's why, even though I wanted to tell him not to take his frustration with the situation out on me, who was not at fault, I didn't. Instead, I felt compassion for him and wished to be his friend and ease his burden.

"Thank you so much for putting my things away," I told Calliope as I looked around.

The room had a king-sized bed and two wooden side tables, which were simple and minimalistic. There was an elegant couch in royal blue, matching the trim on the sheets on the bed. There was a coffee table shaped like a leaf. Some original art on the walls that did nothing for me—they were Viv's style. Gray and brown landscapes that looked pretty but had little soul. I enjoyed art that was modern and abstract, colorful, and vibrant.

I walked into the huge walk-in closet. It looked even larger because my few clothes and shoes only occupied a small space.

"You're going to need to go shopping soon," Calliope informed me. "When Miss Vivian lived here, she needed two closets for her clothes, which were much needed for all the events she and Mr. Declan...."

She trailed off as she realized she was talking about my predecessor. "I'm so sorry, Miss Esme."

I waved and shook my head. "*No hay problema!* Don't worry about it. And call me Esme. Miss seems...well, I'm not a *miss*."

Calliope's eyes warmed. "Okay. Esme. Are you hungry? Or do you want—"

"I'm just going to get some sleep," I cut in. "I'm drained. I got on a flight at five in the morning, and last week was hectic. Ah...is Declan going to be home for dinner?"

Calliope seemed to stiffen at that. She was uncomfortable. "He told me he'll eat with friends tonight, and I should cook whatever you want."

I nodded and didn't let her see that it hurt that my husband, on our wedding day, didn't want to be with me. If he wanted me to know what he thought about our marriage, he was being crystal clear.

"No need to cook for me. Go home...take the day off. Seriously. I'll take a walk and find something to eat."

The older woman seemed horrified. "But...."

"When do you normally leave?" I asked.

"By seven in the evening, unless Mr. Declan or Miss Vi...unless I'm asked to stay longer."

"Well then, take the day off. I'm going to sleep. And he's probably not going to be home until much later."

Calliope shook her head. "Take a nap. I have a few things to take care of. I'm going to do some grocery shopping now, but I'll be here when you wake up.

I put the flowers on the coffee table shaped like a leaf. They immediately lifted the energy in the room. I wanted to explore the house but didn't because I would go into Declan's bedroom and invade his privacy. I would not do that. He had been clear about not being interested in me and thought I was...well, a nuisance. I was too tired to wallow in self-pity, so I undressed and crawled into bed naked. Within minutes, I was asleep.

Chapter 3

DECLAN

I came home after ten at night. I had purposefully had dinner with Mateo, one of my closest friends, and a few others in West Hollywood. My goal had been to come home after my wife had gone to sleep, but I found her sitting in the living room, spread out on the couch, reading. She had a glass of white wine on the coffee table beside her. She looked comfortable, and it grated on my nerves. She'd made herself at home in Vivian's house.

She looked up and smiled. "Hi. How are you? Did you have a nice dinner?"

She was so cheerful and polite that it irked me.

"That table is a Boca do Lobo. Please use a coaster." I didn't give a shit about coasters or stains on wood, but Viv did, and I was repeating something I'd heard her say to me.

Esme immediately picked up her wine glass. "I'm sorry. I'll be more careful."

She was wearing a pair of jeans and a loose T-shirt. Her feet were bare. She was sitting sideways on the couch, her feet up, and a book titled *We Want to Do More Than Survive* on her lap. She sipped her wine and set it on the floor next to her.

I walked out of the living room and went into my bedroom. Why wasn't Esme more upset? Why wasn't she demanding anything? Viv was not such a doormat. She was fire and passion. She'd have kicked my ass.

I took a shower and got into bed, but as I hovered by my bed naked, I changed my mind. I had a wife who I needed to talk to. I put on a pair of jeans and a T-shirt and walked to the living room. The first thing I saw was that she had found a coaster, and her wine glass was on top of it.

She looked up at me and smiled. Her ability to bounce back no matter what I said irritated me. I sat down across from her in a red swan armchair.

"Did you get settled in all right?" I asked lamely.

She set her book down and sat up a little. "Yes. Calliope is wonderful."

"You ate?" I was making stupid small talk, but I felt something...anything needed to be said.

"I went to a wine bar on Olive and had something to eat there...would you like a glass of wine? It's a nice Chablis I picked up today."

I shook my head. "No, thanks." I had a wine fridge with some terrific wines, and she'd bought her own? Why?

She looked at me expectantly.

I took a deep breath. "We're married."

She nodded.

I stood up and sighed. "This is no one's fault. Well, maybe Viv's, but... I'm glad you said yes."

She said nothing, just waited.

"How are you feeling about this marriage?"

She shrugged. "My mother explained that this is something my father's company needed, and they asked me to fill in for Viv."

"And you didn't care that you were marrying your sister's fiancé?" I demanded harshly.

She took a deep breath. "I did. I do. But I was told I had no choice. And since the Hartley company bylaws caused this predicament, and...Viv married someone else, I felt I had to step up. My mother said it was for a year, and the prenup we signed clarifies that you go your way in twelve months, and I go mine."

The prenup was rigid. I had refused to give anything to Esme out of spite. The Hartley lawyers had not objected. Why hadn't they? Why hadn't Esme?

"You get nothing at the end of the year...well, whatever you already have from your parents, but nothing from me."

"Yes, I know. I read the contract."

There was something about the way she looked that stirred me. She seemed at peace with this. Well, why wouldn't she be? She wasn't the one who had her heart broken.

"You want nothing?"

She looked at me in question. "What would I want?"

"Money."

She smiled and shook her head. "No, thank you."

"You have a trust fund, I assume."

She shook her head. "No."

"Viv has one."

She nodded. "Yes."

"Oh, for god's sake, can you talk in full sentences instead of one-word answers?" I was taking my anger out on her, which was damned unfair, but her attitude, her serenity, made me want her to choke on it and show me some spirit, some *hutzpah*.

She bit her lower lip, and my heart hammered. No, she wasn't a beauty like Viv, but there was something about her: a calmness that was... desirable. A part of me wanted to shake her out of it, but the other wished I could bask in it and find peace within.

"You're angry about this situation. I understand. I'm not happy about it, either. But there's nothing I can do to fix it or change it. So, I accept and try to make the best of it. If being unhappy or angry would change anything, then I'm all for it, but I've learned that bending with the wind helps me survive without breaking." Her eyes were bright now with unshed tears. I felt like an asshole. I was an asshole.

I walked up to her and looked down at her. "I'm sorry."

She shook her head and got rid of her tears and sadness. "You're hurting. What Viv did was...well, she hurt you, and I'm sorry for that. Can I do anything to make you feel better?"

I crouched in front of her to be at eye level with her. She confused me. "I'm being a complete jackass, and you want to make me feel better? Who the fuck are you? Mother Teresa?"

She laughed then. "No. I'm not *that* good. But I saw you with Viv. I saw how happy you were, and I can't change that you're hurting, but maybe I can make you feel better. Give you some respite. I know you don't want a marriage, but we could be friends."

Who the fuck had I married? Who was this woman?

"You can't make me feel better," I whispered. "We need to talk about how this marriage will work."

"Okay," she nodded like a student waiting to take notes.

"I don't expect sex," I blurted out, and as soon as I did, I knew I may not expect it, but I wanted it with her. The idea was so ludicrous that I jumped up and took a few steps away from her as if stung. I sat back down on the armchair. I was flustered and uncharacteristically allowed her to see how I felt. I gave very few people that privilege. I didn't even let Viv see it because she was always so in control that I felt I also needed to be.

She smiled her serene smile. "I understand."

"Do you?" *Because I fucking don't.*

She bit her lip again, and all my blood drained to my cock. *Fuck!* Of all the things I had imagined, this was not one of them.

"I know how Viv looks." She didn't think she could compete. "I know you have other women who would be happy to..." she was stumbling on her words.

"Are you saying you'd be okay with me fucking other women?" I asked deliberately and crudely.

She cleared her throat. "If that's what you want. A year is a long time to be celibate."

"And you'll fuck other men?" I asked. *No, she will not*; I wondered where this possessiveness came from. I was here to tell her we'd live separate lives and put on a show for the media and then divorce at the end of the year. But here I was, suddenly talking about sex and wanting to have said sex with her...with Esme? I was losing my mind.

"Oh no," she was emphatic. "I don't do that."

I narrowed my eyes. "Do what? Have sex?"

"I have a vibrator." She groaned then. "I don't know why I told you that."

I smiled. I couldn't help it. Esme Knight *nee* Hartley was a fucking train wreck.

She put her feet down on the floor and looked at me. "I know how I look. I can see how you look. I'm not an idiot. I assume you've been loyal to my sister for the time you've been together."

"I don't cheat." No, that's something Viv does, apparently, without me knowing.

She ignored me and kept speaking, "...You're probably used to getting sex on the regular. If you find an opportunity, go for it."

Go for it? Did she not understand that I had opportunities all the time? I'd turned down the hostess at the restaurant where I just had dinner.

"And you'll make do with a vibrator?"

She blushed. "I don't know why I told you that. I have one. It was a gag gift from a friend. They wanted me to lose my virginity."

"You lost your virginity to a battery-operated device?"

"Oh, mine doesn't have a battery. I charge it...." Esme let out a long breath. "What I'm saying is, bang whomever you want. It's all good."

"And what if I want to bang you?" I asked, and the words jolted me as much as they surprised her. *Where the fuck had that come from?*

"Excuse me?" her voice was thin.

"What if I want to have sex with you?" I enunciated each word. *Shut up, Dec. You don't want to sleep with Viv's little sister.*

"You want to have sex with me?" she croaked out.

Did I?

She bit her bottom lip again, and I had to admit I wanted to taste that lip. I wanted to kiss Esme—my wife. *Viv's sister*, a voice inside my head, reminded me, and I froze. What was wrong with me?

"I don't want anyone outside this house to know what's happening in our marriage. Not even your parents." I didn't want to talk about sex anymore because if I did, I'd be asking to see her vibrator and making her come both with and without it.

"And what is happening in our marriage?" she asked tentatively.

"We sleep in separate rooms. We don't have sex. We're divorcing in a year. I want it to be clear to anyone who sees us that we have a genuine marriage."

"Why?"

"Because I have my pride," I confessed. I didn't want people to pity me because Viv left me, and I had to marry her sister. The uglier…, the lesser sister.

"Okay."

"We have to go to a gallery opening this Friday and after that dinner with some people at Melisse. Be ready by six." That was two days away; it should be enough notice—and was what Viv expected from me.

"Okay."

"Thank you." I left the living room before I could say something else that would make her realize I was pretty unhinged and wanted very much to fuck her senseless and prove I could do a better job than her vibrator.

Chapter 4

ESME

I want to have sex with my husband.

I was twenty-three years old. I was inexperienced. The one time I'd done *it*, *it* had been a disaster for all involved, putting me off trying again.

I wanted to make love with Declan.

Especially now, when he wore jogging shorts and was drinking water in the kitchen after working out in the gym on the top floor. I was waiting for Declan to leave so I could use the gym and then put on my swimsuit and maybe take advantage of the pool. Everyone thought that because I was curvy, I didn't work out. I did. It was because I did; I was only what people called voluptuous and not overweight. In university, I used the gym five days a week, which wasn't easy with two jobs and a full course load so I could finish my masters in a year and a half rather than two years to save money.

Instead of gawking at my husband, I started the coffee machine and made myself a cup of coffee, black.

"How do you take your coffee?" I asked.

"Black."

"Me too." I pushed the cup I just made toward him. "Would you like some breakfast?"

"Calliope takes care of that," Declan told me. "She'll be here soon."

"I like to cook," I confessed. "How do you feel about scrambled eggs and bacon?"

His phone buzzed, and he picked it up to read a text message. "Sure," he said absently as he walked away. He called someone, and I heard him say, "*Viv*, you can't be angry that I married her," before disappearing into his bedroom.

Since I had said I'd do it, I made him breakfast. Fluffy scrambled eggs, the way my *abuela* taught me. Crispy bacon cooked to perfection in the oven. Toasted English muffins. A fresh cup of coffee and orange juice. I had set the table for both of us to eat together. I arranged the food on the plate to mimic the presentation of a high-end restaurant, complete with a garnish of strawberries.

I shouldn't have bothered.

He was in a foul mood when he came out of his bedroom dressed for work. He wore a suit and looked ready to rule the world.

He ate without commenting while he went through his phone. When he was done, he didn't put his plate away, just left for his home office. He came out a few minutes later with a backpack and left.

He didn't thank me for breakfast. He didn't say have a nice day.

I had eaten about half of what was on my plate but lost my appetite and pushed the plate away. I was cleaning up when Calliope arrived. She admonished me for both cooking and cleaning.

"He never leaves this early," she scoffed. "I wonder what happened."

I wanted to tell her he got married and didn't want to hang out with his wife, so he ran away after conversing with my sister, his ex-fiancée, whom he wanted to marry and was still in love with.

I worked out and got ready for my day. I had a job interview at the Keck School of Medicine at eleven. As a Hartley, they expected me to have a high-flying career, a lot like Viv did. When I did not have a high-flying career like Viv, my parents were embarrassed but not surprised.

Do nothing to embarrass the family.
Why are you wearing that? It's hideous.
Why can't you have your hair done?
Get some contacts. Or better glasses.

It was primarily cosmetic—so all I had to do was hide in Seattle, and no one cared what I did and who I did it with. I had learned early in my childhood to disappear. I had figured out that if I lived in the shadows, I'd have the freedom I wanted.

"How do I look?" I asked Calliope when I came out to the living room in a dark burgundy pantsuit I bought four years ago to wear for my bachelor's degree graduation.

"Uh...nice." Calliope seemed confused.

"What?" I asked, looking at my outfit to ensure nothing was out of place.

"You're very different from your sister."

"Oh?"

"She'd never ask if she looked nice."

I laughed. "Because Viv doesn't have to."

"I think you look much better."

Calliope was lovely, and I was grateful. I needed the confidence boost.

"I have a job interview." I walked up to the coffee machine and turned it on. I held my hand when Calliope wanted to take over. "Please, I can make my coffee."

"What is the job?"

"It's at the Keck School of Medicine. I'll work with mothers and young children if I get this job. It's what I want to do, what I specialize in. I just graduated with a Masters in Social Work."

The older woman looked even more shocked now. "You're going to be a social worker?"

"Yes." I took a sip of coffee. "This is such a great coffee machine. I've been drinking crap coffee for years; this is a gift."

"Does Mr. Declan know you want to be a social worker?"

"Yes, he does, and he's fine with it," I repeated. "I have to work, Calliope. I don't have a trust fund like Viv. I had a small inheritance from my grandmother, but that disappeared quickly to pay for university. Luckily, I won't have to pay rent for a year here."

Her eyes widened, and I realized I had spilled the beans. Declan had said he didn't want anyone to know about our marriage—she knew we slept in separate rooms.

"You know, don't you, that this marriage is ...well...you know?"

Calliope nodded. "Mr. Declan, let me know."

"You've been with him a long time. I can tell he trusts you."

She flushed. "Nearly a decade now."

"He's heartbroken," I said thoughtfully. "What does he like? How can I...I don't know, make him smile a little."

Her eyes became sad, as if she was pitying me. "Mr. Declan likes jazz and Cajun food, and in that order."

"Excellent." Food, I could cook. I had to learn significantly when my *Abuela* fell sick and couldn't do much around the house.

Chapter 5

DECLAN

"**A**sk her to go fuck herself," Mateo advised. "She dumps you, and now that you're married, she's got the nerve to bitch about it?"

Mateo Silva was one of my closest friends and the Chief Technology Officer at Knight Technologies. We met in Harvard. I was studying business, and he was getting a degree in computer engineering. It was a match made in heaven. When I took over Knight Tech, Mateo became my right hand, and we'd diversified from industrial electronics to security software; and were now unbeatable with the merger with Hartley Industries.

"She's hurt that I married her sister." I scrolled through my email.

Viv had called in the morning in a panic. She'd never imagined I'd marry Esme. I don't know why, when she knew that this merger required a marriage, and the only other Hartley available to me was her younger sister.

"Who else would you marry?"

"I asked her the same thing. She was crying, Mateo."

Mateo never liked Viv, even though he never said it until we broke up. He admitted she was an excellent corporate lawyer, but beyond that, he didn't think she had much to redeem herself.

"Viv is just spoiled. How's your new wife, Dec?"

I looked up at him from my computer and shrugged. "Fine, I guess."

"Are you going to make this marriage work?"

"Why?"

Mateo sighed. "Come on, Dec. This young girl married you to save her parents' company. Show some compassion."

"She seems fine." The way he put it made my hackles rise. I wasn't being compassionate. Instead, I took my anger out on her because she was there.

"Have you spent any time with her?"

"Sure. We talked last night. It was pleasant." *And I wanted to fuck her.*

"You had dinner with me and the other morons we call friends. You stayed at the restaurant until past ten, Dec."

"Mateo, what the fuck do you want from me? She knows we're getting divorced in a year. This is not a marriage. It's a business agreement that will be moot in 364 days."

Mateo rose from the chair he was sitting in across from my desk. "Is she coming this Friday?"

"Yeah. I told Esme we'd go to the gallery and then for dinner at Melisse."

"I look forward to meeting her. She seems interesting."

As he walked away, I stopped him to ask, "Why?"

"Because she seems untouched by your big society nonsense. She's a social worker. I had some great social workers help me. Without them, I'd have ended up in a gang or worse. It's a noble profession."

I thought about Esme after Mateo left. I agreed with him, she was interesting. There was a grace about her. She didn't make a fuss when things didn't go her way. She settled into my apartment even though I had done nothing to make her feel welcome.

My day became busy, and Esme slipped my mind. My upbringing taught me to prioritize work. If Viv and I had a problem, it was that we both put our work first, which meant we missed some birthdays and anniversaries. I didn't mind so much, but for Viv, it was the end of the world. Mateo's observation was correct; I had spoiled her myself.

And while I was doing everything I could to make her happy, she'd been balling some other guy. I knew his name. I had a complete dossier on him but didn't want to give him an identity; it would tear my heart out of my chest to do so.

I had just finished a lunch meeting when my mother entered my office. Nina Knight was a force to be reckoned with—and I had fallen in love with Viv, as the cliché went, because she was so much like my mother. She'd retired as a California Supreme Court Judge two years ago and had been relentlessly working with the Democratic National Committee to support political candidates nationwide.

She was an elegant woman with not a single hair out of place. Today, she wore a Chanel suit that made her look about a decade younger than her sixty years. Her short bob blonde hair was expertly coiffed, and the diamonds on her neck, ears, wrists, and fingers sparkled. She clutched a small light blue Chanel bag that matched her suit. Viv had been the same. Coordinated, confident, and classy.

And then, unbidden, I saw Esme in my mind. She wore only her wedding ring and a pair of small diamond earrings. She didn't carry a handbag. She'd used the pockets in her dress for her phone and the key fob I'd given her. Her phone had a case that included a wallet.

I kissed my mother lightly on the cheek and ushered her to the seating area in my office. She sat on the leather sofa, and I sat across from her on a matching armchair.

"Your wife is looking for a job as a social worker," she hissed.

"Yes."

"Well, if she wants to do charitable work, we have several foundations she can work with. Julien got a call from the Chairman of the Board at Keck, and he wanted to know why a Hartley was interviewing for some low-level social worker job there."

I leaned back on the chair. "What do you want me to do about it?"

"Get her involved with the Knight Foundation."

"I'll ask her."

"Dec. You tell her what to do. This isn't Vivian, who has a career. Esme is...well, according to Julien, she's a bit of a flake." My mother headed many charities but never got her hands dirty. Regardless, she did a lot of good, and I was proud of her.

"How is she flaky?" I wanted to know. I hadn't seen a flaky woman, maybe one who was not assertive, but also not foolish.

"Julien got her some earrings for Christmas, and she sold them to raise money for some women's shelter. This is why he's not set up a trust fund for her."

"Because he's worried she'll give it all away? That's noble, not—"

Nina waved her hand as if it didn't matter. "She's going to be married to you for a year, and in that time, she needs to behave as expected. I don't know why Julien hasn't managed her better. Monica has some of that...you know—"

"No, I don't know." I didn't mind that my mother was a snob, but how she talked about Esme, who had done our families a huge favor, didn't sit well with me. It was one thing to think that Esme was not as desirable as Viv to be my wife, quite another to say it out loud as my mother was.

"Monica didn't grow up with the money," my mother announced haughtily.

"Mom, I have to get to a meeting." I looked at my watch.

"Get her to stop this job nonsense. If she wants a job, she can run a foundation. No Knight is going to have some eighty thousand dollars a year government job," she announced and added, "I've made sure she won't get this job."

"Mom..."

"And make sure she's presentable this Friday. Did you see what she wore to the wedding? I get it was in chambers, but...it was some off-the-rack nonsense. If there had been time, I'd have ensured she wore something decent."

My mother loved Viv—and it was apparent she didn't care for Esme. It didn't matter to me. I was married for a year, and after that, Esme was out of my life. I'd keep the peace with my mother.

I kissed her on the cheek again and assured her that Esme and I would be at Melisse for dinner after the gallery opening, and that Esme would be dressed as required for a Knight. We would have dinner with Mateo, my parents, Senator Rivers, and his wife. We had business with Senator Rivers, so this was more of a business-plus-pleasure affair.

I had thought about not taking Esme, but the Knight PR team would announce our marriage in the media, so the all-about-family values Senator Rivers would expect her there. The PR head had tutted at the dress Esme had worn and declared that we'd have to go with a close-up because she didn't know how to *salvage that dress*, so they had published a close-up photo.

The dress was simple, but it wasn't offensive. It probably wasn't designer wear, perhaps because Esme didn't care about such things. However, she would have to learn if she wanted to survive my mother and the media.

Chapter 6

Esme

"How did it go?" Mark asked as we sat at Verve, a coffee shop, after my interview at Keck.

I took a sip of coffee and shrugged. "I don't know."

He raised his eyebrows. "The job description seemed designed with you in mind."

Mark Caruso was a neurosurgeon and had moved from Seattle to LA for his residency at UCLA. We were neighbors in Seattle who'd become friends. He knew more about my life than anyone else, and I knew about his. He was my best friend, and I was his. It was because he was in Los Angeles that I applied for jobs here. I'd never thought I'd have no choice but to move here because my husband lived in LA.

Husband.

"The chairman of the board came down for the interview," I told him. "It was *so* weird. He was difficult and...I don't know; it was like he'd decided that I wouldn't get the job even before he spoke to me. He was almost hostile. He kept bringing up why I wanted to work as a social worker when I was married to Declan Knight. I don't know how he knew about the wedding because it's not public yet. He told me I should stop *dabbling* and work at a Knight Foundation."

"Esme, it's not *so* strange. He probably called your father."

"Why would he do that?"

"Because...my innocent Esme, this is how the world of networking functions."

My shoulders slumped, and I wondered if I should even waste my time with the UCLA interview. If I hadn't married Declan, Daddy wouldn't have cared where I worked, but now he did, so he'd expect me to do what he wanted me to do.

Be a good wife in public and private, Esme, he'd warned me as we drove to the courthouse the previous morning.

And none of your shenanigans with helping kids or women or dogs or whatever the fuck you do.

As a Knight, you'll be expected to... well, I can't imagine you showing the same sophistication as Viv, but at least try not to embarrass the family.

Mark put his hand on mine and squeezed. "How's the marriage?"

"A total fucking disaster," I confessed. "It's been a day, and keeping the pretense that this isn't tearing me apart is exhausting. It's not helping that Declan is angry and frustrated."

"And he's taking it out on you?"

I nodded. "He is lost and confused. And I get it. Imagine loving someone and then finding out on your wedding day that they were cheating on you. Knowing Viv, Nick was not the first person either."

"Tell him that," Mark encouraged. "Why are you protecting Viv?"

I laughed. "I don't want to hurt anyone needlessly. And if I told him she was sleeping around throughout their relationship, it would only hurt him. It's only for a year, Mark. I'll find another job. I have a few other interviews; something will work out."

It wouldn't be easy, but I would persevere until I got what I wanted. My personal life was a disaster; I wanted my professional life to be fulfilling.

"If you don't want to live with him, you can come live with me. I have two bedrooms...now that Francois left."

Mark and his partner of three years had recently broken up. They'd grown apart, and the move from Seattle to LA had not helped. Francois could not adjust to LA. He went back to Seattle, and as breakups went, theirs was amicable. There was sorrow that it didn't work out, but not grief. Their relationship had changed over the years, and in the end, they'd been just roommates.

"He wants to show the world we have a proper marriage. And honestly, my parents would lose their shit." I drank some more coffee, which had become lukewarm. I looked at my watch, a present from my grandmother when I graduated. It was a used Rolex. She'd saved up to buy it for me. It wasn't shiny and not a fancy vintage—but I loved it.

"And you? What do you need?" Mark asked, surprising me.

I closed my eyes, terrified of where my life stood right now. "I need to find a job. I need to have a life that's my own. Declan doesn't *want* a real marriage—only one that looks like it. He's going to keep doing what he's doing. And I don't want to get too dependent on his lifestyle. It'll all be gone in a year."

"I still think you shouldn't have signed that contract," Mark admonished. He hadn't been happy that I would get nothing from Declan at the end of the marriage contract. The morning of the wedding, the Hartley family lawyer had told me that Declan Knight himself had demanded a stipulation be put in that I receive no compensation for the year-long marriage. I told him that was fine and signed on the dotted line. My mother was proud of me and told me so. I felt like someone sold me off like cattle.

I looked at Mark's handsome face and smiled. "Money will not make me happy."

Mark laughed. "True."

And he'd know. Born and raised as an heir, he'd turned his back on his father's company to become a doctor. His sister now ran the company. The siblings were close, but his father still had not forgiven him. His mother was a gem. Judith Caruso, artist extraordinaire, treated me like a daughter, and I got from her, Mark, and his sister Maria the love and affection I never got at home.

"I need to buy some groceries. I want to cook dinner. Calliope mentioned Declan likes Cajun food, so I thought I'd make him Louisiana barbecue shrimp," I said.

Mark made a face. "Why waste that on him? Seriously, Es, your heart is too big."

"No such thing as a heart that's *too* big. Want to walk with me to Whole Foods?"

"Sure," Mark sighed, giving up. "If he hurts you, Es, come home to me, okay? Or to Maria or my mother. You've done enough for your family."

I hugged him tightly. I needed it. It had been a tumultuous week, and he was my safe space.

"I love you," I whispered.

He put his arms around me and held me. "I love you too."

Chapter 7

DECLAN

I would never have seen them if I hadn't looked up from my computer. The driver was taking me back to my office after a meeting in West Hollywood late in the afternoon.

I didn't notice her at first. I just saw a woman in a burgundy pantsuit hugging a tall man with blond hair. When she stepped away from him, the Escalade moved a few inches in the LA traffic, and I saw her smiling face. That's my *fucking wife*, I thought and just like her older sister, she was screwing around...a day after the wedding.

I wanted to stop the car and make a scene but resisted. No, I'd find out what the fuck she was up to. I called Raya, the Knight head of security.

"I need someone to check up on my wife," I said without preamble.

"The *new* wife?" Raya asked.

"The *only* fucking wife."

"*Fucking* being the operative word?" She knew about Viv. Raya and Mateo not only worked with me but were also my closest friends.

"Yes."

"Okay. I'll put someone on her. Mateo mentioned you're coming to poker tonight. I thought you'd be home cuddling up with the new missus."

Raya, Mateo, Daisy, another friend from Boston, and I played poker every Thursday night. We usually played at Mateo's apartment, a few blocks from where I lived. The three of us had known each other for many years. I'd always thought Mateo and Raya would get together as a couple. But years passed, and neither of them ever seemed to make it click. When I asked Mateo, he looked at me like I had asked if he wanted to date my mother. "I'm her boss."

"I *may* skip poker," I told her *because I needed to interrogate my new wife about the blond asshole she was seeing on the side.* I needed to make it clear to her that she would have to be fucking *celibate* through this marriage because she wasn't having sex with anyone but me, and since I would not fuck her, she would have to keep her vibrator busy.

I finished my last meeting at seven and returned home. Throughout the afternoon, I kept feeling pressured to call her and ask where she was. Had she fucked him today? At his place, or did she bring him to mine?

I stepped into the apartment and was greeted by a smiling Calliope. She took my backpack and whispered, "I'm so glad you came home. She's cooking."

"Cooking? Didn't you tell her I play poker on Thursdays?"

Calliope's face fell. "I thought you'd come home" She didn't add because you just got married.

"I need a shower, and then I'm heading out." I knew I was being willful, but I couldn't help myself.

"She's making Louisiana barbecue shrimp. I told her you like Cajun food." Calliope's eyes blazed with anger, which I'd never seen before.

I raised an eyebrow. It looked like Calliope and Esme had become friends. Why on earth was Esme cooking my favorite meal? Especially since she was fucking some other guy this afternoon.

"You can go home, Calliope," I told her and walked into the kitchen.

Cuban jazz accompanied the smell of Cajun spices. She wore a pair of denim shorts, a T-shirt, and an apron. As she cooked, her hips swayed to the music. I'd never seen Viv cook.

She turned around and smiled. "I'm so glad you're home. Dinner will be ready in no time."

"I play poker on Thursdays," I told her blandly. "I'm afraid you'll be eating alone." *Or maybe you can invite that asshole you were hugging.*

Her face fell for only an instant, and she went back to her calm and cheerful self. "I should've asked." She took the blame on herself, and I felt something move inside me. "It's okay. I can cook another day."

She turned around to face the stove. I grabbed her arm and turned her to face me. "Who the fuck were you with this afternoon?" I wasn't a violent man, but I was vibrating with anger, and I didn't care if it scared her. I wanted her to be afraid. Never fucking again was a woman cheating on me.

She blinked. "What?"

"This afternoon? I was driving by and saw you with a man."

There was no guilt on her face, just a sense of realization. "You were on Main? You should've come by. You could've met Mark. He's my friend from Seattle. He's doing his neurosurgery residency at UCLA. He's the reason I was applying for jobs in LA. We thought we'd live together...but then...." She waved a hand around the house.

"I know we didn't discuss this, but let me make it very clear. You're not fucking other men. You're not making a fool out of me like *she* did. Got it?"

I expected her to say something angrily, but she smiled sadly. "You think I'm sleeping with Mark?"

"Are you?" My hold on her arm tightened.

She shook her head. "No. He's a friend. We've been friends for six years and...no, we'd never."

"You were hugging him. It looked like it was more than friendly."

She removed my hand from her arm and stepped away. She licked her lips and then looked me straight in the eye. "I know you don't know me well. Maybe you'll feel better if I tell you a little about me. I don't lie. Well, I'll tell a good old white lie like anyone else, but not about something important. Mark is my best friend. I know him, his sister, and his family well. Declan, Mark is gay. *Completely* gay. Even if I walked around him naked, he wouldn't care, and before you ask, it's the same for me. We are friends. True friends."

My heart pounded. I wanted to believe her. Trust but verify. That was my new motto. Raya would find out everything that needed to be found out about this Mark guy.

"Okay."

"Thank you."

Her sincerity almost undid me—but I was still working through my mad, so I continued in the same tone. "My mother came by the office. She said you're interviewing for social worker jobs, and she'd prefer if you didn't. You can look at what needs to be done with the Knight Foundation and design your job. I've asked Baker to set up a meeting for you with the head of the foundation."

The serenity slipped, and I saw something I hadn't seen until now: irritation.

"I'd prefer if your mother stayed out of my business."

Her tone was still the same, but there was fire behind the words. She seemed almost docile and so willing to put up with all the crap I was throwing at her that it was unexpected.

"What did you say?"

"I said I'd prefer it if your mother didn't interfere in my professional life."

"Professional?" I smirked. "Honey, it's a social worker job that pays 80k a year. Let's not make it more than it is."

She turned off the stove and looked at me sternly.

"I've studied for six years to become a social worker and I intend to work as one. I'm not interested in some glorified foundation job. I want to help people, and I'm going to."

"The foundation helps a lot more people than you can as one social worker." *And you'll do as you're told.*

"Then you run it. I'm not interested. Like I said before, you don't know me well, so let me tell you something else about myself. My job is important to me. In a year, you'll go your way, and I'll go mine, so I can't just give my life up any more than I already have for this marriage."

I frowned at her stubbornness. This was some low-level grunt job, and she wanted to fight for it. Well, she wasn't winning.

"Esme, I don't want trouble with my mother, and *you* don't want trouble with Nina Knight either," I warned her. I looked at my watch, and my jaw tightened. "I don't have time for this. Just meet with the foundation—"

"No."

I shrugged. "Fine. You will get none of these jobs. My mother and your father have ensured Keck won't hire you. That's where you interviewed today?"

Her eyes filled with something close to agony. "Declan, please—"

I raised my hand to silence her. "Take it up with my mother if you dare. I'm telling you to take the path of least resistance. Looks like you know how to do that well."

"What does that mean?"

I snorted. "You married your sister's fiancé without complaint. You do as you're told by your family. You're...well...."

"Well, what?" she asked softly.

"A bit of a doormat," I finally said and saw her physically step back like I struck her. I wanted to apologize, but I held firm. I didn't need my temporary wife and my mother fighting and if they were, I knew whose side I was on, and it wasn't Esme's.

"I have to go." I walked away from her.

She'd looked devastated, but she needed to understand what it meant to be a Knight. It appeared her parents indulged her and let her do as she pleased. What did mom say? Her father thought she was a bit of a flake. Maybe she was. She didn't dress right; and didn't know how to behave in society if she was running after some low-level job. It was time to educate her. Even after our marriage ended, she could use some of that wisdom to lead a better life.

I took a shower and went to Mateo's place. Esme wasn't in the kitchen or the living room. Probably sulking in her bedroom. I hoped she would get in line, otherwise, this was going to be a long year for her because I would not lose this silly battle or any battle with her.

Chapter 8

ESME

It had been a long time since I had a good cry. He thought I was a *doormat*. Here I was, trying to make the best of a shitty situation, and all he saw was a pushover. I didn't blame him; how could I? Hadn't I been doing this my whole life? Trying to be as unobtrusive as possible. As pleasant as I could. Giving my family everything they could want without asking for anything in return.

I couldn't, wouldn't, work for the Knight Foundation to enable the rich and famous to get together for charity balls so they could feel better about their wealth. *No way.*

I looked at my phone and made my decision. I called Maria Caruso, Mark's sister.

"Hey, sweetheart, how are you?" she immediately answered, as I knew she would.

"I need your help."

"Shoot."

Maria Caruso was the CEO of an investment bank with a network that could achieve impossible things. If I needed to fight the influence of Nina Knight, I needed someone with similar or more social power.

"I need a job," I told her. "As a social worker."

"Mark said that the Keck job was in the bag."

"The Knights don't want me to work," I revealed. I got up from my bed and walked up to the tall windows. The city's lights blinked, and the opulence of my fake marriage made me grind my teeth.

"Why not?"

"It's beneath me *blah blah blah*. They want me to work for the Knight Foundation. My father and Nina Knight sabotaged my opportunity at Keck."

"And you want it back?"

"Not Keck. That'll be a fight. You said there was a women's clinic in Skid Row that you supported?"

"Safe Harbor, yes. Do you want to work there? They don't pay as much as Keck would, Esme." She knew I needed money like a regular person.

"Well, I don't have to pay rent for a year," I scoffed. "I get to live on top of the world in a six-bedroom apartment with a pool and a gym. I can go to work for less money. After the year is up...well, then they won't care where I work, so they won't interfere."

"You worked in some of the lowest-income places in Seattle, so I don't think Skid Row will scare you," she remarked. "My assistant will send you the details. We can finish the paperwork on Monday, and you can start immediately. We desperately need a clinical social worker. It's chaos out there. The head of Safe Harbor left a few months ago, and everything has been disorganized since then."

I felt relief wash over me. "Thank you, Maria."

"Don't thank me, sweetheart. It's you I should thank for doing the work you do. You and Mark make up for people like me who're chasing after money," she admitted, and I knew she was sincere.

We talked about this and that for a little while, and then I hung up. Maria and Mark knew the truth about my marriage, but I had told them I didn't want their mother, Judith, to know. It would break her heart that I wasn't marrying for love as she knew I wanted to. She wished that for all her children. Maria was too busy working to even date, and Mark, well, he'd recently ended a relationship. I had always thought he'd marry before I did because he was in love with someone. Of course, I'd never imagined that I'd have an arranged marriage in this day and age.

I stopped sulking and decided to get out of the house. If he was playing poker, maybe I could find a wine bar where I could find good wine and spend my time people-watching or reading my book. I couldn't get myself to eat the dinner I had prepared, not after he called me a doormat.

As someone who had grown up in a hostile home, I had become good at keeping my own company. I loved to be alone and hardly ever felt lonely. It came from years of practice, eons of numbing the heart to affection and companionship.

I'd had enough therapy in the past six years while I was in Seattle to understand these things about myself. I wouldn't let Declan's behavior change who I was. I wouldn't become mean and cruel because he was. I would not let unhappiness swamp me. I had only one life to live. This was it. I would not allow a man who had no respect for me to stop me from living my life to the fullest, even if it meant spending one year out of a lifetime with him. I couldn't change his mind—but I wouldn't change who I was because of his prejudice.

I put on a pair of ballet flats and grabbed a scarf. My phone rang as I reached the door. It was the front desk.

"Mrs. Knight, Mr. Julien Hartley is here to see you."

I froze. My father never came to me. He usually *summoned* me.

"Please send him up." I looked around the apartment and made sure I had left nothing out of place. I had cleaned up the kitchen, so he wouldn't be able to complain about that. I was wearing shorts and a T-shirt, which couldn't be helped. But it was a casual Thursday—he wouldn't make an issue out of that, would he?

I waited for him at the elevator door.

My father was a tall man, well-built, and had a full head of silver hair. Julien Hartley was a good-looking man; Vivian took after him and her mother, who had died in a skiing accident when she'd been three years old. Two years later, Daddy met my mother, and they married. I came along a year later. An accident, he always reminded me because he hadn't wanted any more children after Viv.

"Hello, Esme." He walked into the hallway and looked around. "Where is Dec?"

I smiled. "Hello, Daddy. Declan has a standing poker game every Thursday."

He raised his eyebrows. "I want to talk to you."

I nodded and walked into the expansive living room. He sat on the red swan chair, and I felt a shiver run up my spine.

Why was he here? What had I done wrong?

"Can I get you something to drink?" I asked politely.

"Scotch. You know what I like."

I nodded. I walked up to the bar at the other end of the room and poured him two fingers of Macallan 12 with one giant ice cube, just as he liked it.

I took a coaster, set the whiskey glass on it, and sat across from him on the couch.

"I spoke with Nina today, and she's not happy with you," he announced.

The job interview.

I wanted to pretend I didn't know what he was talking about, but he would see it on my face. He could always tell when I lied, so I had stopped doing that long ago. Now, I schooled myself to behave in a manner that didn't need me to lie.

"Daddy, I can't work for the Knight Foundation," I whispered. "My education—"

"You'll do as you're told. You're already an embarrassment to us; don't become one for the Knights. They won't tolerate it."

"Daddy—"

He cut me off with a sharp, "Esme, I don't want to hear your excuses."

I felt shriveled inside. Declan was right, I was a doormat. I did everything he asked me to do, and for that, I could study what I wanted. But now I was back in his circle of influence.

"No excuses, Daddy," I cleared my throat because it was closing up on me. "I have found a job with a foundation that Maria Caruso runs." It wasn't exactly a lie. It was a foundation—though not the kind that threw galas and charity parties to court donations. Maria's foundation was funded by the Caruso family, and 100% of all the money they gave went to support various charities, Safe Harbor being one of them. Here, women found shelter from abusive homes, drug addiction, assault, poverty, and other societal cruelties.

The one thing about me that impressed my father was my friendship with the wealthy Caruso family. Javier and Judith Caruso were a power couple. He founded one of North America's most influential venture capital companies, and Judith was an artist whose paintings hung in famous galleries and museums worldwide.

My father nodded. "Caruso Foundation? Okay. I think that would be alright."

"Thanks, Daddy."

He drank some more whiskey. "Have you talked to Viv?"

The question surprised me, and it showed. "No."

He shook his head as if disappointed. "You married her fiancé, and you've not had the decency to reach out to her?"

But she cheated on him, was what I would've said if I wasn't, as my husband of two days pointed out, a *doormat*. Instead, I said, "I'm sorry. I'll call her."

"She'll be joining us for dinner with Senator Rivers at Melisse. This is an important deal for our families," he warned me. I understood without being told.

Behave yourself. Don't embarrass us.

"Yes, Daddy."

"If you can find a way to not show up, that wouldn't be such a bad thing," he continued. "I think it might be better if Dec and Viv presented a joint front."

It hurt. I didn't let it show. I expected it, but it hurt.

"I'll ask Declan," I replied demurely. I'd stay home if my husband didn't want me to come along.

He finished his whiskey and then rose. "Esme, don't get on the wrong side of the Knights. Nina and Dec are good people—and I don't want them upset by anything you do. They're not like us letting you go off to Seattle and do what you want. These are serious people. And Declan...well...Viv married in haste, and I'm still hopeful she'll come to her senses, and after this year is up, we'll be able to celebrate a *proper* wedding."

He left after that.

No, how are you doing? Are you okay? Do you need anything?

I felt tears crowd my eyes, ready to swallow me whole, but I didn't give in. There was no point. This wasn't the first or the last time my father would make me feel small and inconsequential.

If I cried each time this happened, I'd spend my life unhappy, torn apart.

As planned, I left the apartment and walked around downtown LA. I didn't know the city well, but I loved how alive it was. I found a wine bar and went inside. It was a lovely place with a large patio and the promise of good French wine.

I ordered a glass of white Burgundy and a plate of cheese. Thanks to growing up in wine country, I learned to appreciate wine at an early age. I would drink just one glass of wine if that's all I could afford of the good stuff. The ten-dollar bottles of wine in the grocery store were not for me. Wine was one snobbery I allowed myself.

I let the day disappear into the Los Angeles evening as I watched people, overheard conversations, and became part of the bustling city for a short time.

The year would fly by, I told myself. I'd be free after that to live my life the way I wanted. I just had to get through this one year as Declan's wife.

Chapter 9

DECLAN

"You're such an asshole," Daisy, a redhead with a cliched fiery temper, said when Raya told her how I was making her investigate my new wife.

A successful film producer, Daisy, had joined our group in Boston when we were all in university. After nearly a decade of friendship, we spoke our minds and didn't bother with filters.

"Give him a break," Mateo defended me. "His ex cheated on him for the entire time they were together."

"Viv's marriage, I doubt, will last long," Raya announced. "Nick Steele is a bit of a philanderer."

"Match made in heaven then," I muttered.

Raya sighed. "I know we said nothing, but Dec, Viv's a cold bitch. I think you saw too much of your mother in her."

"Another cold bitch," Daisy piped in.

"Daisy, she's my mother," I protested half-heartedly.

"Please," Daisy raised her hand, "I don't know how you can't see through all the crap your mom puts you through."

"She means well," I shrugged. "And the fact is she's never made me do anything I didn't want to do. She overlooks my foibles, and I do the same for her."

We'd abandoned the poker game because I was in no mood to play. Raya had a preliminary report on Esme, and according to that report, Esme was an honors student and valedictorian. They had invited her to a PhD program in social service at UC Berkeley, which she had deferred to get more work experience. Esme was an accomplished student—and she had graduated with a Master's degree at twenty-three.

"And she's right; Mark is gay. You know his sister," Raya informed me.

I raised an eyebrow.

"Maria Caruso."

I nodded. Yes, Maria and I played in some of the same social circles; and I knew that her brother, a neurosurgeon, was gay. It had been a scandal when he'd not gone into the family business.

"Anything else?" I asked.

"She doesn't have a trust fund. She had a small inheritance from her grandmother, who raised her from when she was eight years old. She owned a vineyard. Your girl is into her wine," Raya said, looking at a report. "Spends a decent amount of money on it every month."

Mateo shook his head. "One thing to see if she's sleeping around, quite another to look at how she spends her money. This is too invasive, even for you, Dec."

"All of it is invasive," Daisy admonished. "Raya, next time, ask him to go fuck himself."

"He pays the bills," Raya grinned.

"*I* am your boss," Mateo countered.

Something flared between them, and I once again wondered if they'd crossed that line from friendship to something else. I knew she was attracted to him; it was plain to see if you knew Raya. Her eyes followed him. But who knew where Mateo's heart was? I'd never seen him go beyond a few weeks with one woman. He wasn't what I used to be—fuck them, and leave them—he was into serial monogamy.

Maybe that's what I needed to do again—fuck a few or several women to get the taste of Viv out of my mouth, so to speak.

Viv and I used to be friends until, one day, she seduced me. I'd thought it was the best day of my life until a few days ago. After just six months of dating, she asked to move in, and I was happy to let her. She helped me redecorate the penthouse. We officially lived together for three months, but she was mainly in San Francisco, working on a case. I never suspected she was unhappy until she told me she was done. She'd gone to Vegas and married Nick Steele, a quintessential tech bro who could give Elon Musk a run for his money, both in finances and personality.

She didn't explain herself, and I was too proud to ask. When she told me what she'd done, I told her that Baker would wipe her existence out of my apartment. So, if she wanted something of hers that was at *my* place, she should talk to him. And that was that. Since then, she'd called and texted to apologize, and when I married Esme, to rail and rant. I hadn't blocked her. I couldn't. If she kept calling and texting, there was hope I could marry the right sister someday.

"The good news is that your wife is not cheating on you," Raya let me know.

"What's the bad news?" I asked.

"For you? Nothing. For her? She seems like a softy, Dec," Raya said sadly. "Gives to women's shelters. Takes care of people. Volunteers while she's working in a bar and a women's clinic *and* going to school."

"She's a Hartley; I don't understand why she needs so many jobs," Daisy said.

"Julien, it appears, has written her out of his will. Viv inherits everything," Daisy revealed.

"What does Esme get?" Mateo asked.

"Nothing." Raya turned off her iPad. "From what I can tell, she's on her own, always has been. Her mother, now she's a piece of work. Monica Hartley spends a ton of money on clothes and jewelry; she just bought a Bulgari diamond choker for a million."

"But she didn't pay for her school?" It baffled Mateo.

It almost seemed like Esme was a tool for her parents. They ignored her until they had a need. Is that why she had become so complacent? Is that why she didn't seem to have a will of her own? Unless I said, she couldn't work. No, then the fire came out. Maybe I should talk to my mother and let Esme have her job. Perhaps I should speak to my lawyer and make sure that Esme gets some money at the end of our marriage. I could afford it. And she'd fucking earn it living with me and dealing with my mother.

I stayed, finishing a bottle of red Burgundy with Mateo after Daisy and Raya left.

"I'm treating her like shit," I confessed to Mateo. "She makes me angry. Not because she's demanding or anything, she's just so fucking pleasant, no matter what."

"Looks like her family trained her to be like that." Mateo filled my glass up.

We had food delivered from Maestros nearby, and the steaks went well with the full-bodied wine. I wondered what kind of wine Esme liked. We had a love for wine in common. Maybe I should take her out for dinner, and we could get to know one another a little.

"Most of the time I feel like she doesn't give a shit. Like no matter what I say, she's determined not to change how she behaves. It's frustrating. I called her a doormat, and I think I hurt her."

Mateo winced. "No one wants to be called a doormat."

"But she behaves like one. Viv would've kicked my ass fifty times by now."

"Viv also cheated on you and jeopardized your and her father's company. Viv is selfish as fuck. Esme doesn't seem to be that type. Give her a chance to at least become a friend, if not a wife."

"Maybe." I wasn't sure what I wanted from Esme. Her entire presence exasperated me. I wish she'd stop smiling all the time and fight back a little.

Chapter 10

DECLAN

S he made me breakfast again. I wanted to leave early to avoid her, and I had woken up at five and worked out, and there she was with a smile on her face and crêpes.

"Thanks." I put some syrup on the crêpe and rolled them. They were delicious and could easily compete in lightness and texture with what you would find in a crêperie in Paris. "But you don't have to do this. Calliope cooks, and if I leave early, I get something in the office."

"I have to eat as well, and I like to cook," she assured me pleasantly.

She was wearing a yellow maxi sundress with a thigh-high slit. She'd just taken a shower, and her hair was damp, curling softly around her shoulders. She wore a silver anklet on her right leg with small bells. Had she always worn that? She smelled of jasmine—something earthy, not like Christian Dior or Chanel as Viv did. Her glasses were metal-rimmed and suited her.

We sat next to one another at the kitchen counter. Viv and I never had breakfast together. If she didn't have an early meeting, I did.

"Do you have a busy day today?" she asked like I hadn't called her a doormat and insulted her the night before.

"Every day is a busy day." I drank some coffee. "My assistant will set up time for you to talk to the Knight Foundation—"

She beamed at that and interrupted me. "I know your mother doesn't want me to work for Keck or any other...well, I talked to a friend of mine, and she runs a foundation that focuses on women's health. I can work there. I told my father, and he thought your mother would be fine with it."

I glared at her. "You told your father? You and I are the ones who are married. You talk to me first."

She nodded. "I'm sorry. He came here last night. It wasn't intentional."

"He was here?"

"Yes."

What the fuck was Julien doing in my house? He knew I played poker Thursday night, which meant he wanted to talk to Esme alone.

"What did he want?" We would not pretend that he wanted to check in on his daughter—not *this* daughter for sure.

She took a deep breath. "He wanted to talk about the job. He also mentioned that Viv would be at the dinner tonight with Senator Rivers and...," she paused for a moment as if trying to figure out how to say what she needed to say, "I'm a straightforward person, so I'll just tell you what he said, and you can let me what you want to do. I'm fine either way, so please don't think I'll be upset. I won't be."

"Why don't you tell me what he said, and then we can decide how you feel?"

She flushed, and I smiled at her. She looked all of eighteen right now with her fresh make-up-free face. I felt like a goddamn pervert for thinking about her sexually. That slit on her thigh was tantalizing, and I wondered how she'd react if I put my hand on her smooth brown thigh.

"He said he'd prefer it if I didn't come for dinner tonight. He wants me to make an excuse so that you and Viv...that you are free to present the plans of what you're working on to Senator Rivers. And it makes sense. I know nothing about your business or—"

I raised my hand, and she fell silent.

"Your father told you he preferred if I went with Viv to dinner with Senator Rivers?"

She nodded unsurely. "He said it wouldn't be a bad thing if I made an excuse. And I'm happy to do that."

I felt something move within me. Her family had taught her to tolerate such abhorrent behavior that she expected nothing from anyone. Instead, she was happy to find ways to live her life and, as she said, make the best of it. So, even though I hurt her, she'd made me breakfast. She'd found a way to appease her father and my mother. She wasn't a flake, I realized, no, she was a shadow who had put up walls around her to survive because the people who were supposed to love her didn't.

"I would not prefer that, Esme." I reached out and covered her small hand with my large one, startling her. "For whatever time we have together, you're my wife."

She bit her bottom lip, and I felt a spark of desire and something else, something akin to affection, flow within me.

"Okay. I'll tell my father—"

"I'll tell him." No way was I going to let Julien intimidate her more than he already had. It was apparent she was afraid of her father.

"Thank you." She gave me a sweet smile, and I didn't resist the urge to lean across and kiss her softly on her cheek.

She pulled away, and I saw her fear and mistrust. I didn't like that at all.

"What was that?" she asked.

I thought about it for a long moment. "You're sweet, and I wanted to let you know."

"Oh." She was self-conscious now.

"Esme, I want you with me tonight and even if I didn't, Senator Rivers is going to want to meet you."

"Why? No one knows me."

Oh, but they're going to.

"The press release about our wedding is going out this morning, and I'm certain he'll be curious. Now, can you tell me more about this foundation you found a job with?"

She shut down immediately. "It's the Caruso Foundation. It's very respectable."

"Esme, if you want to work at Keck, tell me, and I'll make it happen."

"You would?" She could hardly believe that I had a decent bone in my body. Couldn't blame her. I'd been a fucking jackass.

"Sure. Do you want that?"

"No, that would get complicated. Mark's sister, Maria, manages the Caruso Foundation, which supports a women's shelter in Skid Row."

"Skid Row? What the fuck, Esme? Do you know how dangerous that place is?"

She shook her head. "It's not dangerous, Declan. It's poor. I can help people there. I want to. Please, please, *please*—"

I raised my hand to stop her again. I hated that she was begging—that I had made her feel she had to. "I won't stop you. *But* you'll probably have someone with you to make sure you're okay."

"Like whom?"

"A bodyguard."

"No. That would scare the women and children." She stood up, alarmed. "Please, don't do that."

"Calm down. You won't even know they're there, okay? It'll be discreet. You're a Knight now. Do you understand what that means?"

She shook her head.

"It means that you're free game for the media and anyone else who can get access to you."

"I think they're more interested in Viv."

"Yes." Viv appreciated the media attention. My guess was that Esme would hate it.

We'd just finished breakfast when Calliope arrived. She insisted she'd clean up and patted my shoulder affectionately. She liked Esme, and the way Esme talked with Calliope, I could understand it. Viv behaved as if Calliope didn't exist. To her, she was just staff. To me, she was someone who took care of me, and I never took her for granted. Esme had the same values.

She was in the kitchen laughing with Calliope as I was leaving. I paused and looked at her—she looked like a sunflower in that yellow outfit and shone just as bright. I walked up to her, unable to resist, and leaned down to brush my lips against hers, softly.

"Have a nice day. I'll pick you up at six."

Her breath caught, and her eyes widened. Calliope was grinning as I left, and I had a genuine smile on my face for the first time since Viv told me she'd married someone else.

Chapter 11

ESME

“**W**hat the fuck are you wearing?” he demanded when he saw me.

I was wearing the best dress I had. A sleeveless black Tahari sheath dress that went very well with a suit jacket that I put on when I had defended my master's thesis. I bought the dress at Nordstrom Rack, and I thought it looked good. I ad paired it with black heels I had also gotten at Nordstrom Rack, Stuart Weitzman on sale for fifty bucks. *Beat that!*

I bit my bottom lip. “I...it's a Tahari sheath dress?”

"What's that?"

"A business suit brand," I responded tentatively.

"Boss is a business suit brand." He looked angry and disappointed like my father did with me. I didn't want him to spew ugly things like my father, so I talked fast, which I did when I was nervous.

"Look, I know you think you married a Hartley but I'm the...you know, ugly sister. Viv is the princess...from both looks and fashion perspectives. I didn't grow up in LA. I don't do Melisse. I don't even know what Melisse is. You said gallery opening and dinner, so I put this on. It's what I wore for my thesis defense, and everyone said I looked good. *Really good.*"

"What does this have to do with anything...you look like a secretary, not a Knight who's going to meet a Senator.

"I grew up in Santa Rita with my *abuela*. My grandmother," I blurted out, speaking over him.

"Why?"

"My parents were too busy traveling," I responded simply. "Anyway, what I'm saying is I haven't gone to many of these society things. The few times I did, I borrowed something to wear from my mother that was loose on her and not so much on me. I'm a social worker and a student. I don't have money to buy the kind of clothes Viv wears."

He closed his eyes for a moment and then let out a breath.

Why, oh why, did he have to look so good while I...well, I looked like me.

"You're married to me. You have money to buy whatever the fuck you want."

I stared at him like he'd lost his mind. My father would never have said, "Here's some money; go buy something nice," he'd just have said something about my poor taste in clothes like Declan had.

"Declan, I'm sorry. This is the best I can do. What I wear is not important to me. But these things are important to you and your family. I'm willing to learn, and I'll do better in the future. Why don't you go without me this time? Just make an excuse. Say, I'm not feeling well. You know with all the excitement of the wedding and my thesis and all that." *And that would make my father happy, and I wouldn't have to look at Viv who would look like she was made to stand next to Declan.*

I didn't wait for him to respond and just turned around to return to my bedroom. I was depleted. I didn't know why people cared so much about what or who I wore. Why was I never enough the way I was?

"No. This is a business meeting, Esme. And I want you there."

"But, Declan," I pleaded.

"Esme, you're a fucking Hartley, and you're behaving like—"

"Someone who grew up on a small vineyard in Santa Rita with her grandmother," I finished.

"We need to up your wardrobe. Today, PR chewed me out because your dress for the wedding wasn't what we could show in the pictures we sent to the media."

My face darkened with pain, but I hid it immediately. I was embarrassing him as well. No surprise there. I gave him a small smile. "I don't think it'll change anything."

"What do you mean?"

"Because this is as good as it gets, Declan. You know, I worked hard at looking...you know what?" I lost my patience and threw my hands in the air. "Go without me. My father will be happy. Viv will be happy, and obviously, you'll be happy not to be embarrassed by your wife." I was about to walk away when he grabbed my arm.

Chapter 12

DECLAN

I hurt her feelings. She looked good. She looked good enough to eat in that black dress, but I came from a world where I could tell within seconds if a dress had a designer label on it. And so could my mother and everyone else. She'd be ridiculed; couldn't she understand that? I had to use a different tactic if I needed her to comply.

"What?" she demanded sulkily.

"You look good, sweetheart."

"Yeah, right," she said sullenly. "You look at me like my father does. My mother is half Mexican and half Irish. She got all the Irish genes, but I got the Mexican ones. My skin is dark. My eyes are dark. My hair is big and wild and needs to be tamed. My ass is as big as a house, and my tits...well, I think they're fine, but who knows anymore? I'm not tall like Viv. And I can't wear heels above two inches without tripping and breaking my neck."

Her eyes filled with tears, and she looked forlorn. My gut clenched. I realized I'd just joined the many people who'd told her she was not good enough. Her father, her mother, Viv, and now me.

"It's just an outfit, Esme, nothing more."

I could find something of Viv's that was left behind. Would she be able to fit into it?

"What do you want me to do?" she asked, as if giving up.

I picked up my phone and called Baker. I asked him to send some clothes appropriate for a gallery opening and dinner at Melisse ASAP. We would be 30 minutes late, which was acceptable.

"What's your size?" I asked her while I listened to Baker's list of questions.

She pulled away from me and looked like I had struck her.

"Six," she replied quietly.

Viv was a size two. No way Esme could fit into her sister's clothes.

"Shoes?"

"Six as well."

I let Baker know and hung up.

"We'll have something new for you in a half hour and...."

She looked at me bewildered. "This is my *best* dress. It's a little black dress. How could I mess up an LBD?"

"You didn't mess up anything," I tried to console. "We must consider our status. Do you understand?"

"Of course," she replied. "I'll be in my room. Just let me know when the clothes arrive."

Baker was, as always, supremely efficient, and by the time we made it to the gallery, we were only twenty minutes late. My wife wore a royal blue Marchesa cocktail dress with black Jimmy Choo strappy sandals. Her makeup was still off, but I couldn't fix that, and we didn't have the time for a makeup artist. I'd done my best to make her look like she *could* belong to our family and make sure my mother wouldn't blow a gasket when she saw her.

She was quiet in the Escalade as the driver crawled through Friday evening traffic to Santa Monica from DTLA. Most people I knew would look through their phones while on a drive like this, but Esme looked out of the window. She'd set the Prada purse matching her dress next to her. I had seen her put her glasses, phone, and a Chapstick in it. Viv would have put makeup in her bag because she'd keep touching it up throughout the evening. Not my wife. *She'd never fit in*, I thought. They'd eat her alive for her simplicity. And yet, without professional makeup or hair, and even that business suit black dress, she'd looked...well, like a bright star. Clean and fresh. Authentic.

"The gallery opening is for an up-and-coming artist gaining a lot of attention. He's also a good friend," I informed her. "Are you into art?"

"Yes." She turned to face me. She smiled, but it didn't quite reach her eyes.

"What kind of art?" I was trying to make a conversation to get to a place where I could ask her what the fuck was wrong because something was.

"I love Joan Miro and Wassily Kandinsky," she told me.

"Why?"

I could feel her irritation now, though she masked it. "It's evocative."

"Do you know Senator Rivers?"

"I know of him."

I could talk to a wall if I needed to—that was part of being the C.E.O. of a company, but this woman wasn't making it easy.

I put my hand on hers and felt her hand tighten into a fist. "What's wrong?"

"Nothing."

"Esme, we have to live together for a year; we need to communicate. Something has upset you. Can you tell me what it is?"

She looked at me, her dark eyes brimming with emotion. My heart clenched. I didn't want her to cry. "Why do you care?" Her voice was a whisper.

"Because you're my wife."

"The wrong wife."

I tightened my grip on her hand. "No."

"No?"

"Viv was cheating on me, which makes *her* the wrong wife. You, Esme, are the right wife at the right time. So, please tell me what's bothering you."

She waited a long moment as if determining if she could trust me. "It made me feel small and cheap to change my dress; I felt like you were saying my choices are beneath you."

She turned away. Tears were flowing down her cheeks. I turned her face to me with my hands and looked into her eyes as I wiped the moisture away. "I'm so sorry, Esme. I...you..." I closed my eyes momentarily and tried to be authentic and honest like her. "I didn't want you to be embarrassed; I didn't want *them,* my mother and Viv, to make you feel you were less. And I took the wrong approach and did so myself. Next time, I won't make that mistake. In the future, wear whatever you want."

She was my wife, and as my wife, she could do whatever the fuck she wanted. Wasn't that the privilege of being a Knight? I didn't abide by the rules; why should she?

"Really?" Her glossy pink lips quivered. I couldn't help it; I leaned over and brushed my lips against hers. And she opened her mouth in a gasp, allowing me entry, and I tasted her slowly. I shifted my hands to dive into her silky and lush hair. I angled her head so I could go deeper and explore her mouth. She was spice and mint, and the scent of jasmine was sweet and intoxicating. She was giving and generous. She playfully tangled her tongue with mine, and I was *gone.* I used one hand to hold her head, and the other slipped over her dress. I squeezed a breast and found it to be more than a handful. *Delicious.*

She moaned, and her hands wrapped around my neck. She leaned closer.

I nibbled on her lips, and my hand dipped to her lap and under her dress.

I found her wet and wanting.

"Spread your thighs; let me in," I grunted.

She did as I asked, and I cupped her soaking panties.

"*God*," she moaned.

"You're so wet, sweetheart."

"I am?" she whispered.

"Yes." I moved her panties aside and slid my finger over her. She shivered. I entered her, and she clasped my urgent digit. "You're so soft, so tight, Esme."

I returned to her mouth because I couldn't resist that expression of pleasant surprise like she didn't know it could be like this.

"Please tell me you've had sex before," I groaned when I got two fingers inside her and pumped gently. She'd mentioned something about losing her virginity to a vibrator. And she was so tight.

"Yes."

I leaned back and looked at her. Something about how she reacted told me she was enthusiastic but not experienced.

"How many men?"

"One."

"Just one."

She nodded; her eyes were glazed over because my fingers had found her clit. I wanted her to come.

"Just once," she said.

"You've only had sex once?"

She nodded. "I didn't have time and...oh, *god*." She came suddenly, and her entire body shook. I leaned back to look at her. Her eyes were closed, and tears were rolling down her cheeks. Her lips were open in a moan of pleasure.

"Declan." She opened her eyes, filled with lust.

I pulled my fingers out and tasted her. "Next time, I want a proper taste."

She blushed, and I brushed my lips against her. "Taste yourself, sweetheart."

She did, and my erection throbbed, demanding release. If this were anyone else, I'd have asked for a blow job, but Esme had sex just once, and I didn't know how far I could take this.

"You're so sensual, sweetheart." My heart was pounding in my chest, and I felt something I had never felt before, nearly uncontrollable desire. The only reason I was holding back was her inexperience. No woman had turned me on this way, to the point of violence. Not even Viv, who was a dynamo in bed. The sex we had was fantastic, but this was...different, purer, and dirtier, all at the same time.

"Esme, are you okay?"

She nodded, and then her lips stretched into a smile. "I've never had an orgasm without my vibrator before."

Because her pouty lips were designed for it, I kissed her again. "We'll make sure you don't miss your vibrator."

She didn't smile this time and pulled away suddenly.

"Esme?"

She shook her head. "Will we have sex?"

I could still smell and taste her orgasm. It was driving me out of my mind. "Oh, yes. After what we just did, don't you want to?"

"Yes, I want to. But, Declan, I...am not," she stopped talking and seemed to despair.

"Not what?"

"I don't know how to make you come like you did for me," she confessed. "I don't talk dirty...I mean, I'm happy to learn, but I...I don't know how to do for you what you did for me."

I grinned. "Esme, you're sexy as fuck, and you have nothing to worry about." I took her hand and put it over my erection. "Feel that? I'm just about ready to come in my pants."

She stroked me, and I groaned.

"Can I make you come with my hands?" she asked.

I looked out of the Escalade window and determined it would take another fifteen minutes to reach our location, enough time for a hand job. Hell, the way I felt, it would take her two strokes to make me come.

I unzipped my suit pants and took her hand, putting it on my underwear.

"Make me come, Esme."

She was eager and unpracticed, which only added to the eroticism of the moment. She pulled me out, and her thumb touched the tip and rubbed my precum. She brought her thumb to her mouth, and I just about came.

"You taste like me," she said in awe and then bent down to take my erection in her mouth. She tasted me slowly, and it was agony not to pull her down hard and ram my cock to the back of her throat. The combination of sensuality and inexperience was heady. I buried my hands in her hair, not directing but enjoying her.

She took me deep, and my head was about to float off. She pulled away, coughing.

"That looks way easier in porn films."

She used her hands on me, and I leaned back, closed my eyes, and enjoyed the naïve manner in which she jerked me off. Her technique was not great, but her touch was incendiary.

"Declan, am I doing it right?" she asked tentatively.

I smiled. "Harder, Esme. Just a little harder." When she did as I asked, I sighed. "That's right. Just like that."

And then, as if in a dream, I felt my orgasm climb up from the base of my spine and explode into her hands.

"You are beautiful," she said almost reverently, her eyes wide with knowledge and excitement.

I leaned over and kissed her.

"That was wonderful," I told her because I already knew that Esme needed a lot of positive reinforcement.

We'd made a mess. I pulled out a handkerchief and cleaned up.

She wore a secret smile as we got out of the car. Her lipstick was long gone, and I didn't give a shit. Esme didn't care about clothes and makeup, and I would not be the one to change her.

Chapter 13

ESME

I had an orgasm with Declan. My feelings of insecurity had floated right out the window as I'd felt his fingers inside me.

I held on to the arm he offered because my legs were wobbly. I dug my nails into his forearm when I felt the first sting of camera lights.

"It's just some photographers," he whispered, brushing his lips against my ear.

I nodded, feeling unsure.

"I must look terrible."

He tucked my hand in his arm tighter and shook his head. "You look beautiful."

I ignored his comment. "Keep holding on to me because I'm going to break my neck in these shoes."

"Next time, we'll let Baker know you prefer a shorter heel."

"Or flats?" I asked wistfully.

He laughed and kissed me, brushing his lips against mine. "Or flats."

The photographers went wild, screaming his name and mine.

Esme, please look this way.

One more kiss, Declan.

He didn't comply, and we walked into the chic Santa Monica gallery. It was a dramatic space with glass walls on the far side with a view of the Pacific, gently frolicking on the sand.

My father was there, as was Declan's mother. Their spouses were absent. Gerald, Declan's father, was still in Asia, and my mother was under the weather. Had he asked Monica not to join as he'd suggested I didn't either?

"Hello, dear." Nina did the air-kissing thing, and I responded in kind.

My father nodded at me and then took my arm. "Excuse us."

He all but dragged me away. "What are you doing here?"

"Declan said that he wanted me here," I replied meekly. He was angry, and I could feel it flow through his fingers onto my arm. I was glad the dress had long sleeves; otherwise, the marks would show.

"You weren't supposed to tell him I didn't want you here. You were supposed to have a fucking headache," he retorted.

"I'm sorry, Daddy."

He leaned closer to me. "The damage is done. Wear some makeup because you look terrible, and keep your mouth shut. Let Viv and Dec lead the way during dinner. Got it?"

I nodded.

He let go of me and went back to Nina. I looked around, seeking Declan, and found him beside Viv. She wore an ivory silk dress that looked like it was made for her, which it probably was. She stood nearly as tall as Declan in white strappy sandals and held a small white clutch. She was dressed like a bride.

I decided not to go to him while he talked to his ex-fiancée and instead walked the gallery halls to enjoy the art.

The brochure told me that artists like Picasso and Oswaldo Guayasamín influenced Phoenix Blackwood. I loved the art of Guayasamín, an Ecuadorian painter, and the influence was apparent. Phoenix, however, had a more playful style that should've been inconsistent with the starkness of his black and brown paintings—but he made it work.

"Hello," a voice said behind me, and I turned.

"Your paintings are lovely." I immediately recognized the man wearing black pants and a black shirt from the brochure photo.

"Thank you." He held out his hand, and I shook it.

"I'm Esme Hartley...well, Knight."

"Dec's wife. I heard."

Phoenix looked toward where my husband stood with my sister and smiled. "Quite a scandal. Engaged to one sister and married to another. So, who dumped whom, Mrs. Knight?"

I felt my shoulders slump. I had hoped we'd talk about his art, but he, like everyone else, was interested in the gossip.

I turned to the painting I was standing in front of. "I like how you have the lovers fighting in this painting, but it's just a small fight; their relationship will not be impacted."

"Yes," he smirked, "I wanted to paint the end of a fight right before the makeup sex."

The way he spoke made me uncomfortable. First, the gossip, and now the sneer about sex.

I wish I could've walked away, but who could I go to? Not my husband, who looked like he was enjoying his wine and the conversation he was having with his ex-fiancée. Not my father. I touched my arm, still sore from his grip, or my mother-in-law, who probably disliked me just a little less than my father did, and only because she hadn't known me very long.

"Mr. Blackwood, are you trying to make me uneasy?" I asked bluntly.

Amusement was apparent in his eyes. "Yes. I'm sorry. It was petty, but I'm friends with Dec *and* Viv, and I don't know what went down because they're both pretty tight-lipped about the whole thing. I care for both of them, and I know he loves Viv. Are you pregnant or something?"

Loves not loved.

"Something," I whispered, looking to see how I could escape.

"When I saw you come in together, do you know what I thought?" He didn't wait for me to respond, "That you seem incongruous together. Now, those two," he inclined his head to Viv and Declan, "look like they were made for each other."

"You think he married the wrong sister?" I was to meet another friend and colleague of Declan's at the dinner, Mateo Silva—that meeting, I feared, would probably be like this. Their friends would rally around them, painting me as the villain who stole Viv's future husband. They hadn't made the news of her quickie marriage public, but they had announced my marriage to Declan.

"*He* thinks...or maybe knows he married the wrong sister. Don't you agree?" He tilted his head toward Declan and Viv again. They were now looking at art, her hand resting against his forearm, her body leaning toward him. He seemed comfortable holding her, much like Declan had held me when we'd stepped out of the car *after* he'd given me an epic orgasm.

It shouldn't have hurt because I was so used to being second...no tenth or fifteenth best to Viv, but it did; and not just because of the intimacy we'd just shared, but I was starting to like Declan, beyond the childish crush I used to have. I had begun to genuinely appreciate and want him.

Stupid, stupid, Esme. Always wanting things she can't have.

"Since you're such a good friend to Declan and Viv, maybe you should discuss this with them. I barely know you, and as much as I appreciate your art, this conversation is inappropriate."

He seemed surprised by my response, stuck his hands in his dress pants pockets, and eyed me carefully.

"Phoenix," a female voice called to him.

"Excuse me, that's my agent. It was nice meeting you, Esme Knight."

I didn't reply likewise because meeting him hadn't been *nice* at all. I turned my attention to the painting in front of me, now blurred because of the unshed tears in my eyes.

Chapter 14

DECLAN

I was still in love with Viv. It was a harsh realization, if not surprising. What was astounding was that I'd just had one of the best make-out sessions since I was a randy teenager in the backseat of a car with Viv's little sister. I was having trouble navigating the dichotomy of my feelings.

What also was startling was the pinch of jealousy I felt when I saw Phoenix talk to Esme. I would've walked up to them, but Viv leaned against me, and her closeness was a comfort after strenuous days.

"Do you hate me, Dec?" Viv asked as she snuggled closer.

I felt her breast against my arm, and I thought about the fullness of Esme's breasts in the palm of my hands.

"No, Viv. I could never hate you."

"I still love you."

"I know. I still love you too."

"I'm such a fool, Dec. I got confused. I was afraid we were together for the business merger and not because we were in love. I was in San Francisco for that case these past months, and you were traveling. I was vulnerable. I'm so sorry."

She was sincere, and I patted her hand. "What's done is done, Angel."

"You married Esme," she accused.

"You knew I'd have to."

She nodded and burrowed closer. "I miss us, Dec."

"I miss us too."

"What's it like to be at home with her?"

"Nothing like it was with you," I confessed. It was different—not bad or good—but different, peaceful. No rushing around. No competing phone calls at the dinner table.

"I don't want to lose you."

"You could never lose me."

"Even though I cheated on you?"

I felt my heart contract. "Yes." Because love was all-consuming and all-forgiving, and I loved Viv. No, I couldn't have sex with Esme, *I thought as I held the love of my life close to me, ignoring Phoenix chatting up Esme at the other end of the gallery.*

"Give me some time, Dec," Viv pleaded. "Please."

*"You have a lot to make up for, Viv. It won't be like it was,"
I warned her. She'd have to fucking grovel. "You'll have to
convince me you love me; this time, it's forever."*

*"Oh, I will, Dec. I...already talked to a partner at the law firm.
We're going to work on an annulment. It wasn't very smart of
me. Reckless. I regret it so much."*

*"Let's take it one moment at a time, Angel." I held her close,
inhaling her scent. I had her again where I wanted her, and yet,
it was the smell of jasmine that filled me from within.*

·❤·❤·❤·❤·❤·

Esme drove with her father and my mother, while I went with
Viv to Melisse. Mateo would meet us at the restaurant with
Senator Rivers and his wife.

I felt guilt course through me as Viv sat where Esme just had,
where she'd given me one of the best hand jobs of my life. Viv
and I had sex in the backseat of many limousines and cars. We'd
fucked like rabbits when we'd first started dating, regardless of
where we were. However, after the first six months, I had to
admit, the sex had become relegated to a few times a week. But
that's what happened to couples, right? They got busy with life.
The lust for early sex developed into the comfort of making love
in a long-term relationship.

Viv talked about the merger between Hartley Industries and
Knight Tech—and how she navigated that along with several
lawyers at her law firm. She was capable as a lawyer, impressive.
I felt a surge of pride: my smart fiancée, the one who knew how
to get her clients what they wanted.

Besides that, this was a woman who shone on my arm. The way she dressed and carried herself. Her tall frame and those deep-blue eyes. Her makeup was spot-on and elegant. Her Valentino gown was a beautiful second skin. Esme, in her Marchesa dress, paled in comparison. She'd looked better in that shitty black dress—more comfortable. And that's why the marriage would end when this year was up, and I'd find my way back to the woman who was next to me. This woman who had lost her way—but I'd forgive her. *Oh, I'd make her pay*, I thought with satisfaction, but we'd get back together, and I'd make sure she never strayed again.

Chapter 15

ESME

I felt like I had gone a few rounds with a heavy-weight fighter after I got out of the car. Both my father and Nina Knight had commented on my dress and that it was appropriate; however, the hair and makeup were not. According to Nina, a Marchesa was wasted on me because I didn't carry it well.

She seemed to be egged on by my father, who constantly demeaned me.

"One would imagine you'd know how to wear makeup," he shook his head. "Take a class or, even better, ask Viv to teach you. By the way, did you call her?"

I shook my head. "I'll talk to her today, Daddy, when I see her at the restaurant."

"After dinner," Nina warned, "Not before or during. We need her and Dec to be at their best when talking to Senator Rivers. His wife Cecily is into Native American art, so Mateo will sit beside her—he's very knowledgeable. Esme, you will sit between your father and Mateo. That way, you won't be able to get into any trouble."

What trouble could I get into in a Michelin-star restaurant? I had researched Melisse, and it was a two-Michelin star restaurant that was near impossible to get a reservation at for lesser mortals, not the Knights.

Next time I would come up with a stomach bug or a headache, I promised myself. This was not worth an orgasm in the backseat of a car because as we were driving, Viv and Declan probably did that and more together. My insecurities that had vanished during those minutes with Declan had come right back to eat at me.

Why had he touched me? I wondered. And why had he been so kind and understanding if he was going to make it obvious to everyone that he was with Viv again, regardless of how she treated him? Was this love? It probably was. I loved my parents, and they treated me with the same indifference as Viv did Declan.

Like Tina said, *what's love got to do with it?* Absolutely nothing.

So, I needed to be careful and lay down some rules.

1: Don't have sex with your husband or... have any sexual relations with him, finger orgasms included.

2: Don't fall in love with your husband, even if he's kind, because it's all for show; remember that.

3: Find a job and save enough money to escape your family forever.

Maybe I should've demanded some money at the end of the marriage—but I wasn't a mercenary. I needed enough to pay my bills and do the work that made me happy, and what made me happy was taking care of people. I tried so hard to care for my family and now Declan—but to what end? They didn't even notice. No, I'd help the people at the Safe Harbor Women's Shelter and build my resume. Then, I could get a job with L.A. County, where I could do so much more. I would work with single mothers and help them raise their children with dignity and heal the spirits of battered women and children.

Viv and Declan were laughing as they stepped out of his car when my father grabbed my arm again, and I suppressed a wince because he was hurting me. Letting him know wouldn't do any good because he'd just do it harder. I knew from experience.

"Esme, be careful, and don't embarrass me. Got it?"

"Yes, Daddy."

He walked away, and I put my left hand on my right arm to soothe it. Declan's eyes went flinty as he walked up to me.

"Hi," he said.

I looked up at him, clearing all the doubts and stress of the evening from my eyes. "Hi."

"Are you okay?"

I nodded. Why was Declan asking? He didn't care. What had happened in the car seemed like a lifetime ago—when I had foolishly thought we'd have a chance. But then Viv walked over, and that was that.

"Hi, Esme." Viv approached us and slid her hand into the crook of my husband's arm. He didn't shake her off but looked at me with concerned eyes.

"Viv, you look beautiful." She did, too.

She laughed softly. "Thanks. I feel silk is always a good idea."

"Do you think we could have a quick chat after dinner?" I requested it because I knew my father would ask me.

She shrugged. "We'll see. Dec, we better get inside."

I thought *I* was his wife, and he should escort me as I walked behind them, watching his perfect ass and her supremely tight one.

A man stepped next to me and held the door. From the quick hellos I gathered, this was Mateo Silva, Knight Tech's Chief Technology Officer and a total hottie. He was as tall as Declan, around six-two. His skin was the color of a chocolate latte, his eyes were light gray, and his body looked like it went to the gym often. His nose looked like it had been broken before, making me wonder what had happened. I'd seen such breaks in my career working with battered women and children.

"How are you doing?" He walked with me as we followed the maître d' to our table.

"Very well, thank you. I'm Esme."

"Mateo."

"I believe I'm supposed to sit next to you."

Mateo grinned. "You know Nina Knight, she'll slot us all away as she sees fit."

"And Mrs. Rivers is going to be sitting on your other side. She's interested in Native American art, as are you, so ignore me and keep her company." We took our seats, except for the Senator and his wife, who were running late.

"Ignore you?" He sat down next to me; his shoulder brushed against mine.

"Well, you won't be impolite if you focused only on Mrs. Rivers."

"I would be," Mateo declared and then looked up at the server, "An old-fashioned with rye."

I struggled with the menu without my glasses, but I knew if I took them out of my purse, my father would make me pay for that faux pas. I ignored the menu and asked for a glass of champagne. A place like this should have an excellent selection by the glass. "I'll have a—"

"She's fine with water," my father decided for me. "Let's try not to get drunk on our first important dinner." He sounded playful, like we had a close relationship, and I was an alcoholic.

The server stepped away, and Mateo leaned in. "What would you like to drink?"

"Water is fine." I felt stiff and uncomfortable. I also wanted to have a good cry. Senator Rivers was supposed to sit between Viv and Dec, and until he arrived, they sat together discussing how they'd run the conversation—who'd say what and when. This wasn't the first time they were tag teaming at a social event where business was to be discussed. They were a team, and I was an outsider.

"Come on, Esme, you're of age. I think you can have a drink."
Mateo's tone was fierce, even a little judgmental, and I felt my
shoulders slump. There was no winning. If I ordered a glass of
champagne, my father would be livid; if I didn't, Mateo would
think I was a doormat.

I didn't know Mateo, but I did know my father. I could already
feel his nails digging into my forearm again if I refused him.
He never hit me anymore, and we didn't talk about the past.
Everyone would say that Julien Hartley would never stoop to
domestic violence, but he left marks on me and terrorized me
all the same.

I had been living with little interference except for social
events that my father deemed essential for me to attend. But
now I was married to Declan, and there would be no respite
from my family. I'd have to watch as Declan and Viv got back
together, which looked imminent if I had to go by how they were
cooing at each other. She'd cheated on him, and he'd said she
was the wrong wife, and yet, here we were.

"Esme?" Mateo asked again.

I turned to him and smiled nervously. "Mr. Silva..."

"Mateo."

"Mateo, it would displease my father if I drank alcohol. I
understand you feel I should do what I want, and I do, but I'd
very much like not to upset him for the short time I'm in his
company. I'll also ignore the judgment in your voice because you
don't know me, and you have no business judging me."

I expected Mateo to get upset, but he grinned brightly.

"You're direct."

"It prevents miscommunication."

"I'm sorry if I sounded judgmental. I don't like your father, nor do I like how bossy he was. And since we're being direct, I also don't like how your husband is pretending you don't exist while he canoodles with the woman who was cheating on him for most of their relationship."

It saved me from responding when everyone at the table stood. Senator Rivers and his wife had arrived. José Rivers was tall with silver hair and chocolate brown skin attesting to his Latin roots; Cecily Rivers was African American with naturally curly hair tied away from her face.

We sat once the introductions were made, and shortly after that, the servers brought in the first of the six courses on the chef's menu. My father was too engrossed in talking to Nina Knight, but that didn't give me the courage to savor the white Burgundy served with the Halibut mousse amuse-bouche. If he found out, there would be hell to pay.

"Esme, I hear you studied social work." Cecily leaned forward, and Mateo moved his chair back so the senator's wife and I could have direct eye contact.

"Yes, ma'am. I just finished a Master's program in social work at the University of Washington," I confirmed.

"Impressive. And what are your plans? I expect you'll get involved with the Knight Foundation?"

My father and Nina Knight's ear pricked at that, and I was suddenly at the center of Cecily and Mateo's attention. A place I hated as much as I disliked wearing a designer gown for this dinner.

"I'd love to, but I'm committed to working for the Caruso Foundation. Maria is a good friend of mine, and I will help them with a women's shelter."

"Safe Harbor?" she asked, and I nodded.

Please don't say Skid Row; please say nothing about Safe Harbor, which would anger my father.

"Now, that's a place that's changing people's lives," she attested. I sighed in relief. "The Caruso family is known for their good works."

I nodded. "Hundred percent of all the money donated goes directly to support their projects, which I admire."

"They're so committed to taking care of the community. Do you know Mark as well?" Cecily continued.

I smiled at Mark's name; instant warmth showed on my face. "He's my closest friend, and it's through him that I met Maria."

My father stepped in then and steered the conversation away from me to other topics.

Mateo ignored my father's pointed looks at him to take charge of Mrs. Rivers and seemed blissfully unaware of them.

"How is married life treating you, Esme?" he asked softly, his face close to mine. I could smell the whiskey and wine on his breath.

"I met the artist Phoenix earlier, and he was...well, keen on ensuring that I had not come in between Declan and the love of his life. Is that what you're asking me about?"

"I doubt Viv is the love of his life. A woman who so easily discards a man she promises to love...that woman is not the love of anyone's life," he scoffed.

Viv and Declan were talking to Senator Rivers, who seemed to be enjoying the conversation very much.

"They look perfect together," I whispered enviously. Declan Knight had always been out of my reach and never more so now that we were married and lived together.

Mateo looked at me with narrowed eyes. "Do you want him?"

The question surprised me. "I...I..." I stuttered.

"Do you?" he asked again.

"I don't know that what I want matters."

"Sure, it does. If you want something, get it. If you don't want Declan, who cares who he fucks."

Did I care who he fucked? Yes, I did. He was my husband, and our marriage, as dysfunctional as it was to me, was still something to be revered. This marriage was a business contract, but deep down, I knew I wanted a real marriage with Declan.

I watched him laugh when Viv said something, and I silenced my heart. Viv was good at charming people, and I was good at curbing my needs.

Chapter 16

DECLAN

Mateo was sitting too close to Esme. I needed to catch up on what Viv and the Senator discussed because my attention was divided. This was not who I was. Business always came first, but I was jealous that Mateo sat beside her, enjoying her smiles.

She wasn't drinking wine—probably because her father said she shouldn't. She liked wine; I knew that even though we'd lived together for just a few days, yet she'd done what her father ordered. Julien had been angry with her; that was for all to see in how he talked to her with barely repressed fury. I thought he'd be grateful that she'd married me so he could retire with his business in good hands and his future income secured. But when I'd called him to tell him that Esme would join us for dinner with the Senator, he'd advised me against it.

"Esme is not Viv. She'll say something stupid. Monica is like that as well. I'm careful where I take those two."

The way he'd put down his wife and daughter was cruel, I'd thought then, yet I'd ignored Esme all evening. Especially after what we'd done in the car on our way here. At the remembered feel of her on my fingers, I felt my cock tighten. Viv was sitting on the other side of the Senator. Otherwise, she'd have noticed and attributed it to her. She would not have been wrong in the past. Watching her in powerful lawyer mode always made me hard, but today...there was guilt for how I treated Esme. Mateo had said that I should show compassion. I had failed at that. Fuck compassion: I was humiliating her here at dinner. I should've insisted we sit together. Newlyweds and all that.

"Senator, we will be happy to provide funds for some of the mayor's homelessness programs," Viv said when I returned my attention to her.

"The program needs corporate sponsors," the Senator agreed. "And my wife is a staunch supporter."

"Absolutely," Cecily Rivers said. "Esme, have you worked with homelessness?"

Esme looked like she wanted the earth to open and swallow her, but only momentarily. She gathered herself as I'd seen her do so many times in the past two days. The pressure of continually wearing a mask and not letting the fear or sadness of the moment show must be immense. How did she handle that regularly?

"Yes, in Seattle," she replied and stiffened. Her father leaned toward her and whispered something. I saw his fingers grab her arm. He'd done that before, and I hadn't liked it then or now. There was malice in the way he touched her.

"I've heard good things about the Seattle program. Tell us about it," Senator Rivers demanded.

Esme nodded at her father as he said something to her and smiled as if he was being friendly. "The program in Seattle worked closely with SAMHSA...Substance Abuse and Mental Health Services is a federal program. They offer grant programs and services, which assist in setting up facilities to help men, women, youth, and even families struggling with mental health and substance use issues. And the Housing First program, with targeted rental and housing subsidies, also had a major impact."

"What was your role?" the Senator asked.

Julien once again squeezed Esme's arm, and she flinched but kept the smile on her face. "I worked with juveniles aging out of the system to make sure that they went to a halfway home where they would continue to have supervision and would also gain skills through training programs. The goal is to ensure these children attend community college or get trained for a job."

"How many children did this program work with?" Senator Rivers asked.

"Oh, easily, about two hundred young adults every month, and some months it was more. We always had to make do with stretched funds and resources. We continually had to prioritize what we could and couldn't do."

"That must've been hard." Cicely appeared to be impressed with Esme.

My phone lit up with a text message from Viv that I read discreetly. *Get them off this topic. Esme will keep talking about this, and we need the Senator to support the tech bill.*

I looked up to see Esme in her element. "Of course, working with young adults who've had a tough childhood is never easy, but when you can turn their lives around, that's the reward and fully worth it. And honestly, they've had a harder time than the social worker."

"Esme is going to work at Safe Harbor," Cicely told her husband.

He grinned. "An excellent program. Maria Caruso has been more serious about charity programs than her father. We are very impressed with that whole family."

"The Knight Foundation supports many good causes as well," Nina piped in.

"Of course, of course," the Senator realized that he'd admired another wealthy donor and ignored the one taking him out for a six-course Michelin star dinner. "The Knight family is always at the forefront of innovation. Why are Viv and Dec talking about the tech bill, which will make bringing raw semiconductor materials from around the world easier to the United States?"

The topic quickly shifted back to the bill and the cause of the dinner.

Esme fell silent again. Before the last course, she excused herself. I wanted to follow her, but her father beat me to it. If I left the table too, there would be too few Knights left, so I stayed.

When they returned, Esme's face was drawn. And even though she'd painted that awful plastic smile on her face, I'd already learned to differentiate that from the real deal.

After dinner, I was eager to get into the car with Esme and talk to her, but Viv insisted on a drink at a nearby bar called The Misfit. Mateo said he would leave, and Julien took that opportunity to suggest he drop Esme off.

I watched her get into Mateo's Maserati that the valet had dropped off and followed my ex-fiancée to a bar for a drink I didn't want.

Chapter 17

ESME

M ateo came to the penthouse.

"Would you like a drink?" I asked politely, hoping he would refuse. It was just after ten, early for a Friday night—but I was exhausted and ready to crash.

"Yes. Some wine, please."

I had only a little Chablis left from the one bottle I bought. I had checked out Declan's massive wine fridge that housed over four hundred bottles of delicious wine—how could I not? But it felt wrong to take his wine. The wine I coveted cost at least a few hundred dollars, and I didn't feel comfortable opening it without his permission.

Mateo seemed to sense that and sighed. "Esme, this is your house now. His wine is your wine for however long you're married. Just get a bottle out and open it. Or I can do it if you're too afraid."

That was just the right button to push. I was tired of being afraid...of my father and my husband.

Declan wouldn't even care, would he? He had a lot of money; a few hundred dollars would mean nothing to him. I pulled out my glasses from the little bag that matched with the Marchesa dress and went to look for a bottle of wine in Declan's wine fridge.

I expertly used the corkscrew to open the bottle and smelled the cork with delight. When the world was not making sense, and everything was complicated, one had to search for joy in the small things. This was going to be *the* perfect bottle of wine. I found two wine glasses and poured a taste for each of us.

"Amazing," Mateo said.

I let the wine inundate all my senses. It was a beautiful Pinot Noir from 2018. It still had fresh fruit flavors combined with the minerality *Côte de Nuits* was known for.

"Lovely," I agreed.

I filled our glasses. Mateo sat on one of the bar stools at the kitchen counter, and I stood on the other side.

"You can sit next to me; I don't bite." Mateo winked.

I felt self-conscious. I came onto the other side, removed my shoes, and sat in relief. "I'm not used to wearing heels."

"I guess not. In your profession, you probably wear something comfortable.

"I live my life in sneakers," I admitted. "From a business perspective, how did the evening go?"

"I don't know," Mateo confessed. "They invited me to keep you company."

"I thought you were there to engage Mrs. Rivers in conversation."

"I had instructions from both Nina and Dec. Nina wanted me to care for Mrs. Rivers, and Dec wanted me next to you."

I frowned. "Why?"

"Declan knew that he'd have to focus on the senator and wanted to ensure you weren't sitting alone getting bored."

I didn't like that one bit. "You were my babysitter?"

"Yes." He didn't deny it. "Does that bother you?"

"Yes. I'm an adult. I don't need a babysitter."

"Your father thinks you do. *He* wanted me there to ensure you didn't screw up the evening."

I gasped at his directness. I knew what my father thought of me, and it embarrassed me that Mateo, a stranger, now also knew.

"Do you do that a lot? Screw up social situations?" He sipped his wine.

His gaze was intent on me, and I was confident Mateo Silva didn't like me much. He probably also preferred Viv, but unlike the artist earlier in the evening, Mateo knew the truth about my marriage and the reasons, and yet he was hostile—like I had a choice. I should've said I was tired and called it a night. I shouldn't have been polite. I should've known this man would not become a friend.

"Sometimes I'm known to talk too much about things I'm passionate about." I attempted levity and failed. Both physically and emotionally, I felt exhausted. And my reserves were low. It was taking more and more effort to keep my beatific façade.

"And what are you passionate about, Esme?"

He was condescending me. He made me feel small and inadequate as Declan did, as my father did. Mateo was in an impeccable suit—probably bespoke while I was in a dress I didn't feel comfortable in. He wore soft Italian leather shoes, and my feet were bare, and I hadn't had a pedicure in ages. His eyes were full of contempt and disgust; mine were ready to weep.

"I'm passionate about my work. I'm passionate about public policy and social welfare. And I love wine. I can talk about wine until the cows come home." I had a lifetime of evading hostility without showing my fears—by staying on topic and keeping it light.

"Wine? How come?"

"I was raised in a vineyard. My grandmother grew Pinot Noir in the Santa Rita Hills. She sold the grapes, and I grew up playing in the vines." My mood softened as I thought about my *abuela*. "My grandfather was Irish, and my grandmother was from Mexico. He came to California and learned to grow and make wine. After he passed, *abuela* stopped making wine and sold that part of the business to a neighbor. In all honesty, Grandpa was never a great winemaker—but he loved it all the same."

"When did your parents ship you off to your grandmother?" He seemed angry now, and I couldn't tell why.

"They didn't *ship* me off," I protested, even though that's precisely what they had done. "It was just that my parents were *very* busy. Viv is older than me, and I was a surprise baby. My mother was traveling a lot with Daddy, so they decided when I was eight to send me to my grandmother. I had an amazing childhood."

Mateo nodded. "And you don't mind that your family didn't want you around?"

I closed my eyes and set my wine glass down. I stood up then. "Mateo, I feel you're very irritated with me."

"I'm not. Far from it. We're just having a conversation."

"It feels like an interrogation. It's been some very long days for me recently. Would you mind if I went to bed?"

Mateo nodded. "Sure. I can see myself out once I'm done." He held up his half-full glass of wine.

I hesitated. Wasn't it rude to leave him by himself?

"Go, Esme. Get some rest. I'm going to be fine."

"Okay. Goodnight, Mateo."

I was walking away when he muttered. "You don't seem to mind your parents not wanting you, and now you don't seem to mind that Dec doesn't want you. What kind of person are you?"

I felt my temper rise. I turned around; my hands curled into fists. "Exhausted. That's the person I am. I did not create this situation. I'm just trying to make the best of it. And no one is making it easy."

"Why did you say yes to marrying your sister's fiancée?"

"Because my mother asked me," I stated. "I care about my family and need to be there for them. Isn't that what one is supposed to do?"

He came up to me then and stood in front of me. I was probably a sight; my hair was all over the place, my eyes tired, and the makeup I had inexpertly put on was long gone. I stood with my shoes in one hand and a glass of wine in the other.

Mateo put his hands on my shoulders. "Esme, you cannot let everyone walk all over you. I know you're young. Dec, Viv, I, we're all older than you, but you shouldn't let us take advantage of you."

"What would you have me do?" I asked desperately.

"When I was an asshole, you should've asked me to shut up and mind my business."

I gaped at him. "Right! Can you imagine what my father would say? And what would Declan say?"

"He thinks you're a doormat, Esme; show him who you are."

I looked down; my eyes were filled with tears. "And what if I am just what he thinks I am? A doormat?"

Mateo brushed his lips on my forehead. "I'm sorry I upset you."

The front door opened then, and Declan stepped in. He looked at Mateo and me, standing close. I wanted to pull away, but Mateo didn't let me.

He brushed a kiss on my cheek. "Thank you for a wonderful evening, Esme. Have a good night."

Declan was furious, and his anger was palpable.

I stepped away and smiled uneasily.

"Goodnight, Mateo." I turned to face Declan and braced myself, "Goodnight, Declan."

"I'll send our guest on his way and come to your room," Declan said pointedly. "We need to have a conversation."

I felt deflated and walked into my room. I could make no one happy. Everyone wanted me to be someone else, something else. Except for *Abuela*, no one accepted me the way I was.

Don't be a doormat.

Be assertive.

Don't talk too much.

Just shut up and be part of the background.

Dress properly.

What the hell are you wearing?

Stand up for yourself.

Sit down and shut up.

Chapter 18

DECLAN

"What the fuck, Mateo?" I approached him as he sat on a bar stool and picked up a red wine.

"I was enjoying a glass of wine with your wife while you were eye-fucking your ex-fiancée."

"Or were *you* eye-fucking *my* wife?" I walked into the kitchen and pulled out an empty glass. I poured some wine for myself and sat down next to him.

"I like her, Dec," he mused. "She's a nice person getting fucking railroaded by everyone in her life. Her parents, her sister, and now you."

"Why the fuck are you so interested? You just met her, for god's sake." I hated that he was right and that he cared more about my wife than I did.

"I don't know. Maybe because she's a social worker and I have a soft spot for them. Maybe because what you're doing to her is unfair, and it's pissing me off."

"I'm doing *nothing* to her."

"You spent the evening ignoring her, Dec. Everyone could see that. Viv enjoyed that very much."

I drank my wine but said nothing. Mateo was right; Viv had loved how the evening turned out.

"You know she's always had a crush on you, don't you?" Viv said as we sat alone at the bar after dinner; her father and my mother had left us to "reconcile." Subtle as a chainsaw!

"Did she?" I didn't know that.

"Sure," she grinned. "When we started dating, it was a thing. My father and I joked about it."

Which meant they made fun of Esme. Why did they dislike her so much?

"She's nice, Viv," I felt compelled to say. "She's been pleasant, and there's no drama."

"That's because she's hoping she can get you. Tonight, you made it clear to her that whatever may have happened between us, and I get it, I'm at fault; she can't come between us." Viv held my hand.

Since she'd told me about her marriage, I'd been waiting for her to regret it and return to me. And here she was, telling me she was filing for an annulment. I should've danced with joy, but I was conflicted for many reasons, one of them being that Esme was legally my fucking wife.

"She's not trying to come between us, Viv. She's trying to make the best of an unpleasant situation."

"My little sister is good at that," Viv said scornfully. "Always trying to make the best of everything. I know you think she's sweet, but what she is, is dumb. How on earth she thought she'd be able to make you find her interesting is beyond me."

But Esme never thought that. She'd told me she knew how I looked and how she looked, and there was no way we'd be a match—no way I'd see her. She had already decided that I'd never be hers. And, yet, in the car, she'd been passionate and, without knowing it, luscious as fuck. When she came, her face flushed, I'd desperately wanted to part her legs and taste her. I wanted to feel her clit throb against my tongue.

I shook my head to ward off those memories. No way. Viv was here. She was being petty and jealous, but she was here, on her knees, begging me to take her back.

And I would.

Mateo finished his drink and left without saying goodnight or goodbye. He was annoyed with me. He was the better person as he'd always been. He didn't play games. I used to think he was naïve, but I knew now that being honest cost him nothing—but deceiving someone or not being true to himself was too expensive for Mateo.

I finished my wine, left the empty glass on the counter, and walked to Esme's bedroom. I opened the door immediately after knocking, not waiting for a response. She was in a pair of white pajama shorts and a white tank top. I could see her nipples strain against the fabric.

She was standing by her bed, looking at her right arm.

I saw what she was looking at and felt everything tighten within me. There were finger marks patterned one over another. There were bruises, and the skin was broken in several places where Julien's nails had dug in.

She froze when she saw me and pulled a wrap on the bed to cover her arms.

"What the fuck is this?" I pulled the wrap away and examined her arm. "What the fuck, Esme?"

"It's nothing. I'm clumsy and bang into things. Happens all the time."

My eyes bore into hers. "I thought you didn't lie."

She swallowed. "It's not... it's not what you think. I bruise easily."

"Has your father done this to you before?" I demanded. Her arm was mottled in purple, green, and yellow. The broken skin was where nails had dug in. How hard had her father grabbed her?

"No. He just gripped me too hard without knowing the impact."

Yeah, right! I'd seen her father's face when he'd talked to Esme. He *had* meant to do this.

"Be honest with me, Esme."

She pulled away. "I'm being honest with you. Daddy didn't mean to hurt me. I'm just sensitive, is all. Declan, I'm drained. Would it be okay to talk tomorrow? I need to get some sleep."

I ignored her tired plea. We needed to discuss what we did earlier in the evening.

"Esme, I want to apologize for what happened in the car?"

Her back straightened. "We both were equally responsible for that."

"No. You're inexperienced, almost a virgin, and I'm not. I carried a higher responsibility. I'm sorry. Please know it'll never happen again."

Her tears shimmered for an instant, and then her eyes went clear. She knew how to control her emotions, and I felt pride surge. Not everyone could get a hold of themselves in this way; I had learned, but it had taken years. I could never have pulled it off when I was twenty-three.

"Then I'm sorry, too." Esme picked up the wrap I had discarded onto the bed and pulled it around her. "I should've resisted, which I didn't. I promise it'll never happen again."

Never happen again! Is that what I wanted?

"You think you can control yourself around me?" I wanted to push her buttons. Mateo had just torn me a new one for mistreating her, and here I was doing it again.

"Yes." Her voice was a whisper, and her gaze fell to the floor. "I have to."

I lifted her chin to look at me. "What do you mean you have to?"

"You're hers." She smiled weakly. "You're not mine to keep. If I'm not careful, I'll get hurt. I'd much rather not do that."

"How would you get hurt?" I coaxed. I wanted to kiss her again. Those lips she'd been licking and biting were ripe and pouty as if waiting to be claimed.

"I... I'm not experienced as you said, and I may mistake sex for an emotional relationship which would—"

I dropped her chin with a jerk. "You know what we did in the car was physical release and nothing more." She was right. I didn't need her to become some lovesick puppy. That had happened a few times before. I could ignore those women and block them from my life; I wouldn't be able to do that with the woman living in my home, wearing my wedding ring.

"I know."

Since I wanted her to feel that way, I wasn't sure why I felt something die inside me for her to think that making her come and having her bring me to a climax was only some bodily function. When her hand was stroking me, pulling my cum out, I hadn't felt detached from her. It was Esme's hand that aroused me—not some random woman helping me scratch an itch.

And she was right; I was not hers to keep.

Chapter 19

ESME

B y the time I woke up Saturday morning, Declan had already left, and according to the sticky note taped to the coffee machine, he was gone until Sunday evening.

I was alone at home. Calliope didn't work on the weekends as Declan was hardly ever home, either traveling for business or pleasure.

"He and Miss Vivian always made plans for the weekend," Calliope explained. *"They went sailing to Catalina, flew to wine*

country in Napa, or drove to Santa Barbara. Mr. Declan likes
to surf, so he sometimes goes to Baja California."

My phone rang, and I sighed when my mother's name flashed
on the screen. Monica Hartley was going to grade my perfor-
mance from last night.

"Mama, how are you?"

"Esme, what did you do? Daddy is so upset with you. Did you
talk all night about homeless people at dinner?" she demanded.

No, how are you? Hey, we forced you to marry this stranger;
your sister was fucking five minutes ago, is that working out for
you?

"The senator's wife asked some questions."

I knew it was a waste of time to explain myself. She wasn't
calling to hear my side but to tell me *his* side and how much of
a disappointment I was. Didn't they ever tire of beating up on
me? How could they keep at it with such diligence? I was too
exhausted to feel this frustrated with anything or anyone, even
if I had a valid reason. It was unfair that they couldn't see I had
put my life on hold for a year to save Daddy's business when
Viv fucked up. I didn't expect gratitude because I was not an
idiot, but even so, they could at least acknowledge that I did
something for them.

I listened to her mention my dress and makeup and moved on
to how I seemed to talk too much to Mateo, who was supposed
to pay attention to Mrs. Rivers and not me.

I took the phone with me to the gym, happy to have the
penthouse to myself.

I put her on speaker by my yoga mat and started to do push ups. I tried to do a 100 a day and then move on to cardio with a thirty-minute run on the treadmill.

"Viv is getting an annulment, Esme," my mother announced, and I paused for a moment and then continued to lift myself off the mat. It didn't surprise me, and I chose not to be affected by it.

"Hmm."

"Daddy says that if that happens, we can do the same for you and Dec, and *they* can get married."

How nice of them!

"Did you hear me, Es?"

"Yes, mama." I finished fifty pushups, my arms burning, and lay face down on the yoga mat.

"You never thought this would become an actual marriage, did you, Es?" I knew she wasn't exactly concerned about me; she didn't want any drama.

"Of course not, mama," I gasped. I was trying to catch my breath.

"Good, good. You'd never have a chance with him anyway, so it's a good thing you know your limitations."

Did she ever hear herself, I wondered. The way she spoke to me like I was nothing, someone nobody would want. Maybe she was right. My parents didn't want me, so why should it be a surprise that they felt no one else would? Not Declan, who had clarified that my giving him a hand job had been *just* fun and games. Right! Because I gave hand jobs to every man I ever sat in a car with. It was my thing. I was short, ugly, *and* slutty. *Yeah!*

"Mama, I have to go."

"Yes, yes. Just make sure you don't do anything to upset Dec. Or Viv. They must reconcile."

"Yes, mama." *And who cares how I feel?*

"And think about it; you won't be trapped for a year in that penthouse."

I wondered how they'd spin it to the media. *Two weddings and two annulments!* But people like the Knights could buy stories in gossip magazines. They'd say Declan came to his senses and went back to the love of his life. And since no one cared about me anyway, I'd disappear into the background as I always did. Heartbroken for sure, but that would be my dirty secret, which no one would know.

After I worked out and showered, I took an Uber to West Hollywood to meet Maria and Mark for lunch. They'd promised that Restaurant A.O.C. had an excellent wine list. I didn't always go to fancy places because my budget didn't stretch that far, but I needed something nice to happen to me, and I'd decided to splurge.

It was always a pleasure to spend time with Maria and Mark. They were lovely people from a tight-knit family that I wish I had. They'd accepted me as their own, and I'd always been grateful. They hated how my family treated me, but they never judged me, understanding that familial relationships were complicated. They'd prefer that I managed my "please everyone all the time" personality trait better so I would not get used by everyone, but it also made me who I was, so they were patient with me.

"Any hanky-panky taking place?" Mark asked after we'd ordered.

I decided to enjoy a crisp Carneros Chardonnay with the seabass I ordered. Mark, who was vegetarian, had ordered their black truffle risotto and a glass of *blanc de blanc* champagne, and Maria, who had missed dinner the previous night and breakfast this morning, ordered a steak, medium rare with a wine reduction sauce and big, bold Bordeaux.

"Hanky-panky? Between Declan and me?" I tried to delay answering the question.

"No, between you and Mickey Mouse," he mocked.

Maria whistled softly. "Looks like there might be something there."

I shrugged. "I...Declan... we had some fun, and then he told me that's what it was and I shouldn't get my hopes up like I had the guts to do that. My mother informs me that Viv is getting an annulment, so then Declan and I can do the same, and then they can get married. If Viv had kept her legs together and not married Nick, I'd be living with Mark and getting that job at Keck."

I could be myself with these people, and it was a relief to say what I thought and not hide how I felt.

"Do you like Dec?" Maria wanted to know.

I shrugged.

"She's had a crush on him forever," Mark piped in.

"He's handsome; I'll give you that." Maria patted my hand. "So, did you have sex?"

"No. More of a hand job on both sides in the back seat of his Escalade."

"Nice." Mark clapped. "Finally, you did something kinky. Was it good?"

My face went red. As open as I was with Mark—and as open as he was with me (and boy was he!), I was embarrassed. I was still new to sex.

"You work too hard; you need to get out and have some fun," Maria said supportively.

"I just want to live my life," I moaned. "Declan is a jackass most of the time. And my father is driving me up the wall."

I told my friends almost everything, but I'd never told them about the physical abuse. Declan had looked angry enough to kill when he'd seen the marks on my arm. My father had been putting marks on me since I was a young child...*no, I won't think about this now*.

"Talk to Declan about what you're going through." Mark put his hand on mine and squeezed.

"Yes. He needs to give you a safe space and a break. Just tell him you won't do social events. You hate those things anyway," Maria added. "Just get through the time you have in that luxurious penthouse of his—and tell him you'll both be pleasant and friendly to one another. No hand job required if you don't want it."

"The gym is very nice. And the views *are* stellar."

"And the rent is free," Mark reminded me.

"Always a good thing," I agreed. "Maria, thank you for hiring me at Safe Harbor."

"Oh, stop," Maria protested. "I'm so grateful that you want to work with us. With your qualifications and education, you could be running the place. Would you want to?"

"I don't want to do admin work...but let's see how it goes. I'm excited to start working there this Monday. It's going to be glorious."

As I always did, I focused on what was working, and so much of it was.

Chapter 20

DECLAN

I found myself at the sprawling Hartley home in Newport Beach. I was going to surf, so I thought I could drop by and confront Julien.

Esme's arm had been bruised, and from what I could tell, this wasn't the first time. There was no way Julien wasn't doing this on purpose. He was doing this to control her.

The housekeeper opened the door and led me to the back patio, which extended into a private beach. At a large table under an umbrella, Viv was with Monica and her father. They were eating lunch.

"Welcome, son." Julien was overly solicitous.

Viv rose and came up to me; and like the previous weeks hadn't happened, put her arms around me and went on tiptoe to kiss me on the mouth. I moved my head, so she caught my cheek. I may want her back, but I wouldn't cheat on my marriage vows, no matter how they were made.

"All okay, Declan?" she asked, sensing a storm under the calm.

"Yes. I need to speak with your father." I walked up to Monica and kissed her cheek. She was a delicate, frail woman, so skinny that I suspected she had an eating disorder. She was always well put together, not a hair out of place—and hardly spoke. Did Julien put marks on her as well? She wore a pale blue sundress so I could examine her arms—no bruises.

"Let's go into my office," Julien suggested.

I followed him to his office. I found it heavy and dark—like something from an old movie with big leather sofas and shadowy teak furniture.

"Drink?" he asked as he led us to the dark brown leather sofa.

I shook my head. I also didn't sit when he asked me to take a seat.

"What's going on, my boy?"

I put my hands inside the pockets of my jeans to stop myself from punching Julien. "If you ever, and I mean ever, hurt Esme again, I'll break every bone in your body." I spoke calmly and without inflection.

"Excuse me?" he was shocked. "What the fuck has that stupid girl been telling you?"

"I saw what you did to her. You grabbed her arm so hard that she had bruises. You dug your nails into her and broke her skin. I guess this isn't the first time because there are scars from before. But this is the last time."

"Declan, I've never physically hurt anyone, and I find it offensive that you accuse me of something so heinous. You can ask Monica and Viv...and they'll tell you that Esme is...well, we didn't have a choice but to have her marry you, considering the situation, but she's a nut job. She cooks up stories."

He was lying and doing it with such great ease that I wondered if he genuinely believed what he was saying.

"Esme didn't tell me anything. I saw the bruises. Julien, let me be as clear as I can; do not touch my wife *ever* again."

"Your wife?" he scoffed. "What's going on, Dec? Are you slumming it with that young thing? I see the attraction. I married the mother. Monica is much better looking, but that dusky south of the border appeal is there, isn't it?"

She was his daughter, and he spoke of her like a prostitute. During the years I dated Viv, I'd thought Julien was an arrogant snob, but he loved his daughter, which redeemed him. Viv and her father were close friends and confidantes. But *this* man, this father of Esme's, was a monster.

"Julien, you're not listening to me. Do not touch Esme again. Am I clear?"

"Sure, if that makes you happy. *But* I assure you, Dec, I've never hurt Esme."

Yes, you have. Both physically and emotionally. All the time. And now you've drawn me into your circle of abuse, and I am also hurting Esme.

I walked out of the office and banged the door shut. Viv was waiting for me—heightened concern on her face.

"What's going on, darling?"

"Did you know your father hurts Esme?"

"Hurts?"

"Yes. He grabs her arm and squeezes so hard that there are marks on her skin. He broke her skin in many places by digging his nails into her flesh."

Viv's face hardened. "What are you doing looking at Esme's arms, Dec? Are you sleeping with my sister?"

"She's my wife, Viv." I didn't want to concede that we had separate bedrooms and just one sexual encounter under our belts.

She took my hand and led me to her bedroom, which her parents kept for her when she visited, the one she'd grown up in. *Where was Esme's bedroom*, I wondered? Oh yeah, she didn't have one. They sent her off to be with Monica's mother.

"What's going on, Dec? My father is the gentlest man I know. Sure, he's firm with Esme, but you've spent time with her; you know she's a total flake and needs to be constantly told what to do; otherwise, she's a disaster."

Viv looked beautiful in a pair of denim shorts and a tight T-shirt. Her casual, off-day look. She had legs for miles, yet she didn't shine as brightly as Esme did for all her physical attributes. *Shining as bright? What was going on with me?*

"Esme graduated top of her class with a Master's in social work, Viv. She's not dumb. She's not a flake."

Viv's eyes flashed with jealousy. I enjoyed seeing that. Why shouldn't she feel these stabs of pain as I had about her and that asshole she'd shacked up with?

"Are you falling for my little sister, Dec?"

"Why do you and your father hate her so much?"

She seemed stunned by the question. "Trust me; you'd feel like we do if you knew her better. Between Monica and Esme... it's been...you do not know how hard we've had to work to maintain the Hartley name. We don't hate her. You haven't had to live with her."

"I *live* with her now," I countered. "But *you* haven't. Her grandmother raised her."

"That was Monica's decision. And a good one because Monica is right up there on the list of people you can't rely on. Daddy doesn't even let her cook—she's likely to burn the kitchen down."

There was no point in this conversation.

"I have to go."

"Stay the day with me, Dec." She came up to me and rubbed her breasts against my chest. "We can stay in bed all day like we used to."

I had been greedy with her. I had wanted her again and again. And, now, she was offering herself to me, and my cock refused to respond.

I stepped away from her. "I'm not like you, Viv. I don't cheat."

"It's a *fake* marriage."

"But our engagement was real, and yet you seemed to have no compunction in sleeping with other men."

She flushed. "One other man."

I could see she was lying. I knew there were others. How could I not have seen any of this? How blind had I been? Or just too busy. I was pushing myself to make something out of Knight Tech and hadn't paid enough attention to my relationship with Viv.

"Fake or not, it's a marriage. I will not fuck you, no matter how wet your pussy is, darling, because you left me, and I'm now married to your little sister."

I left her room, feeling confused. I didn't want Viv, I realized. The epiphany was like a thunderbolt.

Last night, I'd been confident that I'd take her back with open arms, even if I made her grovel some. But now I knew we were done, and there was no going back. Even after the year with Esme, I'd never be with Viv again. I'd never trust her again. It was over. It had been over for a while, but I'd not seen it or wanted to. I'd not noticed what she did because I didn't want to, not because I was too busy. Viv had been convenient, hadn't she? The merger, the marriage—everything I wanted. And Viv was a prize, just look at her. But she wasn't for me. Not anymore.

I felt a sense of freedom as I drove to the waves of Baja California on the Pacific Coast Highway. I was done with Viv—the heart that had been hurting had stopped and was instead beating healthier and faster.

Chapter 21

ESME

I spent the afternoon at the Los Angeles County Museum of Modern Art, LACMA. When I returned to Declan's place, it was late evening.

As I got off the elevator, jazz music filtered through the air, the crooning voice of Samara Joy. Also, there were smells of food. I had thought it was Calliope's day off, but maybe she'd come over.

I entered the expansive kitchen, dining, and living room space to find Declan cooking. A lovely *Château Mouton-Rothschild* bottle was breathing on the kitchen counter. There was an empty wine glass standing next to it.

"Hi." Declan smiled broadly and picked up his glass of wine as a toast.

"You said you wouldn't be back until tomorrow night."

"I know. But...do you want a glass of wine?"

"A *Mouton-Rothschild*? Hell, yes."

He poured me a glass. I pulled my phone out of the pocket of my jeans and set it next to my wine glass on the granite kitchen counter. I swirled the wine and then smelled it. It filled my senses with dark fruit, oak, and forest floor. I took a sip and let it satisfy my taste buds before swallowing the wine.

"Wow."

He was watching me, waiting, and he grinned when he saw I was happy with the wine. "Sit," he invited.

I sat on a barstool and looked around. Declan had set the dining table for two. There were even a couple of white tapered candles glowing. I'd think he was courting me if I didn't know any better. But I knew better. He probably wanted to celebrate the end of this marriage that had barely started so he could marry the *right* woman.

"How do you eat your steak? Do you eat steak?"

"Medium rare."

"I wasn't sure if you'd be home for dinner, but I hoped. Steak with scalloped potatoes and asparagus. I don't bake, so the dessert is from Republique. A chocolate gateau."

"What's the occasion?"

"I want to apologize for being an asshole these past few days. You deserve better. You're doing my family and yours a favor, expecting nothing in return, and I've not had the decency to treat you with respect. I'm sorry."

Knock me out with a feather!

I barely managed a "Hmm?"

He wore a white dress shirt with jeans. Businessman at rest on a Saturday night, cooking for his wife. It was eerily domestic and made my heart flutter.

Stop it. This is a business deal to him, not a marriage. Look at him. Do you think he'd be interested in you, ever?

I shifted my glasses up my nose to have something to do rather than eye fuck him. He had such a beautiful face, and then there were those beautiful blue eyes. He'd kissed me with those full lips, and I'd touched his high cheekbones. And that's all I'd have of him, a memory that would fade as time passed.

"My mother told me that Viv was getting her marriage annulled and...that...well, that you and I would do the same so, you and Viv...." I trailed away, leaving the words unsaid into my wine glass as I took another sip of the brilliant wine.

"I'll never, ever marry Viv," he announced. "*Ever.* And I have no plans to end our marriage until the contractual time ends. I will not risk the merger. If you're okay with it, that is. Are you?"

I nodded like a fool, unable to form words.

"This means that you and I have a year together. How do you feel about that?"

"Free rent," I blurted out and then flushed, embarrassed.

He smiled. "And that's the other thing. At the end of the marriage, I'll give you three million dollars as reimbursement."

My eyes widened. "Why? And what would I do with all that money? I don't want it. And reimburse me for what?"

"For taking this year out of your life to do me and your father this favor. You can do what you want with the money. Maybe even start a foundation to help people.

That made me excited. Three million dollars was a lot of money. I could work with Maria and Mark to find the best way to spend it to help single mothers and their children, maybe help juveniles who age out of the system, or fund programs to eliminate homelessness.

"Until then, I'd like you and me to have a... relationship. Friendship. Companionship. If you don't want to go to social events, then we won't go. Some I cannot avoid."

Social events? Like the one last night where I was humiliated repeatedly by him, my father, Viv, and even, to some extent, Mateo, who was trying in his own fucked up way to help me be more assertive. I don't know why people thought I couldn't be equally mean and cruel; of course, I could. We all have all sides within us, but I refused to let how others treated me change who I was or compromise my values.

"It won't be like last night," he continued as if reading my mind. "That was a shit show, and it was my fault. Esme, you said you like being direct and honest, so I will give you that. For a moment, a long moment, last evening, I thought I'd get back with Viv, and if that was the case, then...."

"I didn't matter?" I offered.

He took my free hand in both of his. He bent his head and brushed his lips against my knuckles.

"I'm sorry."

"I didn't say that to make you apologize, Declan. I get it."

He set my hand down on the counter but didn't let go. "I'm sorry, Esme. I was insensitive and worse, cruel. Mateo all but punched me last night. Here is a promise: that kind of thing won't happen again. You and I will be together if we go to a social event. Okay?"

I looked at his large hand holding mine. "Yes, of course. But why the change in heart?"

"You think I'm being insincere?"

I pulled my hand away from his. "No, I'm worried that you think you have to persuade me. You don't have to. Tell me what you want, and we can discuss it like grownups. No subterfuge required."

He seemed hurt, but he covered it by drinking some wine.

"I'm not persuading you. I'm following your advice and making the best out of the situation. And what do I want? I want to fuck you. Hard. I can't stop thinking about what we did in the car, and I want more of that."

My heart sank. He wanted sex. He was doing all this to fuck me.

"Look, I don't care if you have sex with someone else. Feel free. I told you last night that I'm not experienced, and sex is complicated. It's not just a tab A into tab B situation. My emotions are involved, and yours are not. It'll create a dynamic that will end up hurting me."

He leaned and brushed his lips against my cheek. "You, Esme, are a breath of fresh air. I don't want you to hurt. If you feel that us having sex may cause you pain, then we won't do it. *But* I would very much like for us to at least be friendly roommates if we cannot be married lovers. Would you agree to that?"

"And what's all this?" I waved a hand at the wine and the food.

"Peace offering, sweetheart."

He got up then and announced it was time to cook the steaks.

"Do I have time for a shower?" I asked him.

"No rush. Take your time."

"Maybe I'll take a bath then."

"I'll wait."

He confused me again. I didn't know what to expect from him. I undressed in the bathroom, and my phone rang. I didn't want to take the call from Viv, but I did and put her on speaker as I stood naked, gazing at myself in the bathroom mirror.

"Hi, Viv."

I desperately needed a bikini wax if I wanted to have sex. Viv probably took it all off and had a smooth pussy. Good thing he didn't go down on me in the car; he'd have been disgusted with all the hair.

"What are you trying to achieve, Es?" Viv demanded.

"Hmm."

"Dec was here today. He threatened Daddy. You've now told people Daddy beats you. Es, this is just horrible."

Declan stood up for me against my father. Why?

"Viv, I know nothing about this."

"I made a mistake, and I'm making amends. Dec and I are together. We'll always be together. Just stay out of everyone's way, and you can get on with your life."

I wanted to say *no; right now, you are not together. Right now, he's my husband.*

"Viv, I'm trying to navigate this the best I can. I didn't ask Declan to talk or say anything to Daddy."

"I know you've always wanted him, haven't you?"

My heart beat faster. I thought I'd hidden it, but I obviously needed to do better. Who wouldn't want Declan? He was handsome and funny. He had been kind and generous with Viv. He had been romantic. I'd watched him with Viv—watched how his eyes lit up when she walked into a room and how he relaxed when she kissed him. While Viv ignored the staff, he was kind to them. Declan remembered Jean, our cook's birthday, and brought her flowers. He'd given Carlos, my father's driver, money for his son's school. I'd kept track of him since he'd been friends with Viv. I read about him online. I watched his videos.

It had been a crush.

It turned sexual a few months ago when, as I was walking past Viv's room, I heard them having sex. "*Viv, you ready for my cock, baby girl?*"

Viv sounded breathless and moaned, "Dec, please, please, please."

"*You begging, Angel?*"

"*Yes.*"

"*Are you mine?*"

"*Yes.*"

"*Always. Always mine.*"

I ran away. I didn't even tell Mark about what I heard. But I wondered how it'd feel if he said these things to me. *Always. Always mine.* I wasn't jealous of what my sister had; I wanted someone to feel that way about me.

"I don't know what you mean, Viv," I replied. *Yes, I wanted him, but I'm not a fool. I have no chance. I never did. Not when I had to compete with her.*

"He was here this morning, Es. And we made love. So whatever dreams you're weaving about having a real marriage are never coming true."

He had sex with Viv and then came home and told me he wanted to fuck me. What kind of man was he? And what kind of woman was I that, despite this, I wanted him to make love with me?

"You want your sister's sloppy seconds, is that it?" Viv demanded.

"Viv, Daddy, and Mama asked me to marry him because the business needed it and I have. Once this year is up, we go our own ways." *And I'll find the love of my life. I will. I need to guard my heart while I'm with Declan.*

"Good. Remember that. And once my marriage is annulled. You'll be out of that penthouse and his life sooner than a year. I promise you."

"Okay, Viv."

"You don't have what it takes to keep a man like Dec, you know that don't you? You're fat and have some low-level job. Dec and I, we're the power couple."

I wanted to end the call because horrible things were clamoring to come out of my mouth. I tried to call her on the "power couple" and "made for each other" statements when she banged other men while engaged to Declan. If I were engaged to Declan, I'd never even look at anyone else.

"I understand, Viv." My voice became smaller, and I felt like I was shrinking right in front of my eyes in the bathroom mirror as I listened to Viv.

"Oh, and next time there's a social event, don't bother showing up. Dec and I will go as a couple. It'll be good for the media to see us again. I wonder why Dec announced your wedding publicly. If he'd just kept it quiet, we could have managed this without the media drama."

She wasn't talking to me anymore, I realized. She was making plans.

"Viv, is it okay if we talk about this at another time?"

"Whatever," was her response before she hung up.

I turned on music on my phone and showered as I listened to Ella sing *Blue Skies*.

Chapter 22

DECLAN

I brought her a glass of wine to her room, so she'd have it with her in case she took that bath she'd mentioned. It had jarred me to hear Viv talk to Esme—not just her tone but how she easily lied about having sex with me today.

I heard the defeat in Esme's voice. Why didn't she fight back? Why didn't she ask Viv to shut up and take a hike? I heard Mateo's voice in my head that her family had trained her to be this way. Julien had threatened her physically and emotionally to become this person. And, yet Esme wanted to do good in the world. Be a social worker, not some social butterfly running a foundation and throwing parties. She wanted to work on the streets and make a difference. Only someone with an enormous heart could see past the bad they experienced to want to do the right thing.

She was not a doormat; she was strong and courageous.

I heard the shower start, and I left the wine glass on her bedside table and left.

Esme and I were going to have a pleasant meal with some good wine, and we were going to talk.

Foremost, I had to clear up Viv's lie. Esme must be disgusted with me, thinking I slept with her sister and then came home and asked to fuck her. The idea of her naked in her shower sent the blood straight through to my cock, tightening my pants. She turned me on. Not because she was the most beautiful woman I'd been with—because there was a light she emanated, maybe because she was always trying to be happy and trying to make others happy.

I brought our plates to the table as she entered the dining area.

I'd lit the candles and dimmed the lights to create a cozy atmosphere. Even in the dimmed lights, her discomfort was obvious to see.

"I thought maybe you'd want your wine with you, so I came to your room," I explained once she was seated.

"I forgot it..." she attempted to rise, but I held my hand up.

"Have a fresh glass." I poured wine into the empty glass in front of her. "When I was in your room, I heard you speak with your sister."

She looked at me in panic as if going through the conversation to ensure she had said nothing wrong.

"I did not have sex with Viv. Our marriage may be unconventional, but I *am* married and don't cheat. I won't."

"You're okay being celibate for a year?" she asked.

"Why not?"

"It's just...the media emphasizes you are used to having a new woman under you all the time until Viv a year ago."

"I'm not a hormonal teenager. So, yes, I can go without sex. My right hand may get a lot of action, but I won't ride some faceless body. I like sex. I like to like the women I have sex with."

"You like me?" She sounded like a child when she asked that question.

"Very much," I confessed. "You're smart, authentic, kind, and good. What's not to like, Esme?"

She didn't say it, but I knew her family had never said these things to her, and she didn't believe me.

"I know your family has been harsh with you, but you have friends. Don't Mark and Maria think you're wonderful?"

She shrugged. "They're my friends. And, honestly, I'm grateful that they are. I don't have many friends."

"I'd like to propose a new deal." I raised my glass, and she did the same. "Friends, Esme? Can we become friends?"

"Yes." She licked her lips, and my cock went on high alert. "I'd like that."

This was going to be a long year, I thought, *if she didn't give me access to that petite body of hers.* But if she didn't, then she didn't. I wouldn't pressure her. I'd let her decide how she wants to maneuver our relationship. Her family had taken away many of her choices—I would not do the same.

"This is great," she told me.

"We have that in common, a love for cooking. We can cook together. Have some friends over?"

"Yes," she beamed.

I realized that some of her previous smiles might have reached her eyes but not her heart because right now, her eyes shone bright, and I felt like I was ten feet tall because I'd made that happen.

She was fun to hang out with. Intelligent and thoughtful, well-read, and curious. We talked about a paper she was working on for a journal, and I told her about my plans to expand our offerings to customers. Viv and I talked about work all the time; after all, her law firm managed the merger, yet it had never been relaxed like this. There was harmony in sharing without planning the next move and the next, which is what Viv and I would do.

"May I ask what made you...well, do all this?" she asked after we finished our meal.

I refused to let her help clean up and did it while she watched me from the kitchen counter.

"The cooking and cleaning?"

"And the change in...well, earlier, I felt like you wanted me to blend into the wallpaper for the next year. Now you want to get to know me."

She seemed fragile as she waited for me to answer. I dried my hands on a towel and came toward her. I rested my elbows on the counter and my chin on my fists so my face was the same height as hers.

"I realized I didn't love Viv anymore. I always thought love never died, but I realized it could be killed: death by a thousand pricks. Viv and I have been on this course since we started, and I can see that now. And Mateo has been hammering me about being a better person where you're concerned. I went surfing today in Newport Beach after I saw your father—and yes, I told him not to touch you ever again, and if he did, I'd break all his bones. That's a genuine threat, Esme."

"It isn't—"

I cut her off. "If someone in your care were experiencing this, you'd call it abuse. Your father is a bully. And that Viv...I expected better from her. Seeing her values are so close to your father's destroyed whatever last bits of love and desire I had for her."

"Okay, what now?"

"Now, we eat dessert."

We sat on the balcony with the chocolate gateau, the sounds of the city soothing from sixty-three floors below.

"I start working tomorrow," she told me almost shyly.

"At Maria's place?"

"Yes. Safe Harbor."

"What will you do there?"

"I'm going to work as a Clinical Social Worker. I'll provide clinical case management services to help women find housing, do an ongoing assessment of their needs, build skills, and offer mental health support. I'll run coordination meetings for women on the streets so we can move them out there. It's a lot of things: trauma support, de-escalation, crisis intervention, abuse assessments, and ensuring that the facilities are safe because some of these women have walked away from abusive relationships."

It was obvious she loved this. I'd never seen Viv this passionate about justice—definitely about making money and doing right for the business, but never about taking care of people.

I had to stop comparing Viv to Esme. I had to stop thinking about Esme constantly in terms of Viv. But she was so different from any woman I'd ever been with that a contrast was inevitable. I dated models, actresses, influencers, lawyers, and corporate executives. Regardless of her parents and their wealth, Esme was down to earth and talked about money like regular people did, people who were not born into millions and grew those millions into billions. I'd never had to worry about money. I never had to think, *oh, free rent*. I wanted that for her. I wanted her not to worry about such things and focus on what she loved to do.

"Esme, I don't know what your family told you about yourself, but here is what I've learned in the short few days we've been together. You're kind, beautiful, charming, knowledgeable, and have a heart the size of Montana." I looked into her eyes when I spoke. "And I'm humbled that you agreed to help my business by marrying me."

She flushed with pleasure. "Thank you." And then her eyes hooded like she wondered why I was saying these things.

"I'm not trying to get you into my bed," I added. "I will not lie and say I don't want to because I do, but that's not the goal of this evening. I want to get to know you better and make this year pleasant. Make the best of it."

"Okay," she said. "I want to tell you something. I've been using your gym and your pool. But I didn't want to overstep. I—"

"While you're my wife and you live here, everything that's mine is yours. Use the gym whenever you like. Use the pool however you want."

"Whew! I was feeling guilty."

"You work out?"

"Almost every day. My body type will go big if I don't, and unlike my mother, who hardly eats, I love food and wine."

"What's your favorite kind of wine?"

"Pinot Noir...Burgundy, to be specific. Yours?"

"I'm a left bank kinda guy. Bordeaux, deep, big, and bold."

We talked about wine and many other things and started building a friendship I had no doubt I'd cherish.

Chapter 23

Esme

We fell into a pattern in the next few months. We worked out in the morning together and swam. He was a better swimmer than me. He didn't rush to work in the morning anymore to avoid me, so we had breakfast together, which Calliope made.

For dinner, if he was home, we'd either go out, or I'd cook something. On weekends, when he wasn't traveling, he cooked, and we'd talk, watch a movie, or sit together in the living room reading. I suspected he was avoiding social events because Viv called me to ask what was happening, as Declan wasn't returning her calls or going to the places where he usually hung out. She'd assumed that I had done something.

I met Declan's poker friends and even joined them in what they called charity poker. Whoever won the pot would give it to a charity of their choosing.

Mateo had softened towards me and soon became a friend who came by with food or a bottle of wine when Declan was traveling. Raya, their head of security, kept her distance from me—she seemed like an introvert who took time to warm up to people. Daisy was a delight who immediately brought me into her circle, insisting that I join her book club. Mark and Maria had come to the penthouse for dinner and had become friends with Declan. In a few months, I'd gotten settled both professionally and personally.

Declan kept his promise and did not insist I join him for this gala or that party. I knew he'd been to a few without me—I'd seen pictures of him in the media, usually with Mateo or his mother, a couple of times Viv had been with him. I'd not asked him about it. I waited for him to invite me to come with him, but he didn't, and I was too afraid of rejection to pursue it.

We had become roommates. Not intimate but friendly. Not invasive but companionable.

My vibrator was getting a workout almost every night because I was falling for *this* Declan despite my best intentions. He was funny, fun, and charming. He was engaging and engaged. He knew how to laugh at himself.

He'd not brought up sex with me again. There had been that one time when I'd walked into his bedroom to hand him his ringing phone, he'd forgotten in the kitchen and caught him naked. I'd averted my eyes, but not before I got an eyeful. He had a powerful naked body designed for romance book covers and sin.

There had been another time when I thought I was alone in the gym and had dropped my sweaty clothes on the floor as I headed into the shower. He'd walked in then and, unlike me, did not avert his eyes. He said nothing, but his gaze had darkened, and I'd wished he'd joined me in the shower, which he didn't.

Work was consuming more and more of my time and energy. I was coming home later as the caseload kept increasing, and we were only two clinical social workers at Safe Harbor. The budget wouldn't permit a third.

I was dragging my tired ass home at nearly ten in the evening when I saw Declan sitting at the dining table, working on his laptop, a glass of wine next to him.

"You're back." I felt such relief that he was home. He'd been gone for nearly a week to London for a conference and meetings.

He smiled at me. "And looks like while I've been away, you've been burning the midnight oil."

"Both ends of the candle," I admitted and sat beside him on a dining chair. I picked up his glass of wine and sipped. "Nice."

"Should I pour you one?"

"Yes, please."

I watched him bring me a glass. He wore gray sweatpants that hugged his hips, and a snow-white T-shirt hung loose on his muscled torso. He was barefoot and smelled of cologne. His hair was damp. He must have just taken a shower. I inhaled him when he set my glass in front of me.

"You look exhausted," he said. "And I'm the one who just flew back from London an hour ago."

"Everything hurts," I confessed, closing my eyes and leaning back on the chair, my wine glass in hand.

I didn't hear him move but felt his hands on my shoulders. He kneaded gently, and I moaned as he found a knot and broke it into submission.

"*Oh*, that's nice." I set my wine glass on the table and enjoyed the impromptu massage. He slipped his hands under my white peasant blouse and squeezed my shoulders. *How could an act so innocuous as relieving pain be so sensual?*

"Are you eating properly? Calliope mentioned when I called, you were skipping too many meals."

"Calliope is a snitch."

"Anything to report in the week I was gone?"

"No."

He always asked—and what he wanted to know about was my family. He'd taken me under his protection, it appeared, and it was frustrating my family. Viv thought I was fucking him—but then she also told me he'd never be interested in someone who looked like me. *Decide, woman.*

In no uncertain terms, Viv expressed her confidence in getting Declan back. She believed he still loved her and would forgive her. He was angry and deserved some time off. Declan shared nothing about Viv with me. He talked about his work and asked me about mine.

When my paper got published in a peer-reviewed journal, he made a big deal out of it, taking me out for dinner. He made me feel special—and as someone who'd never experienced this before, it made the barriers I had half-heartedly put around my heart crumble.

"How was your trip?" I asked, wanting to change the topic. What was the point of telling him about the phone calls or the one visit from my father?

"You know I know who comes to our home, right? Even when I'm not around."

I stiffened.

"Relax," he whispered, his mouth close to my ear. He kissed my cheek. "Don't lie to me, Esme."

I sighed. "Then why do you ask?"

"Because I'm waiting for the day you kick that asshole of a father out of our home."

He'd started calling his apartment *our home*, which thrilled me each time he said it. And, yet, this was all temporary, I valiantly reminded myself.

"He's my father, and that's not quite my style."

His hands moved to my lower back, and I winced. "Too hard?"

"No. I was climbing a ladder and slipped. I think I twisted something."

"Okay, let's go to bed."

I spun around. "What?"

Amusement was clear in his eyes. "So, I can give you a proper massage."

"You know how?"

"I'm an expert. You have to be when you play soccer. And I played a lot of soccer in my misspent youth."

Chapter 24

DECLAN

I came home early because Raya told me Julien had come over the previous evening and stayed for an hour.

"Take off your blouse," I requested when we got to my bedroom. I wanted her here. I wanted to see her lying on my dark blue sheets, her hair spread on my pillow.

She didn't question me and just took it off with her back turned to me. "And your bra." My throat was dry as I watched her unhook her bra. I took the sensible white bra and tossed it aside. "And now your pants, sweetheart."

I thought she'd say something, but she didn't. Her hands shook as she unbuttoned and unzipped. The pants fell at her feet. She wore a pair of white panties that hugged her tight brown ass, the contrast brutally erotic.

"Lie on your stomach, gorgeous."

She did as I asked. She was not looking at me, but I could feel her stiffness and tension.

She snuggled into the pillow as if inhaling my scent.

I found some massage oil in my bathroom that someone had used in a similar situation before. I had not been the masseuse then.

"Sweetheart, where does it hurt?"

"Declan," she whispered, her eyes closed.

"Yes." I leaned close to her face, her lips an inch away from mine.

She opened her eyes, and I saw desire, regret, and fear all combining into lust.

"If we have sex, what will change?"

"I'll stop jerking off in the shower as much as I do."

She smiled. "You've been traveling...I thought you'd find...."

I kissed her then, slowly, gently. "I told you I wouldn't cheat on you."

I turned her on her back and kissed her again. Her lips were soft and delicious.

"Declan," she gasped when I trailed my mouth across her jaw and caught her earlobe in my teeth.

"Yes, sweetheart." My hands couldn't stop touching her, feeling her. I now knew she could do a hundred push-ups, and that's why her body was so toned. Her breasts were agonizingly soft, her nipples hard with arousal.

I kissed her again, and my hands went over her stomach, and I was about to part her thighs and see if she was wet when she pushed me away.

I moved away instantly. "Esme?"

Her hands moved to pull at the comforter to cover herself. "No."

"Okay." I had gotten carried away. I stepped away. "I'm sorry."

"No, it's not that." She seemed afraid, and I felt my heart wrench. No, I didn't want her to fear me. What had I done to make her feel this way? Did I touch her that reminded her of something else?

"Tell me, my love."

My love?

"I...meant to, but I... didn't."

"Esme, you've got to talk in full sentences."

She swallowed. "I wanted to go for a bikini wax but didn't have the time. And...I also didn't think we'd end up this way."

It wouldn't do to smile now, but god, she was adorable.

"Sweetheart, I love your pussy." I kissed her on her nose.

"But it's...I know women do the whole...." She closed her eyes, obviously embarrassed.

"Okay, I understand. Let me look, and I'll let you know how it looks."

I gently pulled the comforter away and kissed each hardened nipple. It would take some work to distract her. I let my hands go between her legs as my mouth went down the curve of her soft stomach.

"You're so wet, Esme." I pulled her panties down and threw them aside.

"Declan, I'm sorry," she whimpered, her eyes closed.

"Don't be. I'll lick it off." I deliberately misunderstood her.

I could smell her sweet arousal and feel the tremors in her thighs as my fingers stroked her clit. I parted her thighs and looked at her. She was pink, dewy, and swollen. Her clit begged to be sucked, and I couldn't resist any longer. I went down on her like a starving man.

I put two fingers inside her to open her up as I sucked her clit. She was tight, and my cock throbbed to find out how she'd feel. Wet, wanting, clasping, milking.

Her fingers were in my hair, pushing and pulling.

"What do you want, Esme? Tell me what you want."

"Please," she moaned.

"Please, what?"

"I need to come, Declan. Please."

I needed her to come as well because I couldn't wait to taste her and see pleasure fill her eyes.

"Open your eyes, Esme." She languorously looked at me, disoriented and aroused.

"Watch me, my love. Watch me take you. I need you to watch me."

I was a wreck. I felt like I was fifteen again with my first girl, unable to control myself. I could already feel the precum making my underwear wet.

I sucked her clit hard and inserted three fingers inside her.

She flew apart. I kissed her labia as she came down from her height, panting.

"Your pussy is gorgeous," I told her as I rose to remove my clothes.

She licked her lips when she saw my erect cock.

"Can I taste you, too?" she asked.

My penis jerked in response. "Not this time. I need to be inside you. I'm clean. Are you on birth control?"

"Yes."

"I want to take you bare."

"Yes."

I lay on top of her and drove into her. As aroused as I was, being inside her filled me with a sense of peace. This was not sex. This was heaven. I lifted her thighs and placed them on my shoulder to go deep. I wanted her to feel me inside her womb.

"You're so beautiful." I kissed her and drove my tongue inside her mouth, keeping pace with my erection. "Can you come for me again, sweetheart? Can you come with me inside you?"

My fingers went to where we were joined, and I pinched her clit. She tightened around me and came. Her thighs on my shoulders shook, she gasped out my name, and I lost control. I slammed inside her repeatedly until I couldn't tell where she ended, and I began.

I came with a violence I had never experienced. It had never been like this. Peaceful and hungry; a storm and a calm sea; arousal and...love. *Fuck.*

When did I fall in love with Esme?

Chapter 25

ESME

He held me after. He stroked my hair and back, my head resting on his shoulder, a thigh resting between his legs, touching his damp semi-erect penis.

"I still owe you a massage," he mumbled, kissing my hair.

"All my aches and pains seem to have gone away."

"Orgasms can do that, I hear. They've done clinical studies to prove that."

I had sex with Declan Knight and enjoyed two incredible, breathtaking, and heart-stealing orgasms.

"Declan?"

"Yes, my love."

My love! Again?

"May I ask an inappropriate question?"

His hold tightened on me. "Ask me anything, Esme."

"Will this change anything?"

"Yes."

My heart hammered, and he nuzzled my head with his chin.

"What?"

"I want you to move into my bedroom. Make it ours."

I raised my head to look at him. "This is feeling like...well, not a roommate situation but a relationship."

"You're catching on."

"I don't understand."

He kissed my forehead and settled me back against him. "I don't either. But it feels right. I miss you when I travel. I think about you all the time. I want to text you, but I worry I'll bother you."

"You'd never bother me."

I felt him smile. "And now that we made love, I don't think I can go without it for long."

Fear consumed me. I wanted to ask how long this would last, but I didn't want to know. Whatever time I had with Declan; I'd take it. Grab it with both hands. I was in love with my husband. I had been falling in love with him from the start, and now...after this, how would I let him go when he inevitably would want to leave?

"What's going on in that pretty head of yours?" He hauled me up, so I lay on top of him. His penis nestled between my thighs.

I looked at him. "I heard you once."

"Hmm?"

"With Viv."

Realization warmed his face, and I saw regret move in his eyes. "I'm sorry, sweetheart."

"I...you called her Angel."

"Yes."

"Okay." I lay my head back down and winced at my silly gauche question.

"What do you want to know, Esme?"

"Nothing," I squeaked.

"Are you asking me how it was to have sex with Viv?"

"No," I lied.

"It was different. It's always different. But, sweetheart, just as I wouldn't talk about what it's like to make love with you to anyone else, I can't talk about her with you. Just know that's in the past. This is in the present."

And what about the future, Declan? What happens, then?

"I'm sorry for being insecure."

"Speaking of which, what the fuck was your father doing here?"

"Do we have to talk about it?" I groaned.

"Esme," he cautioned.

"He just... he's upset that you haven't called Viv. They're hoping for a reconciliation. Her annulment should come through in the next month, and he wanted...well, he asked me to...." I trailed off.

"Since I'm not asking for an annulment, they're trying to pressure you to get one. Is that it?"

I nodded but didn't respond verbally.

"I'll take care of it."

I looked up at him unhappily. "Please don't get into a fight with Daddy."

"I won't fight." But I could tell he was losing interest in our conversation. He shifted under me; his erection turgid like he hadn't only just come a little while ago.

"I'm hard again," he murmured.

I shifted so I could straddle him, and as I did, he slipped inside me. I was still wet from the last time, from my orgasm and his.

"Ah," he groaned. "You feel so good, love."

It wasn't easy to move—they made it look so natural in porn films, but I didn't have any purchase to ride him. I put my hand on his chest, rose, and fell, but my movements were jerky, hardly expert. His hands moved under my ass, and he gently lifted me and dropped me back down.

"Like that, Esme. Ride me, sweetheart."

I did, and he watched me hungrily; his hands helped me move atop him. "Your tits look amazing. Look at how well you take me, Esme. *Ah, god.*"

Looking down where we met enchanted me. I'd never imagined it could be like this. Dirty and erotic, and yet sweet and loving.

I found my rhythm and rode him faster.

"Like that, just like that. Squeeze me inside you, Esme. I need you to milk me." His voice was hoarse, almost unrecognizable.

I tightened my muscles. "Is that good, Declan?"

"Yes," he muttered, and then suddenly, I was on my back again. "I need to fuck you hard, Esme."

He rammed into me and groaned. "Sweet-heart"—thrust—"you are perfect"—"and mine"—thrust—"Say you're mine."

"I'm yours." *I've always been.*

I came again as he did.

He rolled off me and held me tight as if he'd never let me go. "Esme, I'm addicted to your pussy."

All thoughts of Viv scattered as we got comfortable against each other. For the first time in a long time, I slept peacefully, feeling loved and well fucked.

Chapter 26

DECLAN

I whistled as I entered my office, where Raya and Mateo were waiting. I was late for a security meeting. It had been inevitable that once Esme and I had sex, we seemed to be at it like horny teenagers. The morning got delayed because she got on her knees in the shower and practiced how to deep-throat me. She told me she had a long way to go before becoming an expert, but that she'd practice with me as much as she could. I had no problem with that.

"Someone got laid." Raya raised an eyebrow.

"You don't say. He has that well fucked look about him," Mateo agreed.

I cheerfully gave them both a finger.

Baker, my assistant, showed up as soon as I was settled at my desk with my morning coffee and my printed schedule for the day.

"Isn't he looking all flushed, Baker?" Raya teased.

"Excuse me?" he asked primly in his proper British accent.

"Your boss has been balling someone," Mateo explained. "And we're giving him a hard time about it."

"When one sleeps with one's wife, it's not called balling," Baker protested.

"Wife?" Mateo made an appreciative sound. "And how do you know it's his wife?"

Baker looked at me, and I nodded; I also wanted to know.

"Well, when he got the report that Julien Hartley visited his daughter, the wife in question, Dec wanted his jet to get a flight plan back home approved ASAP. And this morning, he texted me to send flowers to Esme at Safe Harbor. Two dozen yellow tulips. Roses aren't her jam."

"She's probably going to give the flowers away to the women there." I grinned at that thought. Esme was a giver. Her big heart would not allow her to keep and enjoy the tulips; it'd make her happier to see a smile on the face of a woman struggling with life to get flowers.

"So, you slept with your wife?" Raya leaned back on her chair.

"How the fuck is who I'm fucking any of your fucking business?" I drank some coffee. "Baker, thank you for being so astute and indispensable."

Baker nodded in acknowledgment and walked out of my office.

We went into work mode after that.

I had back-to-back meetings until lunch. I wished I could find time to go to Skid Row and check out Esme's place of work, which I'd never been to but had been assured by Raya was just the hell hole I thought it would be and that she'd done all that she could to make it safe for Esme. *But* she'd also warned me that the influx of crazies into the shelter was high—and since she couldn't do anything about that, there was a risk of something going wrong. Since there was no way I could convince Esme to stop working at Safe Harbor, the only option was for Raya's team to do their best.

I had just finished a Zoom meeting when Baker suddenly stepped into my office without knocking. He stood at the door, blocking it with his back to prevent it from being opened.

"Okay, who's outside with a gun that's got you running?" I mused.

"Dec, it's Viv, and she insists—" there was a hammering on the door, "on seeing you."

"Let her in. Next time we'll tell security downstairs not to let her up and avoid this situation."

Baker looked relieved. He's probably wanted to do this since Viv broke our engagement but hadn't wanted to cross the line. As assistants went, I couldn't do better than Baker.

Viv wore a red dress that went to her knees with a long slit on one side that went right up to her panties. Her black suit jacket complemented the dress. Her heels were sexy as ever. She had legs that went all the way up. My penis didn't stir. It thrilled me that my body had finally caught up with my brain.

"Dec, what is with you?" she demanded as she approached my desk. "You don't respond to my text messages. You don't call. And now Daddy is saying that Esme won't file for an annulment. I thought we'd annulled our marriages to get back on track."

"Hi, Viv. I'm doing well, thank you. And how are you? In a mood, I see." I leaned back on my chair, making no attempt to get up to receive her.

She walked around my desk and stood in front of me, pouting. I used to think her pouts were adorable. Now...well, now they were irritating and plastic.

She sat on my lap and put her arms around my neck.

"Darling, tell your Angel what's going on."

I grabbed her hips and lifted her off of me.

"No touching, Viv. I'm another woman's husband."

"What the fuck is wrong with you?" Her hands rolled into fists, resting on her hips as she got into fight pose.

"I don't cheat. You can't sit on my lap and try to whisper sweet nothings in my ear."

Especially since I just found out I'm in love with my wife. The wife who, in eight months, will leave me if I don't find a way to keep her. Because I wanted forever with her.

In the past, that would've made me sweat bullets. Even with Viv, I'd been a little uncomfortable about everything from living together to getting engaged. I had thought I loved her but had not contemplated forever. With Esme, I wanted it. I wanted to watch movies with her. Take a walk with her in downtown LA. Go to a wine bar or restaurant. Cook with her. Fuck her every day until she'd miss having me inside her. Have a baby with her. *Fuck me; I was done for!*

"Are you getting your marriage annulled or not?" she demanded.

"No, I'm not."

"Dec?"

"Viv, you and I are finished. I tried to tell you that earlier, but you chose not to listen to me. When you first came back, I thought that was what I wanted, but I quickly realized I didn't. You cheated on me, Viv. You married another man who you'd been fucking on the side. We're done. I will *never* marry you."

Her face contorted in pain. A part of me that used to love her felt sympathy. I didn't want to hurt her; however, I wouldn't lie to her to make her feel better.

"Will you stay married to Esme? Isn't she boring the life out of you? Are you seriously saying you'd rather be married to her than me?"

"Yeah, that's what I'm saying."

Viv took a step back as if I physically struck her. "You think Esme will stay with you if I don't want her to?"

"I don't understand what you have to do with her or our marriage." But I understood. Julien and Viv had been manipulating Esme for years, playing her like a fiddle. Not this time. This time, I'd be her support system. This time, she won't be alone, easy prey.

"Esme will ask you for an annulment and, after that, to maintain the bylaws; you'll have no choice."

I smiled. "The marriage is consummated, Viv; there is no going back now."

All color left her face. "You're having sex with her? Her? Dec, your standards have dropped. She's ugly, short, overweight, and... what's happened to you?"

"First, she's not overweight. And second, insinuate that my wife is below my standards ever again, and I'll fucking destroy you. Esme hasn't been doing what you want because you're a good manipulator; she does it because she cares for her family. But you're done taking advantage of her. Please let your father know that security will no longer let him into our apartment. If he wants to talk to Esme, he goes through me."

Viv stared at me like I had grown a second head.

"Now, Viv, get out. We will not permit you to enter this building from now on. You're not my fiancée any longer. You're nobody. I'd say sister-in-law, but considering what a terrible sister you are, I don't think that counts.

Her face changed from shocked to angry in ten seconds flat. "You'll pay for this, Dec."

"And tell your father that if this merger fails, Knight Tech will survive, and his company will go under, so it's no threat to me if my marriage is annulled." This wasn't true. To put it mildly, it would be difficult for Knight Tech to recover from the death knell the merger not being approved by the board would inflict.

"I know the details of the merger, Dec, so don't give me that bullshit."

I shrugged. "I think Esme and I will have a *proper* wedding...in a church with friends and family. I don't think we'll invite you."

That thought pleased me. I'd find out what kind of wedding Esme wanted and give it to her. She asked for so little that I was desperate to give her everything she ever dreamed about.

"Now, get the fuck out, Viv. And don't come back again."

She flounced out of my office.

The incident left a nasty taste in my mouth, especially since I'd have to tell Esme about it. I didn't want to hide things from her. I wanted our relationship to be based on honesty.

My cell phone rang, and I picked it up.

"Forest, what's up?"

"You're coming to my mother's fucking gala this Saturday."

"Am I?"

"Don't fuck with me, Dec. She's driving everyone up the wall. She wanted me to make sure you are going to show up."

Forest's father and mine were brothers—and his mother and mine spent their days trying to prove which one was the better hostess. My money was on Nina Knight. Lena Knight was not organized enough to pull it off, so she'd harass Forest. If she could catch him, she'd also harass Forest's younger brother, River—but he spent most of his time traveling, working as a photojournalist. He happily ignored his mother's calls, and every time he visited would give her some sob story about being stuck at the ass end of nowhere in Iran, hence not being able to cater to her crazy. He usually was in the ass end of nowhere, but even if he was lounging in the Ritz in Paris, he'd pretend he was off the grid.

"Esme and I'll be there." I wanted to take her out, show her off.

"How is the marriage going?"

I smiled. "She's...well, a surprise."

"Now, where's the man who said I want to get done with this and spend a year trying not to kill her before sending her on her way?"

I laughed. "Yeah, how the mighty have fallen."

"And have you fallen?" he wasn't joking anymore. His tone was serious.

"Yes. Head over fucking heels, brother."

"What changed?"

"I began to understand myself better. I like her, Forest. She's quirky and kind. She's sexy and funny. She falls all over herself to be nice to people, including that terrible family of hers. I don't know how to say this without it sounding corny as fuck, but she makes me want to be a better person," I confessed.

"Well, I look forward to spending time with her at the gala. She might be the only one there with real tits."

"Don't talk about my wife's tits, man."

"Saturday at the Beverly Hills Hotel. I'll kill you if you don't show up because my mother will nag me to death."

I had skipped the past two galas Auntie Lena had organized. One was to save some animal that was going extinct, and another was to raise money for some disease.

After finishing the call, I worried about telling Esme she would need a dress. I'd now become familiar with her closet and knew that her penchant for shopping at the Rack meant that her entire wardrobe cost less than the suit I was wearing.

I got an idea and picked up my phone. I called Maria Caruso.

"Dec, what's up?"

"Are you attending Lena Knight's gala this Saturday?"

"Absolutely. She's raising money for a women's shelter in East LA. I convinced her that the endangered spotted owl would be fine without her money. Why?"

"I don't know how to say this without sounding like a down-right asshole, but I don't want Esme to face any...well, *catty* behavior, which she will if she doesn't go shopping for a dress and the last time I got her a designer outfit, she felt I didn't like her the way she is. And I do, I love the way she is. But if she shows up in something weird, the media, my mother, and Viv will eat her alive, and I don't want her to get hurt. I was hoping you'd take her shopping or whatever and...you know, do the woman thing."

There was silence on the other end, and after a moment, I heard a stifled laugh.

"Maria?"

"I'm sorry." Not stifled anymore. She was laughing out loud. "Woman thing?"

"Damn." Now that she said it aloud, it did sound foolish, but I didn't mind sounding like a moron if it meant Esme wouldn't get hurt. "She'll feel bad if I say something. I don't mind taking her in a burlap sack, but Viv will be there...I want her to feel her best, Maria. Buy her something comfortable that's not from a store called Maxi-something, so she feels her best at the event.

"TJ Maxx," Maria informed me.

I did not know what that was. Probably something like the Rack Esme frequented.

"And then you'll owe me."

"Anything you want is yours."

"Two hundred thousand dollars for Safe Harbor besides whatever you donate at the gala."

"Done."

"Really? Damn, I should've asked for more."

"My wife works there, Maria; I'm happy to give money. And it's a damn good tax write-off."

Chapter 27

ESME

I held Nancy's hand as she told me what she'd gone through. The right side of Nancy's face was swollen. Her left hand was in a sling. There was a massive bruise around her left eye. Her boyfriend had beaten her mercilessly. A nurse at the Good Samaritan Emergency Room led her to us. This wasn't the first time her boyfriend used her as a punching bag.

"Will he be able to find me here?" she was frightened, and I didn't blame her.

"No." A select few law enforcement officers and first responders knew the location of Safe Harbor. Most women's shelters had to hide in plain sight, and we always instructed the women never to let anyone know where they were. Sometimes people slipped, and we'd have an incident with a husband or boyfriend trying to break in. The security wasn't perfect—but it held up most of the time.

"What am I going to do? I'm pregnant. How am I going to care for myself and this baby?" Nancy was crying, and my heart went out to her. No matter how many women I met with similar stories, I felt their pain, which broke me. I couldn't afford to crumble and fall, I had to hold myself up so I could do the same for them.

"We're going to take care of you, Nancy. I promise. You'll be safe here, and I'll help you find a place to live and a job to pay the bills. For now, I want you to heal and get strong. How far along are you?"

"Five months." She protectively ran a hand over her belly. "He wanted to have sex, but I wasn't feeling well. So, I said no, not tonight. He got angry—kicked me in the stomach. The doctors told me the baby was fine. But if he finds me again...."

"That will not happen," I told her firmly. "I won't let it happen." I was making promises I knew I might not keep, but I'd die trying.

"Thank you, Esme."

I took her to the room she'd share with two other women. Safe Harbor, a group home, was the result of converting an old warehouse. It had six floors; the bottom two were shared spaces, while the top floors housed women. We'd usually have twenty-five to thirty women in the shelter. But we turned away several others because of a lack of space.

When I get the money Declan offered at the end of the marriage contract period, I could buy the building next door and expand the premises of Safe Harbor.

I came to my office on the first floor and looked at my watch. It was already past seven in the evening. The day had flown by, and there was still so much to do. When Declan wasn't home, I sometimes stayed at work until past midnight; but tonight he was home, and after what happened last night, I couldn't wait to see him again, to hold him again. *And* he'd made dinner reservations for eight.

I was packing up when Maria knocked on my open door.

"Hey." I lit up seeing her.

"How's it going?" She gave me a hug. "Going home?"

"Yes," I smiled shyly. "Declan is taking me to dinner at the Girl & The Goat. He said they have a nice wine list."

"He's picking you up?"

"No. I told him I'd meet him there. I thought I'd walk. It isn't too far."

Maria nodded. "I hear there's a gala this Saturday."

I felt weak at the thought. Declan had texted me to keep Saturday evening free, that he couldn't say no to Forest, the judge who married us, and that he wanted me with him. I was excited to go but afraid I had nothing appropriate to wear, and I wanted to look nice for him. I didn't want to embarrass him. I also wanted to look sexy enough to seduce him instead of vice versa. My bank account couldn't handle the dresses that Viv wore. The Marchesa dress that I'd worn to dinner with Senator Rivers had cost eight thousand dollars. I had looked it up.

"I know. Maria, I need help."

"Of course."

"I have nothing to wear and don't know where to start. I also don't have a ton of money. I don't know what to do."

Maria scoffed. "You're married to Declan Knight; you have all the money in the world. He's given you credit cards, hasn't he?"

He had, and I'd left them in my dresser at home.

"I couldn't do that," I protested. "Maybe I can rent the Runway or something. Then I can get one of those designer outfits."

"Instead of borrowing something from an online store, why don't you come by tomorrow after work? We'll make a Friday night out of it. And you can find something in my closet."

I looked at her, horrified. Maria was a tall, slender woman. "Nothing of yours will fit me."

"Wanna bet? And we are the same shoe size. And, you know I have more bags than I know what to do with. You can get dressed at my place on Saturday. I have someone coming over to do hair and makeup—so we'll play dress up." She winked at me.

I felt relieved. The last time, I'd been entirely out of my depth—this time, I'd do better and be better for Declan.

"That would be wonderful, Maria."

"Excellent." She kissed me on the cheek. "Come by after six tomorrow."

Maria lived in Silver Lake in a townhouse. She loved the area with its cozy boutiques and wine bars. I might live in that area after the year with Declan was up. I could afford it better than downtown, and I'd be able to walk everywhere as I could now.

I was the last to leave the office, so I turned off all the lights and locked up.

"Going home late again, Miss Esme?" Jim, a retired patrolman from LAPD who worked for us as a security guard, told me.

"You know how it is, Jim. How are the grandkids?"

"Real good. And my daughter says thank you for the books you sent for them. They love Captain Underpants."

Jim's daughter lived in Denver with her husband and six-year-old twins. I'd met them a month ago and fallen in love with her gorgeous boys.

"I'll send some more books," I promised. I usually bought books whenever my budget allowed for Safe Harbor's library. It was good for the children to have books in the playroom—and since I always loved to read and found it healing, I hoped it helped the children as well.

I had walked several blocks when someone cried out, "Bitch."

This was Skid Row; someone was always yelling something. I hurried my steps instinctively, my hand going inside my bag to find my pepper spray. Downtown LA was safe—and I'd never needed to use the spray before, but I enjoyed having it with me as a security blanket, just in case.

I heard footsteps behind me, but a hand grabbed my arm before I could turn. "Bitch, where's my Nancy?"

I tried to pull away, but the man was strong. He was nearly six foot tall and built like a linebacker. Nancy was about my height and thirty pounds lighter than me.

"Who are you?" I demanded, anger surging through me even though I knew. This enormous man pummeled his girlfriend who was half his size. What chance did she have?

"I'm Billy. Nancy's my girl. They told me at the ER that *you* took her. Where is she?" He shook me, and I could smell the alcohol on his breath. From my experience, big men who were drunk were not capable of dialog and listening.

He was following me...did he see me come out of the building? Would he be able to backtrack to Safe Harbor?

I held onto the pepper spray.

"Where is my wife and baby?" He brought his face close to me, his eyes bloodshot. I should've been afraid, but I wasn't. Anger was taking me over, thinking about Nancy at the mercy of this large man.

My self-defense classes kicked in. I stomped on his foot as hard as I could. It didn't bother him at all. He slapped me hard, and I felt my vision fray.

My hand pulled out the pepper spray. I closed my eyes and sprayed him. As I did, I screamed. "Help."

He didn't loosen his grip as he cried in agony. Tears flowed down my eyes as well because pepper spray didn't just hurt the assailant but also the victim as it got in the air and splattered. Sure, the spray would debilitate him, but it also slowed me down.

I lifted my knee and rammed into his groin as hard as I could. He slammed his forehead into my nose. I heard something crunch painfully in my face. We both went down. I scrambled up before he did. I was going to run, but an arm came around me before I could.

"Mrs. Knight, are you okay?" I turned to see a man in a suit. A man as big as Billy.

Another man in a suit had turned Billy onto his stomach on the asphalt, his knee digging into his back. He put handcuffs on Billy.

This wasn't LAPD. This was...Declan.

"We're so sorry. We just realized you had left. We're usually always behind you."

I wanted to ask many questions, but I could taste blood. I am sure that my nose was broken. My vision swayed, and then everything went black.

Chapter 28

DECLAN

Raya entered my office as I was preparing to leave, and I lifted my hand to stop her from speaking. "I'm taking Esme out to dinner and am already late. So, don't give me a hard time about missing poker night." My last meeting took longer than I thought it would. I'd texted Esme to get a drink, and I'd join her shortly.

"Dec," her voice was calm, but something was wrong, and I went on high alert.

"What?" I demanded.

"She's in the ER."

My heart pounded, and I could feel a buzz in my head. "Who's *she*? Not Esme."

Raya nodded. "I'm sorry, Dec."

"What the fuck, Raya. I told you to take care of her. What happened?" I walked around my desk. "Which ER?"

"Good Samaritan, and your car is waiting downstairs. I'll brief you in the car."

"Is she hurt?"

"Yes," Raya responded tightly.

I felt nausea climb through me at the thought of Esme hurt. "Not much, right?"

"Dec...it's..."

"Christ!" I all but sprinted to the elevators.

Raya told me what happened as our driver navigated the busy streets of DTLA.

"Where the fuck were your people?"

"They didn't realize she'd left. Usually, they're with her. *But* she handled herself. Kneed him in the nuts *and* pepper sprayed him."

"Then why the fuck is her nose broken?" I demanded.

"I really am sorry, Dec."

"Fuck, Raya. Do you know how small she is?"

"I know."

"How big was this guy?"

"Six two, two fifty."

I blinked. "And she brought *him* down?"

Raya smiled. "Yeah. Don't get on her bad side."

"She works out; does a hundred pushups in one go." I felt admiration for my wife. Esme was fucking remarkable.

But she didn't look like a warrior woman, more like a broken doll when I saw her on a bed in an examination room in the ER. The minute I could, I was going to take her home.

"Where the fuck is her doctor?" I demanded.

"I'm so sorry, Declan." Esme held her hand out to me.

I grabbed her hand and cradled it. She had bruises on her knuckles. "Sweetheart, there's nothing for you to be sorry about."

"I should've gotten an Uber, but I thought I'd walk. It's not too far."

"Raya, can you find out why her fucking doctor isn't here?"

"This is an ER, Declan." Esme tried to smile and winced. They had taped her nose. Her left eye was shut. There was a bruise on her left cheek, the size of my fist.

"They cleaned her up in the ambulance," Raya told me, "but she may need surgery as her nose is broken." She had been keeping up to date with the two idiots standing outside the room, their white shirts smudged with my wife's blood.

"What happened to the asshole who hurt her?"

"They arrested him. Esme will have to make a statement, but the detective in charge said he'd wait until they patched her up."

Esme gripped my hand. "Please don't be angry."

I brushed my lips against her forehead. "I'm not angry with you, darling."

"Don't be angry with anyone. It's not the first time that this has happened."

"What do you mean?"

She moaned in pain, and I stiffened. "I've worked in women's shelters and homes for children before. Abusive spouses and parents...they always like to take it out on the world."

That was it. She was going to find a new line of work if I had to force her to do it. No fucking way she was going to Skid Row ever again.

"You still look angry," she mumbled, then closed her eyes.

"Esme," a panicked voice came from behind me. It was Mark Caruso.

Esme opened her eyes and let go of my hand. He immediately sat on the bed next to her and embraced her.

"My nose is broken, Mark," she said sadly.

"I know, baby doll. I know. But we'll fix it up, okay."

"But you're not a plastic surgeon."

She was crying now, and he rocked her.

That should've been me, I thought. But I was so angry with everything and everyone that I'd not held her, comforted her. I'd let my frustration with letting her down take over. I had put my feelings first, not hers. I knew she needed peace, and since I got here, I ignored her requests not to be angry and barked orders. That I felt like shit, watching another man comfort my wife, was exactly what I deserved.

I stuck my hands in my pockets and watched the two friends. Mark was devastated. One look on his face told me that.

"How is she?" Maria whispered. I hadn't even noticed her come in. She pulled the curtains back to maintain Esme's privacy from the other two patients in the room.

"Her nose is broken," my voice was hoarse with emotion. "And she's sad."

Maria put a hand on my arm. "I should've insisted on giving her a ride. She said she'd walk to the restaurant and—."

"Not your fault," I immediately soothed her because I knew Esme would want that.

The doctor finally arrived, and I reigned in my temper to not fly off the handle with him and demand why he was late. As Esme had said, this was an ER, and broken noses were not a priority; life-threatening bullet and knife wounds were.

They ran blood tests and x-rayed her nose. They cleaned and re-bandaged her. Thankfully, her nose would not need surgery as the break was a hairline fracture and clean. There would be some swelling, but it would pass soon. I was happy about that because having Esme go under anesthesia scared the fuck out of me. It was Mark who pushed her wheelchair. Once we were outside, I picked her up and carried her to the Escalade.

"I'm too heavy," she moaned, loopy from the painkillers she had taken.

"Never." I put the seat belt on her. I slid inside beside her and let her head rest against my shoulder. "Mark, do you want to come along?" I asked because she'd want him.

Mark shook his head. "I'll check on her tomorrow."

"We both will." Maria spoke with concern and guilt in her eyes, "We both will."

As we drove home, I secured her to me with an arm around her shoulder.

"Are you in pain, love?"

"Hmm," she mumbled. "I know there's pain, but it's far away, behind a wool cloud."

They'd given her codeine because her nose would hurt like a mother, the ER doctor had assured me. I hugged her close as she slept.

She slept through when I carried her to the penthouse and put her in my...our bed. I took the hospital gown she was wearing off. Underneath she wore a pair of sensible white panties. There were still streaks of dried blood on her chest. My heart stuttered as I covered her up with the duvet. I watched her for a while, wondering when she'd become so important to me that I was afraid to leave as she slept, worried she'd stop breathing.

Even with her nose plastered and the bloom of a bruise on her face, she looked beautiful. My warrior princess, I thought. How could I ever have thought she was a doormat? She took down a hulk of a man with pepper spray and her knee. Sure, she looked like she went a few rounds with a linebacker, but she'd gotten the best of him.

I left her to sleep and went to my office, which was through our bedroom. This way, if she moved, I'd hear her.

I called Raya because she'd insisted I do that after I settled Esme in bed. She felt guilty, and even though I wanted to be annoyed with her, I knew she was not at fault. Esme worked in a high-risk workplace. And even though I wanted Esme to stop, I knew she wouldn't. She loved her work, and I couldn't change her mind. I would, however, make sure that she had better security—and this time, she'd know about it and not go anywhere without someone watching her back; she'd have to do so for my sanity.

"How is she?" Raya asked.

I heard a rustle of clothing and smiled when Mateo's sleepy voice came through the phone. "It's late, *querida*. Who are you talking to?"

Raya moved away from where she was as I heard her footsteps. "Is she okay?"

"Yes. She's sleeping. We must ensure she knows she has security and they're with her. I'll give her a car, so she doesn't walk to work or take the metro or whatever the fuck she's been doing. This is on me. I should've taken better care of her."

"Esme will not let a car drive her around, and you know that. Security has had one hell of a time keeping up with her because she insists on public transportation."

"I don't know why she wants to live like she has no money."

"She doesn't," Raya reminded me.

"I do. And what's mine is hers."

"Things have *certainly* changed."

"And I guess you'll be well fucked when you come to the office tomorrow," I retorted.

There was a long pause. "Any chance you'll forget what you just heard?"

"That Mateo called you darling, and it seems like he's in whichever bed you plan to climb into after this call?"

I could hear her grit her teeth. "Yes, that. Mateo doesn't want anyone to know."

"Why?"

She sighed. "Because...it's just the way he wants it."

But you don't, I thought, and that was maybe why sometimes there was grief in her eyes. The man she was in love with was not in love with her, or not enough to make it official and public.

Mateo probably saw this as a temporary relationship that would end soon. Also, if it came in the open, HR would have a few things to say about him fucking someone who reported to him. Well, I was the company's CEO, and I was okay with him and Raya having a relationship; hell, I'd been waiting for it to happen for years.

"How long has it been going on?" I asked softly.

"A few weeks."

"On his side, a few weeks. On yours?"

I heard a self-deprecating laugh. "A lifetime. Give my best to Esme."

"Goodnight, Raya. And I'll say nothing to Mateo."

"Thanks, Dec, and I'll take better care of Esme. I promise."

Chapter 29

ESME

E verything hurt.

I groaned as I tried to get up and felt shards of ice go through my face.

"Sweetheart, let me help you." Declan wore jeans and a white dress shirt, his home attire.

"What are you doing here?"

"I live here, honey." He helped me sit up and then, as if giving up, slid an arm under my knee and another around my neck and picked me up.

"I'm heavy," I protested.

"No, you're not, and no, I'm not too weak to carry my wife. Bathroom first, I imagine?"

I nodded and snuggled into him, enjoying the woodsy smell of his body wash and cologne.

He gave me privacy in the bathroom so I could use the toilet. I even brushed my teeth. I put on the T-shirt and pajama shorts that he, or Calliope, had conveniently left in the bathroom. It wasn't too bad, I thought until I looked at my face in the mirror. I looked like something out of a war movie. A sob tore through me.

"Esme?"

"Declan, I look terrible."

He came inside the bathroom and stood behind me, a whole foot taller and way more handsome than anyone had a right to be. "You look beautiful." He kissed my hair.

"How am I going to go to the gala tomorrow?"

"You're not."

I pouted.

"There will be other parties."

"You haven't asked since that first time, and now you finally did. Maria was going to let me borrow a dress and shoes. I was going to look pretty for you." I gulped some air and then bawled like a baby. He picked me up again and took me to bed. Calliope had just finished changing the sheets, and he set me down on the fresh linen.

Calliope quickly came to fluff pillows behind me so I could sit up.

"How are you, Esme?"

"I look like a monster," I whimpered, bursting into tears.

"Oh no, no, you don't," Calliope soothed.

Declan held me in his arms.

"Now, my love, it's just a gala. You would not enjoy it, anyway."

"But I was looking forward to it. I thought I'd look nice, and you'd...be proud of me."

He pulled back and looked at my puffy eyes. "My love, I'm always proud of you."

But because painkillers were still running through my system, I'd have never asked. "Why do you keep calling me your love?"

I heard Calliope snicker before she left the bedroom.

"Because you are my love. My wonderful, beautiful love." He kissed the bruise on my cheek, closed eye, and nose.

"Not beautiful."

"Gorgeous. If going to the gala means much to you, we'll go."

"Looking like this?"

"We'll fix you up. We can appear and leave before your painkillers wear off, okay?"

I looked at him in disbelief. No one, and I mean no one, had offered to do something they didn't want to do because I liked it.

"You can't fix this up," I lamented.

"We'll get the best hair and makeup person. You'll look amazing. But if you want to go, you must rest all day today and tomorrow."

I sniffled. "Okay."

"Good girl." He kissed my lips softly. "You scared me but good, Esme."

His tone was serious now.

"I scared myself a little as well. I didn't know I had security."

"Bodyguards, yes. Raya kept them discreet, but now you must let them be with you. And I want you to take a car and a driver. No more public transportation and no walking late at night."

Hell no. My lips straightened into a revolutionary line.

"Esme, please, for the sake of my mental health. I can't...I can't see you like this again. It's killing me that you got hurt; that I couldn't protect you."

He looked so miserable that I nodded reluctantly. "Can they not wear suits? They'll stand out like sore thumbs at Safe Harbor."

"Deal."

He brought me some fresh pea soup, and he fed me as I sat like a queen in bed being served. I took some more painkillers and immediately went to sleep. According to Declan, healing took time, and I needed all the healing I could get.

I woke up several hours later, feeling sore but better. The clock on Declan's bedside table said it was seven in the evening. I slept for nearly eight hours. Those painkillers were industrial strength.

I sat up and heard raised voices from the living room. I got to the bathroom as that was urgent, and then I brushed my teeth. I wanted to do more, but I was worried about who Declan was arguing within the living room. I walked out barefoot, wearing the t-shirt and pajama shorts I had been sleeping in.

Viv and Julien were in the living room, sitting on the sofa across from Declan, who was in the red swan armchair.

They all looked at me as I came into the room.

Declan immediately rose and walked up to me. "How are you?"

"Okay." I looked at my father and sister. "Daddy. Viv."

Were they here because I'd gotten hurt? That would be a first. But it warmed my heart. Maybe they were finally caring for me.

"Wow," Viv exclaimed. "You look like hell."

"I know." I leaned against Declan.

"You should go to bed." He helped me sit down on the arm-chair he just vacated.

"I've been in bed all day." I was conscious of my black t-shirt and pajama shorts, and as if he could read my mind, Declan picked up the cashmere throw that rested in a basket next to the sofa and draped it around me like a shawl, covering all of me and keeping me warm.

"Esme, maybe it would be better if you were not here," my father said acerbically. "This is a family matter."

"She is my family." Declan sat down on the side table next to me.

"Come on, Dec, be reasonable," Viv interjected. "She knows nothing about Hartley Industries or Knight Tech. She'll be bored."

"Then that's her problem," Declan retorted.

"No, that's okay. I'm tired, and I can—"

"Stay," Declan ordered. He then looked at Daddy and Viv. "The merger will be completed in two months—and I'm not changing my mind. We're sticking to the plan."

"Now, Dec, you know these things take time. Let's extend the timeline to the end of the year. That way, you and Viv have enough time to resolve—"

"There's nothing to resolve," Declan bit out.

I wished I could disappear. Vanish!

They wanted Declan to get our marriage annulled. They'd been pressuring me, and I would do it if my husband agreed, but he didn't. He insisted he'd tell a judge how we were indeed married and that if I wanted to get rid of him, I'd need a divorce, which would take several months and include a separation period, all of which would get us past the one-year contract period mark, anyway. The Hartley Industry bylaws include a mention that a divorce, unlike an annulment, can put the merger at risk.

"Do you want to stay married to Dec, Es?"

Before I could say anything, Declan spoke. "That's between Esme and me, wife and husband, and none of your business."

Daddy looked at me with disgust, and I recoiled. Declan took my hand in his and squeezed.

"My wife is recovering from an attack on her, and I'd like you both to leave." He patted my hand as he set it back on my lap and stood up.

"Dec," Viv pleaded. "Please, don't do this."

"Do what? Ask you to leave my house?"

"Our house. This is our house. We got it together. We decorated it...hell, I decorated it."

"I bought it; we did not. You couldn't afford it. And you didn't decorate it; an interior designer did," Declan corrected her.

Viv shot a glance at me. "Are you enjoying sleeping in the same bed he and I made love in?"

My shoulders slumped. I was tired. I didn't want to fight with my family.

I rose, holding the cashmere throw around me. "I'm going to go to bed."

Declan picked me up like I weighed nothing and carried me to his room.

He tucked me in. "I'm sorry. I'll send them away."

"Wouldn't it be better if we annulled our marriage," I offered. "I can't do this anymore."

"Do what?"

"Fighting with Daddy and Viv; my mother is upset with me. Why not give them what they want?"

He nodded. "And you? What do you want?"

I smiled weakly at him. I knew I wanted him, but there was no way I could admit it to him or anyone else. In fairytales, Cinderella married her Prince; in the real world, they never met, and even if they did, he didn't want her.

"How does that matter?"

"It matters to me."

I closed my eyes. It was too tempting. He was too tempting. "I'm tired, Declan."

"I know, sweetheart." He brushed his lips on my forehead. "Sleep tight, my love."

He was almost at the door when I let my heart break, "Please stop calling me that."

He turned and looked so sad that I cringed. "My love?"

"Yes."

"Why?"

"Because I may start believing it and...I can't let myself get hurt."

He seemed far away suddenly, his eyes shuttered. "I do, Esme. I lo—."

I didn't let him finish. "Please, Declan."

"Sleep well, Esme."

He left, closing the door softly behind him.

I wanted to believe him, but I was afraid. No one had loved me; why should he? All my life, I waited for my family to care about me. I was madly in love with my husband and wanted to build all those castles in the air my father had warned me to stay away from. I couldn't take the risk with Declan because it would destroy me when he walked away from me, as he most definitely would. It was already too late.

Chapter 30

DECLAN

M ateo and Forest came home when I didn't respond to their texts. Esme had taken another painkiller, and from recent experience, I knew she would be out for eight to ten hours. Enough time for me to get drunk because I failed to convince the one woman who had me turned inside out about how I felt about her. Viv had believed me blindly when I said I loved her. She'd had no doubts. My feelings for Viv paled compared to those for Esme—and she wouldn't even let me say the words.

What I used to think was a weakness of smiling through insults and unfairness, was the courage to keep living her best life. I was learning to be a better person with her. To be a happier person. I was learning from her, and my obsession with my work had tempered in her presence. How could it not when my wife told me how she helped a child smile after being beaten by his father? The issues she faced at work were more real than mergers and acquisitions and pursuing dollars.

"Why are you guys here?" I demanded as they walked in without me inviting them. Security reported to Mateo as Knight Tech owned my building, so they let him up to the penthouse without questioning or alerting me.

"You missed poker night," Mateo explained. I was drinking in the living room. I was sprawled on the couch, some ballgame playing on the television that I could not get interested in. I was a quarter of the way through a bottle of Ardbeg 10 and was planning to keep at it and have the mother of all hangovers.

"I don't even play poker with you guys, but I needed a break from the gala craziness my mother has been generating in massive proportions," was Forest's explanation.

They got comfortable in my living room and helped themselves to my whiskey.

"How's she?" Mateo asked.

"Sleeping." *And breaking my fucking heart.*

"Then why are you moping around?" Forest wanted to know.

I sighed. "It's...nothing."

What was I supposed to say? I fell in love with my wife, and she doesn't believe me. Or that when we have sex, it feels like a celebration of life, and I wanted to be inside her all the time? Or that I feared losing her, and seeing her in that emergency room almost killed me?

"That doesn't sound like nothing." Mateo drank some whiskey.

And what the fuck did Mateo know about falling in love? He was going to fuck it up with Raya, but I'd promised her I'd keep her secret, so I kept my mouth shut.

"You know, for someone who hated getting married to the...I think he referred to her as the *ugly* sister," Forest mocked, "you seem fucked up about her injuries."

"She's not ugly," I thundered. "She's fucking gorgeous."

"I agree." Mateo held up his glass.

"Stop looking at my wife, you son of a bitch."

"And he's jealous. Raya tells me he was jealous of Mark Caruso." Mateo was enjoying himself at my expense.

Forest grinned. "And he's gay."

"I didn't know that then, and I wasn't jealous. I just didn't want my wife to fuck around on me after my fiancée had done the same." *But I was envious, not about the non-existent sexual feelings between them but the love. She looked at him like he hung the fucking moon. When he told her he loved her, she believed him. When I tried to say it, she went into apoplectic shock.*

Forest cleared his throat. "From the evidence I have seen, I determine that you've fallen in love with your wife, Dec."

"Yeah, your honor," I didn't bother contradicting him. "And a fat lot of good that's done me. I thought my heart was breaking when Viv left, but compared to what Esme is putting me through, that was a cakewalk."

"What is she putting through?" Mateo stretched his legs. He was still wearing his suit, though he'd discarded the jacket on the back of the armchair he was sitting in.

Forest, who wore jeans, even in chambers unless there was a special occasion, was dressed SoCal style in a pair of board shorts, a T-shirt, and leather sandals. Off duty, and sometimes even on, Forest looked like a surfer, not a high court judge.

"She doesn't believe me. Her family wants me to annul our marriage, and Esme thinks that's a grand idea. She thinks that if she believes I love her, she'll get hurt. She's confident I'm going to walk out on her." I felt grim as I spoke and laid the truth out. I poured myself a fresh glass and drank it like it wasn't whiskey but a shot.

"And what have you done to show her you love her?" Mateo asked.

I stared at him. "What?"

"I mean, what have you done to prove to her you love her?" he reframed.

"Yeah, women are big on this proof thing. Daisy dumped my ass because she didn't believe that I...that's ancient history. Let's talk about you. How do you *show* Esme you love her?" Now Forest looked as grim as me as he drank some whiskey.

He and Daisy had had a red passionate affair for nearly a year, four years before Forest became a judge when he was a District Attorney. Suddenly and without explanation, Forest stopped showing up for poker because Daisy told him she didn't want to see him—and since then, he casually asked Mateo and me how Daisy was without admitting he desperately wanted to know *everything* about her. I had tried to ask Daisy what happened, but she shut down the conversation by saying something along the lines of, *mind your own fucking business, or I'll punch you in the face.*

"I spend time with her. We have fantastic sex, and...what the fuck does it mean to *show* that I love her?" I was doing things with her I'd never done with women. Going on fucking walks, holding hands, kissing in public, watching movies...what else was I supposed to do?

"Dec, all her life she's been told she's not good enough—"

"And I always tell her she's great," I interrupted Mateo triumphantly.

"I think you're going to have to show her what she means to you," Mateo said sincerely and with sympathy. "She's been ignored her whole life—and the only time her family has paid attention to her is when they want something from her. She's probably not good at trusting people, and that you both got married the way you did doesn't inspire confidence."

Forest slammed his glass down and stood up. "Let's go to your game room and play some pool. I can't do this relationship talk anymore."

"You having trouble with a new lady?" I asked.

"Same old trouble. Same old fucking lady. But I've moved on, and she has moved on and on and on. She's sleeping with some golf player."

"Cade Reilly. Four-time PGA champion," I offered.

"Right. And I see...you know, lots of women," Forest said lamely.

Mateo stood up. "Yeah, let's play pool."

"And how about your love life, Mateo?" I couldn't help myself.

"I have a sex life, not a love life. The woman I fuck knows that we're having a good time. She gets an orgasm or two, and I get the same. After that, she goes her way, and I go mine. I won't give her a disease; I'll make sure she doesn't get pregnant, and she needs to go when I say it's over." Mateo tucked his hands in his pockets.

"And what happens if *she* says it's over?" I asked.

Mateo's vision wavered. Ah, he hadn't thought about what would happen if Raya walked away from him.

"Then so be it. No harm, no foul." We could all see that he didn't believe what he was saying.

We men were a bunch of morons, I thought.

Here were three of us, all lying about our relationships. Well, I wasn't anymore. I loved my wife, and I'd have to show her every day so that before this marriage contract ended, she would believe me and we would build the life I knew we could.

Chapter 31

ESME

I stood in front of the mirror in Declan's walk-in closet. It was huge, filled with his suits, clothes, and shoes. And it had a dressing area with mirrors on three walls. A woman had designed this space. Most probably the interior designer Viv had hired.

The dress was a dream. It was a strapless pink Rodarte gown with a tight bodice and a long chiffon skirt.

"It's perfect for your petite frame," Maria announced as she looked at me with appreciation.

The shoes were Miu Miu ballet flats also in the same rose pink as the gown—but the skirt was so long that no one would notice what I wore on my feet, and even if they did, the shoes were beautiful. This hadn't come from Maria's closet; I knew that. But once I put it on, I couldn't make an issue out of it because I wanted Declan to see me. I'd worn nothing this beautiful or *expensive* in my life before.

Maria had got dressed at Declan's penthouse as well, and her hair and makeup person called themselves Chase and did marvelous things with makeup primarily to conceal all my bruises. They also did something to my hair, which hung around my shoulders in soft waves.

"Now, impress Dec, and I'll get ready. Mark is picking me up from here." Maria ushered me out of the closet and gave me a tiny Chanel bag that matched the dress as I reached the door. It had enough room for my phone and ChapStick, which was all I needed.

I was nervous as I walked into the living room. I knew how Declan looked in a tuxedo and dreaded how unmatched we'd look. People would think he should've married Viv. They'd wonder what happened there. I'd heard the rumors and the media headlines.

Esme stole her sister's love.

Is Esme Knight pregnant?

Who is Esme Knight? All the dirt from her high school boyfriend. (And I didn't even have one!)

Trouble in paradise? Is Dec Knight back with Viv Hartley?

There was also a storyline about me being an alien—which amused me. The other headlines, not so much. One thing was obvious, my family, his parents, and the media all thought that Declan and I were not suited for one another—and that he should return to the beautiful and adorable Viv.

There had been an entire story by an influencer about my weight. *She's so fat he has to roll her in flour to find the wet spot.* I was five-three, and a size six. I was not heavy. I just wasn't skinny. I worked out and stayed healthy, but next to the willowy Viv, I always looked like a hippo.

Declan was reading something on his iPad in the living room when I came to stand in front of him.

"Ta-da," I said with all the fake cheer I could muster.

He looked up, and for a moment, nothing happened; he seemed frozen, and then slowly, he smiled. "You look lovely, sweetheart." He set his iPad aside and rose to stand in front of me.

He bent his head and lifted my chin at the same time. "You always look beautiful, you know that?" he said as he brushed his lips against mine.

I pulled back. "I don't know how to do lipstick properly, so this needs to stay, and they said it will as long as I don't go about kissing or giving blow jobs."

"They?" His eyes crinkled as they did when he was holding back laughter.

"Chase. The hair and makeup artist."

"So, no blow job in the car for me?"

"You want one?" I asked.

His eyes went from amused to hot in an instant. "If you let me taste you, sweetheart, I'll let you taste me. Is that a deal?"

"I can't open my jaw too wide, or I'll smear the lipstick," I told him, then closed my eyes as I heard what I'd just said. "I say the dumbest things."

He pulled me into his arms. "You smell delicious, like jasmine. And let's rest your mouth until you completely heal. Now, your pussy, I can stretch wide, can't I?"

I felt the heat pool between my legs. "Declan."

"I love how you say my name when you're aroused." His lips feathered kisses across the jawline.

"How do I...say it?"

"Like you want me inside you." He raised his head. "You feel well enough to let me taste you tonight?"

I didn't know, but who the hell cared? "I do."

"Good girl." He set me aside and looked at me proudly. "Your eyes are so expressive."

"And now both are open. Chase did a great job with the makeup. And that's why my face is off limits to you."

"I'll miss kissing you...but maybe I'll find other lips to satisfy me."

I felt warmth rush into my cheeks.

"Are you wet, Esme? Wet for me?"

Declan put his hands on my hips and pushed my skirt up. He was delighted to find the slit and slipped his right hand under my dress as his left held me, his eyes boring into mine.

His fingers pushed my panties aside, and he groaned. "Esme."

"Yes." I swayed slightly.

"You're so wet. So tight."

It was too much—all of it. I closed my eyes.

"No, look at me when I make you come," he commanded with his voice and fingers. He strummed my clit.

I was on painkillers; I'd had the crap beaten out of me. My nose still felt raw and sore. And, yet, it didn't seem to matter. He touched my pussy, and I was ready to go.

"Come for me." His voice was hoarse—he was as aroused as me.

My glance fell to his crotch. His erection was pushing against his pants. I licked my lips at the thought of tasting him.

"Eyes up here," he growled, and I looked into his eyes; they set me ablaze.

He pushed two, then three fingers inside me, and then just as he touched my clit, several things happened at once—the elevator door opened, and Mark stepped into the penthouse; Maria walked into the living room in a gorgeous Givenchy red dress, and I came on a soft cry.

Chapter 32

DECLAN

She was charming when she was shy. And immensely relieved when I whisked her away from the knowing eyes of Mark and Maria to the car downstairs.

She was flushed. It looked good on her. The bruises had faded thanks to the handiwork of the doctors and makeup artists, but I could feel them still in my heart. The detective in charge told me that Billy would not be getting out for at least three to six years for assault. This was not his first offense. Carolina Vega, the Knight family lawyer, had assured him she'd do everything in her power to make sure that Esme would not have to testify in a court trial.

It had been hard enough to watch her give her statement to the detective the day before. If you didn't know her, you'd have thought she was calm and collected, probably part of her social worker training, but I could see the burden she carried as she narrated the events as clinically as anyone could. My admiration for her only increased. The detective was grateful for her detailed account and was confident that Billy would accept a guilty plea. He would not survive a trial with a witness like Esme and his pregnant girlfriend Nancy, who had her own horrific story of abuse.

"They saw me have an orgasm." It mortified her.

"They were smiling, and I can assure you they were happy you're getting some."

She grinned sheepishly. "Mark has been trying to convince me to get laid for years."

"Why haven't you had more sex, Esme? You're a lovely passionate woman. I can't imagine there weren't men who wanted you." When we'd first met, I'd thought it was obvious why no one wanted to sleep with the boring-looking social worker—but that was when I didn't know the fire that burned inside her. The goodness that was sexier than any woman I'd ever been with.

"Well...I was busy. I had two jobs. And classes."

"I'm sorry your family didn't help you." I knew Viv had lived luxuriously when she attended school; her father paid for everything, and she had a massive trust fund to boot. I'd never had to think if Viv was interested in me for my money—I may have had more, but she had plenty. But she wanted to enjoy the power that being a Knight would give her. Esme mostly seemed bothered by it.

"I didn't mind," she said, and I knew she meant it. Some people would say it as proforma but not Esme.

"Come here." I pulled her onto my lap and held her like she was the most precious thing in my life, and she was.

"May I ask you for something?" her voice was timid.

"Of course." *Anything. You can ask me for anything, and I'll give it to you.*

"Last time we were out...you left me with Mateo, and I like him—but...this time—"

"I'll be with you the whole time." I kissed her cheek gently. "I'm sorry about last time."

She looped her arms around my neck and smiled at me. My heart skipped a beat—I felt like a fucking teenager falling in love for the first time.

"Thank you for taking care of me these past few days."

"It's my pleasure...though I'd much prefer you were not hurt the way you were. I think I have a few gray hairs because of that."

She caressed my hair. "You'd look distinguished with gray hair when you get them."

"Esme," I took a deep breath and tightened my hold on her. "Can you take some time off? I'd like for us to go away for a few days."

She seemed uncertain. "How many days? When? I have clients. I can't just leave, Declan."

There was panic in her voice. I didn't know why.

"I'll give you plenty of notice. Will that work?"

She closed her eyes and nodded. "I'm sorry. I haven't been on holiday in forever. But, yes, I'd love to go away with you. Where would we go?" The excitement was back in her eyes.

"Where would you like to go?"

She thought about it for a moment. "You'd find it boring."

"Tell me."

"If it's in the summer, I'd like to go to the Mojave Desert. They have these eco pods there with glass ceilings and walls. You can see the whole big sky with all the stars. It's stunning."

"And if it's winter?" I had foolishly thought she'd say Paris or Rome. But no, she surprised me again.

"The Finnish Lapland. They have these igloos you can stay in that are made of glass. I desperately want to see the Northern Lights."

"I thought you'd say wine country, what with your love for wine."

"If I had all the time and money in the world...then I'd love to spend a month in Burgundy tasting wine. But after that, I'd get bored and want to return to work. Where would you like to go?"

I thought about it and shrugged. "The usual places. I like London very much. Paris. I enjoy going to the opera—so I go to Vienna and Verona during the season. Maybe Kauai because I like to hike."

"We should go hiking. Topanga Canyon has great hiking."

We discussed her dream plans and places she'd love to go to and cataloged each. I wanted to show her my love. I'd show her by making her dreams come true—all of them. A month in Burgundy? Absolutely. A week in Finland? I'll book that trip now.

She lay against me, and I felt content holding her. I'd never had this before with anyone. Not even my friends.

I love you, Esme. I wanted to shout the words out, but she wasn't ready. But she would be, I'd make sure of it.

I held her hand as we stepped out of the car.

"You look great," I whispered in her ear, knowing she was worried.

"You too. Do you think...we look *okay* together?"

"We look fucking *wonderful* together."

I knew she was thinking of all the photos of Viv and me. I couldn't erase the past, even if I wanted to.

There were photographers and the flashes jolted her. I put an arm around her, and she looked up at me, her eyes in fight-or-flight mode. I bent my head and kissed her. Slowly. Seductively. She moaned as always when I kissed her, and the sound made my semi-erect penis rock hard. I took my time tasting her, letting the world around us dissolve. I knew the picture we made—a tall man with a small woman. I was holding her up, literally lifting her off her feet. When I set her down, her eyes were clouded with desire, not concerned about how we looked and what the photographs on social media would look like.

"Wow." Her cheeks were bright, no makeup could compare to an aroused Esme.

The gala's theme was Female Power, and my aunt had pulled all the stops. They painted the entire ballroom red and pink for power. It somehow looked both flashy and classy at the same time. My mother would comment about how vulgar it was, and my aunt would gush about how the pink and red roses came together to show womanhood. If I told her, it would mortify her that she had chosen the colors of a pussy.

Forest came up to us, a drink in hand. "The whole fucking place looks like someone's vagina."

"Oh my god, it does, doesn't it," Esme exclaimed, delighted with his inference.

"We have a table." Forest indicated to a table at the edge of the room. "Easy to escape if it gets to be too much."

He wore a tuxedo, and amongst all the Knights, he was the one who hated the monkey suit the most and looked damned uncomfortable in it.

"Oh, and Daisy is here," he warned me.

"At our table?"

"Yes. I need another drink." He walked away, and Esme looked at me in query.

"Daisy and Forest had a relationship. Something went wrong, and now they hate each other with the passion of a thousand suns...or at least they *pretend*."

Esme nodded. "Like Mateo and Raya *pretend* they're not together?"

"How did you know?"

"It's obvious. She shines like Christmas lights when he's around, and he can look at no one but her when they're in a room. Haven't you seen it?"

I shook my head. "Esme, you're something else. Raya and Mateo think it's a secret, and from what I can tell, no one, not even their closest friends, know. I found out because I heard him on the phone one night, and Raya came clean. But keep it to yourself. Mateo doesn't want anyone to know."

"Why? If they're in love..." she trailed off as understanding came. "They're not in love?"

"She is. He isn't sure." *Like us. I know I love you, but you're resisting me, resisting us.*

I took her to the bar and got her sparkling water with lime. Her powerful painkillers were not meant to mix with alcohol, and to keep her company, I ordered the same for myself.

"You can drink champagne," she said. "We have a driver."

"I enjoy drinking with you."

"Esme, you should've stayed home with all those bruises," her father mocked as he approached us at the bar. He then looked keenly at her.

All the joy left her face, and her smile became plastic.

"I..." she began, but I cut in.

"She looks stunning. I can hardly keep my eyes or hands off her."

Her face went pink, and I smiled at her.

Her father's lips tightened. "Don't be crude, Dec. It doesn't suit you. Is this Esme's influence? She deals with scum all day. Is that rubbing off on you?"

"Esme *is* influencing me. I've learned so much from her, and I'm still learning."

Viv approached her father; her face wreathed in a tight smile, which I know she gave when she was miserable. The photos of me kissing my wife had probably already hit some social media sites.

"You both look cozy," she murmured, raising her cheek to me. I ignored it.

"Viv, you look beautiful," said my wife, who couldn't read the room when it was hostile or probably could and didn't care. I could hear her say, *why should I change my behavior because people are small and petty?*

"Your face is healing, Es. The dress is nice—a couple of seasons old but looks decent."

"Rodarte made this as a special favor, Viv. It will not hit the runways." Considering how it would freak Esme out, I wasn't planning to reveal this, but enough was enough.

"What?" Esme looked horrified.

Most women would show off, but here she was, wondering how much I had spent, and as she'd said once to me when I told her money wasn't an issue for her anymore, "If you have a hundred thousand dollars to spend on a stupid dress, then you should *not* buy the dress and give it to a place like Safe Harbor. We need all the funds we can get."

"Dec, may I speak with you?" Viv demanded like it was her right.

"I'm afraid not, Viv. I'm going to dance with my wife and then get her off her feet because, as you know, she's recovering."

"Oh, yes, I heard about it. Some woman's boyfriend beat you up?"

Viv could be such a bitch, I thought. This was who she was. I just had been too clouded with her surface to see within.

"You should see the guy she kicked in the nuts. He's in jail and will probably do three to five." I picked up Esme's hand and kissed her bruised knuckles. "*My* Esme is not someone to fuck around with. The guy who attacked her was built like a linebacker."

I didn't ask to be excused but led Esme away from the two people who made her most unhappy—while she did everything she could to make them happy.

"Declan, I can't dance. I never learned."

"You just let me lead you, darling." I took her in my arms and almost immediately felt the irritation that Viv and Julien had caused dissipating. "It's a healing thing to hold you, Esme."

"For me too."

She wasn't as bad a dancer as she thought she was. She let me lead, and we fell into a rhythm. It wasn't until I felt a tap on my shoulder that I paid attention to my surroundings. I broke into a smile.

"Dad." I hugged him. "Esme, this is my father, Gerald. Dad, my beautiful wife. How was Thailand?"

"Excellent. And as were Vietnam and Malaysia. Hello, my dear; I'm this one's father. I'm so sorry, I've been traveling with monks for six months and missed your wedding."

My father disliked such events as much as Esme did and constantly avoided social life by traveling with tribes, monks, thought leaders, sociologists, and philosophers—learning about the world. It was what he was doing with his retirement, not interested in politics like my mother and secure with the fact that Knight Technologies was doing as well as it could under my leadership.

He hugged Esme, and I knew that surprised her. She probably thought my father would be like my mother and thank god he wasn't. I loved my father, but like my mother, I was annoyed with his lack of ambition. *But* now, with what I had learned about living life as a student from Esme, I knew I'd shortchanged him.

Maybe I should hand the company over to Mateo and Esme, and I could travel with my father. Perhaps I could take over the Knight Foundation with Esme. We could partner with The Caruso Foundation to take part in more grassroots activities like women's shelters, orphanages, and juvenile homes.

I surprised myself with those thoughts. I never thought I'd want to step away from the business at the age of thirty-five. I loved the company. I loved my job and the work.

I watched Esme charm my father with her curiosity to learn more about him and his travels.

When Esme excused herself to use the ladies room, my father nodded appreciatively. "I like her much better than that blond one you wanted to marry."

"Yeah, me too."

My father narrowed his eyes. "What's going on, son?"

My face was wreathed in smiles. "I'm a man in love, dad. A besotted fool."

"It looks good on you." My father patted me on my shoulder. "It looks *very* good on you."

Chapter 33

ESME

When I fell into bed after the gala, I was exhausted—but happier than ever. Declan had been with me the whole time. Dancing, holding my hand, carrying me when I was tired. His father had been a surprise, and he would come to Safe Harbor and see if he could volunteer. He was taking a month off from traveling while he made plans for a trip to South America and Antarctica in the winter—and wanted to be productive.

"I had a great time, Declan." I snuggled into him, resting my head on his shoulder. His arm was around me.

"Me too."

"Can we go again for another such event? Especially if your father will be there?"

He laughed. "You liked him, did you?"

"Very much. He's nothing like your mother...not that there's anything wrong with her; they're just different. Your mother is—"

"Cold," he interrupted. "You don't have to like everyone, Esme."

"I don't dislike your mother, Declan. I could never. She has some outstanding qualities. Do you know all the work she's done to help women in business as a judge?"

"I want to apologize for ever calling you a doormat. Because darling, what you are is a force of positivity. And I'm madly in...I...love that about you."

Was he going to say madly in love with you? Was he *really* in love with me?

I felt heat surge through me at that thought. I nuzzled his chest and licked his nipple. I felt his heartbeat go from average to fully aroused in seconds.

"Baby, you're tired, and no matter what you do, we're not having sex."

"But I want you." I kissed his chest and found him with my hand, hard and ready.

"I want you too, love, but..." he trailed off when I put just the right amount of pressure as he'd taught me to stroke him. "Ah...sweetheart, stop."

"You made me come this evening, and I did nothing for you."
I'd never initiated sex, and that I was experimenting with my
sexuality was erotic.

"You're hurt, my love," he said without conviction.

"I want you, Declan." My hand became more urgent, and I
pushed the comforter away.

I leaned down and kissed his belly and went further down.
Declan slept in the nude because he got hot at night—and it
was convenient. I watched him watch me helplessly as I slid my
mouth down, down, down, down.

When I took him in my mouth, he stroked my cheek and
his eyes darkened when I licked the top of his erection where
precum had gathered.

"I now know why you like to taste me so much. It's..."

"It's what?"

"Sensual. I'm as aroused giving as I am taking."

"Yes," he groaned as I took him in and used my hands and
mouth on him.

"Deeper, darling. Take me deeper."

I did as he asked, and tears ran down my cheeks as I struggled
to take his girth and length in. When he tried to pull away, I
shook my head.

Like him, I was aroused and desperately wanted to make him
come.

"I'm going to come," he cried as I increased speed, touching
his balls and squeezing them gently.

He was suddenly spurting inside my mouth, and I swallowed.
I pulled away, gasping, cum running down my chin. He pushed
the cum back into my mouth, and I took his finger in and sucked.

"How did I do?" I asked eagerly.

This was the first time I'd made him come with my mouth. I'd been practicing, but this was a first.

"Amazing, as always."

I came back up to lie next to him, feeling mischievous. "That was great. When can we do it again?"

He laughed. "I'm not a teenager, darling. You'll have to give me time."

He hauled me up to him and kissed me. He tasted himself. I loved that about him. He was comfortable with sex and was game for anything.

"You want to come, my love."

"Yes," I whimpered when he found me. He slid down and put my thighs over his shoulders.

"Oh, Esme, you're beautiful down here. Do you know that?"

"I got a bikini wax," I told him proudly.

"And you look just as beautiful as you did before." He parted my labia and licked me from back to front.

"Declan," I panicked. "Not there. I..."

"This is mine, too." He explored the tight flesh of my perineum with his finger and slid it inside me.

"Declan," I cried out, embarrassed.

"Esme, be quiet."

"But it's...I mean..."

As he pushed his finger further in and licked my throbbing clitoris, I moaned. He slid two fingers inside me.

"You're so tight in here, baby. I will open you up slowly, over days, and then when you're ready, I'll take you here."

I'd done no anal play. I didn't mind that it was forbidden, dirty, and kinky. But it was new, and I wasn't comfortable. "Will it hurt?"

"No, baby. I'd never hurt you. You'll love it. You behave like a good girl, but you're my filthy slut." His dirty talk always pushed me to the edge.

He devoured me, and even before he could gently bite my clitoris, which always made me come, I convulsed, my thighs shaking.

"When we make love, you never hold back," he whispered. "I'm hard again, Esme."

"Come inside me, Declan."

He kept my thighs on his shoulders and drove deep into me. "Am I hurting you?"

"No," I shook my head, my eyes glazed over. "Please, Declan."

"Slowly, my love, slowly. I'll make you come again. I promise. Just let me...ah...let me feel you."

I came again, this time with him, and I felt my universe had never been this perfect. The days on the calendar were moving faster than I wanted. It had been six months since we married. A year would be over in a heartbeat. Then what? And then he'd leave me.

How will I survive without you, Declan?

Chapter 34

DECLAN

"What are you doing here? I thought you were in New York and wouldn't come back until later tonight," she exclaimed when I entered Safe Harbor. I opened my arms, and she walked into them.

For the past two months since the gala, we'd gotten closer, and she was less weary of us, more trusting.

"I came back home early because I needed a hug."

"I missed you," she whispered as she held me close. She pulled away momentarily, took her glasses off, and went back to snuggling against me so the frame didn't come between us.

She's in love with me. I knew that. I'd known it for a while now even if she didn't admit it.

"I missed you too, sweetheart, and I'm looking forward to watching the stars with you tonight." I kissed her nose and then her lips.

She was busier than ever, as was I, with completing the merger between Hartley Industries and Knight Technologies. She'd promised me a weekend to go away to the Mojave. But it kept getting postponed, sometimes because of her and sometimes me. However, this time, I was going to whisk her off in the evening for a long weekend in the desert come hell or high water.

"I still need to pack, Declan. I didn't have time this morning."

"Calliope already did; your bag is in the car's trunk alongside mine. No excuses this time, sweetheart."

"I'm so sorry. I know I've disappointed you—"

"You're many things, Esme, but never a disappointment. We've both been busy. I had to cancel as well because we had that crisis in London," I reminded her.

She tried to step away from me when she heard the snickers from her staff, so I held her in a loose hug. In the past months, she'd taken more responsibility at Safe Harbor, and even though she didn't like administrative work, she knew established processes were critical to helping the women and children who came to the home. Maria had happily stepped back, letting Esme lead. And my wife was born to lead. With kindness and generosity, she'd turned the place around. She still worked with the women as a clinical social worker, but she now also managed all the members of the Safe Harbor team. It made her come home late—but it also made her happy and feel accomplished.

"Hi, Mr. Knight," Betty, the receptionist, said, fluttering her eyes at me.

Esme had told me that Betty, who's just turned seventeen and worked at Safe Harbor part-time as she went to university, had a crush on me.

"Hello, Betty."

"You can't keep coming here. You'll scare the women." Patricia came up to me and kissed me on my cheek even as I held Esme in my arms. "Or they'll want to steal you away. If only I was ten years younger."

Patricia was the other social worker on the team. Esme had hired the veteran away from LAPD County as she looked for more reasonable hours to spend with her new granddaughter.

"You'd still be ten years too old," Gina barked. She was the den mother of sorts and took care of the housing needs of all the women, as well as the kitchen. Gina was the same age as Patricia, and they'd known each other for many years; in fact, Patricia had recommended Gina for the job at Safe Harbor.

I knew my donations through the Caruso Foundation enabled the team to expand. I was already looking into buying the building next to Safe Harbor so they could grow. That would be a birthday surprise for Esme, who would turn twenty-four this fall. Jewelry worked for other women but wouldn't for Esme, so I'd found out what would and was working to make it happen.

I needed a break as much as Esme did. It had been tough navigating the merger with Viv and Julien, who were pressuring Esme and me to end our marriage. Viv's annulment had come through, and she was more persistent than ever. I had given her no encouragement, but she couldn't understand how I could be interested in Esme when I could have her.

She'd been in New York with me for meetings and done her best to get me into bed. I didn't have to resist. I wasn't interested after the magic of making love with Esme. When the heart was involved, I realized the sex was better. Esme had ruined me for all other women. If she ever left, I'd die sexless and celibate. *Scary thought!*

I worked in her office while she finished up.

Mateo sent me an "urgent" message, and I called him. "What's up?"

"We have a security breach with Macmillan."

Macmillan was one of the largest media conglomerates in the world and one of our biggest customers. "What the fuck?"

"Yes. Raya is looking into it; it looks like we were hacked. We've put mitigation in place, but you must get to New Orleans ASAP. Rick Macmillan is shitting a brick."

"Damn it, Mateo, I'm taking Esme to the Mojave. We've yet to make a single weekend work. Can't *you* go?"

There was a long pause on the other end of the line.

"Mateo?"

"I'm sorry. Where is Declan Knight, and who the fuck are you?"

"What's that supposed to mean?"

"This is a contract worth several million dollars for Knight Tech, and you don't want to secure it? The *old* Declan would have already called his assistant to get the plane ready."

Yeah, he was right. "I'll call Baker."

"Thanks. I'll make sure I resolve everything with this account before you get there."

"And Raya is hunting down whoever is fucking with our systems?"

"You know her, she's like a dog with a bone."

I hung up and went to find Esme.

She was in one of the meeting rooms. It was only partly glassed. I watched her with a woman who had marks on her face. Esme was cradling the woman's baby rocking as she spoke to the woman.

She was a natural and looked like a fucking earth mother as she sat there with that tiny pink bundle. My heart hammered against my chest. I wanted Esme to have my baby. A girl. Yes, a little girl with Esme's hair and eyes. I could almost picture the toddler version of our child, wearing a pink dress and running like a two-year-old, unsteady, and unsure, but eager.

Damn it, Dec, you can't make a weekend away happen with Esme, and you want children?

Regardless, I couldn't stop imagining Esme with a swollen belly, and my cock went from half-mast to complete stone. It aroused me to think of her with child, her breasts heavy. I'd never thought consciously of children. I knew I would have them eventually—Viv and I discussed it as a future project. She and I were both busy with our careers. If Viv had a baby, she'd told me it would have to be through a surrogate. She couldn't and wouldn't spend nine months growing large to pop out a baby. A surrogate, according to her, was more civilized. I hadn't given it much thought. Esme wouldn't dream of that—she'd want to get pregnant and have a baby. She'd not be the type of woman who'd hire a nanny as they did in our circles. No, Esme would want both of us to care for her. Suddenly, all I wanted was to knock my wife up.

I knew she had an IUD to prevent pregnancy because birth control pills made her nauseous. Could I convince her to try for a baby right away? A baby would make this marriage permanent.

Even as I thought about it, I knew I didn't want to tie Esme to me through stealth. I wanted her with me because she believed I loved her and loved me enough to overcome her insecurities and controlling family.

I texted Calliope and asked to pack a new bag for Esme, this time with a weekend in New Orleans in mind. It wasn't the Mojave for certain, but we could make the most of it. I'd meet Rick Macmillan at his HQ, calm him down, and spend the rest of the time exploring the city with Esme. We'd eat at Antoine's and Muriel's. I'd introduce her to jazz at Tremé. We'd make love in the Hotel Monteleone and have a drink at the Carousel Bar. I didn't know how Esme would feel about it, and I worried she might be upset that we weren't going to the desert. I worried needlessly.

"Oh, can we eat at Mr. B's Bistro? They make the best Louisiana barbecue shrimp. They serve it with a bib."

We flew to New Orleans that evening, ate dinner at Mr. B's as she wished, and went to The Spotted Cat Music Club in Tremé to cap off the night.

There was something about being away from home and LA—like we were a regular couple with a traditional marriage and life. Like we weren't together because of some corporate bylaw—and because my fiancée had dumped me at the last minute. The media didn't care that we were kissing in a bar called Absinthe or making out at the jazz club in the dark.

"Maybe we should move to New Orleans," I suggested as we got into bed that night. I was tired in the best way possible. Good food, music, wine, and sex. The perfect evening.

"Why?" She rested her head on my shoulder. During the night, we'd detach, but we began the night holding on to one another. It was one of the best parts of my day.

"It's more relaxing."

"I think it's because we're on vacation, and honestly, if I ate and drank like this every day, I'd be three times my size."

"Then there would just be more to love."

Chapter 35

ESME

I walked around the city while Declan met with a customer to soothe their nerves about a security breach. I felt lighter and happier. May was always one of the best times to be in New Orleans when it was pleasant.

My life was different, I admitted to myself. And I was happier...more than I had ever been. Declan had changed me in so many ways. And so had I.

I was learning how to have fun. For the longest time, I'd taken care of myself and had to deal with my family, and I could never just be me. I made new friends. Mateo, Forest, Raya, and Daisy. And even Baker, to some extent. As Declan's executive assistant, I sometimes felt I spoke more to him than to Declan when he was traveling.

I walked into a boutique and, on impulse, bought a new dress. We were going to go out for dinner at Muriel's, and after that, we would go to Tremé for music. Declan loved Cajun food and jazz and seemed to be in his element in New Orleans. The dress had a tight bodice and came above my knee. *Easy access, as Declan would say*, I thought with a smile.

As I returned to the hotel, thinking I deserved a nap, my phone buzzed with a text message. It was my father. I didn't want to look at it, but I did.

"Call me."

I texted back that I'd call in five minutes.

I returned to our suite, sat in the living room, took a deep breath, and called my father. I knew what he wanted to talk about, asking me to leave Declan because if I did, he'd have no choice but to marry Viv to protect the merger. Declan had been firm. There were six months of the contract period left, and he would not file for an annulment.

Half a year had passed—the best time of my life.

"Hi, Daddy."

"Esme, your mother is in the hospital and wants to see you."

"What happened?" I felt panic claw at me.

"She fell down the stairs and has a broken ankle and three broken fingers. She's at UCLA Medical Center. When can you be here?"

"Ah...Declan and I are in New Orleans, Daddy."

"Get here soon," he ordered and hung up.

I knew Declan was in a meeting, so I texted him instead of calling: *My mother is in the hospital. I need to go home.*

He responded immediately: *Take the plane. I'll fly back commercial. Call Baker to set it up.*

I called Baker, and he promised to get the pilot to file for approval for a flight plan back to LA for take-off in an hour.

I had just finished my conversation with him when Declan called.

"I stepped out of the meeting. What happened?"

"Daddy said she fell down the stairs and broke her ankle. And some fingers. Oh, god, Declan."

"I can leave this meeting, Esme, and come with you."

"No, please stay. I don't want to interrupt your work. I can take a commercial flight, Declan."

"Don't be silly, sweetheart. Go home and be with your mother, and I'll be back by tomorrow morning at the latest. Okay?"

He texted me he'd return to LA by midnight as I got to the hospital. The efficient Baker had made sure there was a car waiting for me. For someone who had to hustle as she watched her family sail through life, there was discomfort at having all this at my fingertips because of Declan.

Mark was waiting for me outside my mother's room. I had texted him to keep an eye on her until I arrived. He hugged me and then kissed me on my forehead.

"What?" I asked, wanting to push past him to see my mother.

"I need you to brace yourself. It looks worse than it is...actually, it's probably as bad as it looks."

"Okay. Tell me."

"She requires surgery for her right ankle because the bone broke and splintered, and extensive physical therapy. Three fingers on her right hand and two ribs are broken. She has a rather deep gash on her forehead, and she's concussed."

I took inventory of all the injuries he'd listed. As a social worker, I'd read many such reports. I felt fear go up my spine. "And?" I demanded because I knew he had more to tell me.

He tightened his jaw. "The police were called by the attending doctor, Esme."

But because Mark was holding me, I'd have crumbled onto the floor. "No," I whimpered. But I knew. I'd known since my father had called me. This wasn't the first time, though it was the first time one of us was admitted under our real names into a hospital.

Mark held me tighter. "She's not pressing charges. Monica maintains she fell down the stairs. Your sister says she saw it happen. The police can't do much even though we all know that..."

I raised my head from his scrubs, now damp with my tears. "He did this to her?"

Mark nodded sadly.

"Because of me, right?"

"No," Mark was emphatic, "Because he's a sick son of a bitch. Your sister is protecting him—and honestly, I think she believes he's incapable of hitting your mother. Or you."

"That was a long time ago." I would not dwell on the past.

"It happened just a few weeks ago. Declan told me about the marks on your arm, Esme."

"What? Now you're talking to my husband behind my back?" I pushed him away. "Just go, Mark. I need to see my mother."

I'd never been this rude to him, but fear made you say things you never thought possible.

"Go in, darling. I'll be waiting right here for you." But friends, real friends, didn't punish you for poor judgment. Instead, they continued to be there for you.

I nodded, feeling ashamed of myself.

I took a deep breath before I stepped into my mother's room. There were white roses on a table. My father probably, I thought bitterly, to make sure that people knew he was in the clear on this.

She was as pale as those flowers. Her eyes fluttered open, and she called out, "Esme?"

I went and sat on her bed. And I stroked her left hand where they'd put the IV cannula.

"Mama, I'm so sorry."

"Baby, please do what he says. Please."

"Yes, Mama. I will."

She was crying. "I'm so sorry, Esme, that I never protected you. And...I still can't."

"That's okay, Mama. It's you who requires protection."

It was always her who needed it. I wish she'd left him and freed us of him; however, my mother was too afraid to leave and even more fearful of being alone. He'd controlled her and me through cruelty and abuse, and here was the result. Did I think there would be no consequences for my not getting an annulment? I was so selfish. I'd thought because Declan was with me, I was safe and had not cared for what my father would do to Mama.

"Esme?" she whimpered.

"I'm right here."

"Promise me you'll say nothing to the police. Promise me."

"I promise, Mama."

What would I tell them? Why would they believe me? They'd believe Julien and Viviane Hartley. Was Mark right in thinking Viv didn't know what our father did to us? How could she not know? Didn't she suspect when I moved in with *Abuela*? Or did she buy the story I'd been fabricating my whole life that my parents were busy traveling, not that my mother was afraid that he'd kill me the next time?

"You have to convince Dec to marry Viv. Please, Esme."

How could she ask me to do this? It would be like cutting my heart out.

"I will, Mama."

She smiled weakly and closed her eyes. "Good, good. I'll sleep now. Can you get me my makeup bag? Your father said he'd come tomorrow. I want to make sure I look good for him."

"Yes, Mama."

I held her hand as she fell asleep, my heart as broken as her body was.

Chapter 36

DECLAN

Mark called me as I got into the chartered plane from New Orleans.

"Is Esme okay?"

"No," was his curt reply.

"Clarify," I demanded as the pilot announced we'd take off in ten minutes.

"He beat her."

"Beat Esme?" My heart sank, and everything inside me stilled before going into adrenaline overload.

"No, her mother."

"What?" I nodded when the flight attendant brought me a glass of Scotch. They knew what I drank and had it stocked when Baker booked the charter.

I heard him sigh. "She doesn't talk about it and thinks I don't know. He's been beating them the whole time, Dec. Why do you think Monica sent her away?"

It made a horrible kind of sense. "And now he's making a statement to convince Esme to leave me?"

"I need you to protect her."

"I will not let her go, Mark. I'm in fucking love with her."

"Yeah, we can all see that. Don't let her walk away, because she's going to. She'll do whatever she can to protect that useless fucking mother of hers. She never showed Esme love or cared for her—instead, fuck, I can't stand that whole family."

Mark was voicing my feelings.

"Where is she? And where are you?"

"I'm...well, standing guard outside Monica's room because I don't want her to be alone with her parents. I exchanged shifts with a colleague to be here. She's inside with her mother, probably making promises about not getting the police involved and convincing you to marry Viv."

"I'm not marrying Viv no matter what happens. I'll walk away from the merger, Mark."

"You may well have to."

I heard what he was saying even if he didn't voice it. "I'll put Esme first."

"Yeah, someone should."

After the plane hit cruising altitude, I called Raya. I asked her to ensure she got all the information from the police on the investigation of Monica's alleged accident. I called Carolina Vega, the Knight Tech counsel, to ask her what the consequences of going against the Hartley Industries bylaws would be.

"You mean if you divorced your wife before the year was done?"

"Yes."

"Or if you annulled your marriage and married the other Hartley?" she asked acidly. Carolina had met Viv and Esme and made it clear, as had everyone else in my life except for my mother, that they were on team Esme.

"I'm not marrying Viv, Vega. Just tell me what the damage will be?"

"Well, you'll lose... it'll be significant. The contract is clear; whoever calls for the divorce, Knight Tech, will have to pay remuneration. An annulment not followed within one month with a new marriage contract will lead to the dissolution of the merger, which is going to be a cluster fuck now that both companies have just come together."

It would be a lot of money—and would negatively impact the lives of thousands working at both companies. The stock would take a dive. The board may not fire me because the Knight family owned over fifty percent of the company, but I wouldn't blame them if they did.

"So, we're fucked no matter what?"

"Well, you can annul your marriage; you've been married for just six months, and any judge will grant that, and I'm sure Forest knows enough judges to make that happen for you. Then you can marry Viv, get a new contract, and off to the races you go."

I shook my head. "Who the fuck agreed to such a bullshit contract?"

"You did. I warned you. But you were in *love*," she spat out that last word.

"I'm a fucking moron."

"Not going to contest that."

"Well, counselor, my wife is being pressured right now to coerce *me* to give her family what they want."

"What are they doing?"

I told her what I had learned from Mark.

"These days, the police can go after abusers even if the victim doesn't press charges, Dec. But from what you are saying, their hands are tied if Viv claims she saw the accident. Doesn't she realize that she'll be disbarred if it's proven she's lying?"

"And how will we prove she's lying?"

I drank more Scotch as we flew and tried to figure out how I would save my wife, her mother, my marriage, and my company simultaneously. Yeah, it was a fucking cluster fuck!

Mateo couldn't agree more. He picked me up at the airport and drove me to UCLA Medical.

"Any news on the hacker?" I asked.

Mateo shook his head. "Raya is looking high and low. It's her number one priority."

Sorry, buddy, I think her number one priority is, and has always been, you.

"She's also made sure there are a couple of people at the hospital so Esme will never be alone with *him*. But that blond giant of hers is standing outside the door, scaring everyone away."

I smiled. "Mark is a good friend."

"If only I swung the other way."

"Where are Viv and Julien?"

"Viv is packing up in San Francisco. The marriage is officially annulled, as you know. And from what I hear from sources, her next project is to become Mrs. Declan Knight."

I sighed. "Can't believe how popular I've gotten."

"Not so popular if your wife wants to annul your marriage."

"I don't know how to get through to Esme."

Mateo looked at me as the city lights flashed past us in the Escalade. "She's twenty-three, Dec. Remember when you were that age?"

"Yeah."

"And she's lived in fear of her father for herself and her mother all her life. Be a good girl, Es, or Daddy will beat Mommy."

"Christ." I ran a hand through my hair. The torture my wife had gone through, and yet, she wanted to help people. Now, I could see where her passion for helping abused women and children came from. She'd learned from experience how hard it was to step away from an abuser. Monica was weak, and Esme had to be the adult in that relationship.

"And your mom wants you to call her back."

"She called you?"

Mateo nodded. "Since you won't talk to her, she contacted me. *Esme is not our kind, and blah blah blah, could you go back to Viv?*"

"I feel like a fucking stud, and not in a good way."

"She always liked Viv."

"Because she is like Viv, and I was, as Freud would say, trying to marry my mother. Mateo, how did we get here? I thought this merger would make us one of the most powerful tech companies in the world, and now I'm not sure we'll keep our shirts."

Mateo shrugged. "If we lose it, we'll just start again. Our abilities are not rooted in our bank accounts, Dec; they're within us. A social worker who helped me told me that once."

"Esme would say the same thing."

Chapter 37

ESME

I refused to go home, so Dec ensured I had a change of clothes. He didn't pressure me to go home; instead, he sat beside me on the sofa in my mother's room.

"I sent Mark away," he told me.

"He was here all day, and now he has to work the night shift."

I didn't let Declan hold my hand. I kept a distance between us. I had to tell him something, convince him somehow to marry Viv. But I didn't have the words. I loved Declan Knight and didn't want to let him go. Who would? He was loving and caring, a bright star in my life that had been so often dark. Once he left, it would return to being gloomy and worse than before because now I knew how wonderful life could be, how love could and did make the world go around.

We sat quietly, watching my mother. He didn't make any demands of me, and I felt guilty. But I didn't know what to say to him when what I had to say was, *"Let me go, Declan. Please. And marry Viv. She loves you, and you love her."*

I had to remember how they were together. That would give me strength. I remembered Viv's birthday party one year when I had come down from Seattle. Declan had given her a tennis bracelet. It was beautiful.

"It's a five hundred grand bracelet," one of Viv's friends told me. *"He loves her so much."*

But it wasn't the bracelet that told me that; it was how he put it on her wrist and kissed her, how he nuzzled her when he sat next to her, unable to stop touching her.

"You want my cock, baby girl? Beg for it. Let me hear you beg, Viv."

The memories made something inside me bleed painfully. My eyes closed, and I let the exhaustion claim me.

When I woke up, my head was on a cushion in Declan's lap. His fingers rested on my head, tangled up in my hair. He was asleep as well. I sat up, and he opened his eyes. He languorously smiled at me. "How are you, sweetheart?"

"You should go home," I said sharply. "Please. My father will be here soon." *And I don't want you to be with me when I see him.*

He didn't appear to hear me as he stretched.

I knew how I looked in the morning, with my hair going everywhere. He looked perfect.

"Coffee?" he asked.

"I said *go home*."

"No." He brushed his lips against mine. "Esme, I'm going to find some coffee. It was a long night. With the nurses coming in and out, I hardly got any sleep. So, let's not push my buttons, okay?"

I hadn't woken to the nurses. I had been entirely out, warm and cozy, with Declan's fingers massaging my scalp.

I used the ensuite bathroom to brush my teeth.

Declan returned with coffee and fresh croissants, probably delivered by Baker because they didn't look hospital-issued. I took the coffee but couldn't stomach the pastries. Declan didn't have a similar problem with his appetite.

He refused to leave and became even more adamant when my father and Viv came to see my mother. They spent five minutes with her, and then my father asked me to step outside with him for a conversation.

"No." Declan stood in front of me.

I shook my head and walked past him. "It's okay. He's my father."

Declan didn't respond, but the fury on his face told me how disappointed he was in me. I couldn't blame him. I was choosing my family over him. He knew that. I knew that. And seeing the triumph in Viv's eyes, she also knew that.

As soon as we came out, he dragged me, grabbing my arm in that horrible way to an empty seating area with tables and chairs. He shoved me into a chair.

"Esme, it's gone on long enough, this sham marriage of yours. I understand Dec is upset with Viv, but he'll get over it. So, here is what you need to do. Pack up your bags and leave his house."

He threw an envelope and a pen on the white hospital table. The pen made a horrible sound as it crashed against the linoleum surface. "These are the annulment papers. Sign them."

He saw my hesitation. "Don't you love your mother, Esme?"

He wasn't even going to pretend that he wasn't blackmailing me.

I nodded weakly. I didn't read the papers. I pulled them out of the envelope and with blurry eyes, signed them. He snatched the papers away.

"Now get lost."

"But Daddy—"

"Esme, *go*. I want nothing of yours in his and Viv's place by the time he gets home. Got it?"

I looked at the door of my mother's room. "Let me at least talk to—"

"Esme—" he began, but the rest of his words dropped off when Declan walked out of my mother's room, Viv in tow.

My father handed the papers I'd just signed to Declan. "She's signed the annulment papers, Dec. The ball is in your court."

Declan looked at me with such pain that my heart broke all over again. How is it I was happy with him just a day ago, and now, it was all gone?

"Esme is this what you want?" he asked me, ignoring my father.

"Yes." I kept my head down. I wouldn't be able to leave him if I looked into his eyes.

I saw Declan take the papers from my father. "Vega will have to look through them. I believe I have a month to sign."

"Yes, and if you don't, we'll start divorce proceedings, and if that happens, we all lose Dec."

"I know." His voice was firm, not bleeding with emotion as mine was. I wanted to see his face, but I didn't dare. It would crush me. As things were, I wasn't sure how long I could even stand here when all I wanted to do was curl up and grieve.

"Esme is moving out of your place," my father told my husband.

"I'd like to hear that from her."

"I'm going to go home and pack," I said meekly. What else was there to do?

"No need to pack, Esme. Calliope will take care of it. Just let her know where you want your things delivered."

So, I wouldn't even get to say goodbye to the penthouse that we'd made into our home. He didn't want me in his space. I'd made my decision, and he'd made his. Of course, he had. I was a coward—a doormat. And the evidence was in front of him. Why would he want to be with someone like me?

"Thank you." I was looking at my shoes and the white floor of the hospital.

A part of me had hoped he'd try to stop me. That he'd fight for me. But he was going to let me walk away. Let me leave. End the magic that was us.

Don't think about it. Don't think about it. I repeated the words like a mantra.

"Then it seems like there's nothing else left to say. Goodbye, Esme," he breathed.

I nodded and blindly walked away.

Chapter 38

DECLAN

"**Well**, this is a cluster fuck," Forest said that evening when he came to the penthouse, where Esme didn't live, with Chinese food, Mateo, Raya, and Daisy.

"Where did she go?" Raya used chopsticks to serve herself some noodle nonsense.

We were sitting at the dining table. Calliope had been *so* distressed to hear that Esme was leaving me, I'd asked her to take the week off. I didn't need anyone at home. I wanted to stew in my juices. I'd said as much to the people eating fried rice and *chow mein* noodles in my house, but they'd ignored me.

"She's staying with Mark. He said he'll take care of her."

"And we still have the bodyguards," Raya reminded me.

I couldn't eat. I was drinking Scotch.

"You know she loves you," Mateo told me.

I nodded. "Yes. But she needs to accept it, and she's too afraid right now. I don't want to pressure her. If I do, she'll worry about her mother, and...she's hurting. Mark said she's been crying ever since she got there. Refuses to tell him what happened."

I hurt for and with her. She was my woman, and when she was in pain, I felt it too.

"Are you going to just let her leave?" Daisy demanded, glaring at Forest. "You men give up so easily."

"He can't stop her," Forest protested. "How should he? She decided."

"He could have convinced her otherwise. Maybe she needed him to show her he loved her," Daisy threw back at him.

"Maybe that's because he doesn't love her," Forest responded harshly.

I watched the volley of words between them, and we all knew they were not talking about Esme and me.

"Guys, get a room," I said blandly. "I love Esme, very much. But I need her to come back to me. If I bring her back...she'll always be in doubt."

"What's your plan?" Raya asked.

I smiled for the first time in what felt like a very long time. "First, I'm going to deal with that asshole family of hers, so they'll never hold the proverbial gun to her head again. And then, I will nudge her a little—so she can be free of her fears. There is no guarantee that she'll return in the next month before the annulment, though."

Mateo shrugged. "It will hurt business."

"Big time," Raya's eyes widened.

"We built it up after Gerald left the company half dead; we can do it again," Mateo said.

"Right on." Raya raised her glass of wine to clink against Mateo's.

I had personal wealth outside of the company, which Mateo and Raya didn't have, so that they were ready to battle for me was even more meaningful.

I told them my plan, and they gave their feedback on it. Just like we would for any team project, we honed it and finally laid out the roles and responsibilities.

"What do we call this project?" Mateo wondered.

"Project E for Esme," I offered.

"No," Daisy was looking at Forest, "Call it what it is. Project L. Project Love."

We held our glasses then and cheered, "To Love."

"When do we start?" Forest asked.

"No time like the present." I would not wait. I had a month before I'd need to sign the annulment papers and announce my marriage to Viv, or we'd lose the merger and probably the company's reputation. I had no intention of doing either.

That night I lay in bed, unable to sleep without her. I missed her. The scene in the hospital played in my head in a loop. She wouldn't look at me when we were there. I knew her now, and knew how soft her heart was. If she looked at me, she'd not be able to leave. She loved me. I knew that for certain.

After she'd left, Viv and her father had descended upon me like vultures.

"We have to plan the wedding," Viv immediately said. "And we'll keep it lowkey...the media will go nuts, but we'll just say that you made a mistake, and now we're back on track.

I couldn't believe how mercenary she was. How had I been with this woman for a year? I must've been blind.

"Your mother wants to, of course, plan a big shindig, but I dissuaded her," Julien piped in.

Did my mother know how her friend convinced Esme to leave? Did she know he was a monster who beat his wife and daughter?

"I haven't signed the papers yet, Viv." I tried to stall her. They'd all decided it was fait accompli.

"Oh, I know you're angry with me, Dec." She wrapped herself around me. "But I know you love me. I love you too. I just...lost my way. Can you forgive me?"

I wanted to push her away, but I didn't. I was formulating a plan to bring my life back to order, starting with destroying Julien and Viv Hartley. It would be easier to do if they thought I was playing along.

"We'll announce the wedding to the board at the meeting in four weeks, which should protect us from any repercussions," Julien interjected. "I'm glad you're seeing sense, Dec. Esme, as I told you, is a flake. Look at how she walked away."

I wanted to strangle Esme's father.

*"Well, I have a tee time, so I'll leave you both to plan things."
Julien left, and after a while, so did Viv and I.*

*I knew Esme would come back to be with her mother, her
father and sister would not.*

*I told Viv I was tired and didn't let her enter my home. While
I may pretend to play along, there was no way she would sully
the house that had become a home to Esme and I. Esme had
changed the décor, slowly but steadily. She'd bought new rugs
and curtains from god knows where because they had no designer labels—but they looked just right. She'd added touches
here and there and made it a cozy haven for us. She'd tempered
the starkness with warmth. This was no longer a place Viv had
arranged with an interior designer—this was home. Mine and
Esme's home.*

But I couldn't stand being in that home.

I had bent her over the dining table and taken her from behind. We'd sat on the couch and watched movies while fighting
over popcorn. We'd made love in the gym and the pool. In
the living room. In the bathroom, both in the shower and the
bathtub. She'd given me a memorable blow job on the balcony.
I'd eaten her out in the elevator.

I'd go mad if I had to stay in this place.

I moved into one of the corporate apartments in the Knight
Tech office building. I'd tell Viv that I was renovating or some
such thing. It would help not to smell and feel Esme in the
penthouse.

I texted Baker to have an apartment ready for me and to pack
enough of my things to last me a month there.

I wondered if Esme was still crying, and I felt tears fill my eyes at the thought. She was my miracle. I just had to be patient and let her come back to me.

Chapter 39

ESME

My mother didn't ask me how I felt about leaving what had become my home and the man I loved. She didn't ask me about my red puffy eyes. She pretended everything was A-okay. A part of me that had held our secret for so many years because of my love for her cracked.

"Thank you for buying me new makeup," she chuckled when I put the Bare Mineral cosmetics in front of her. I wasn't going to my father's house to pick up *her* makeup bag. "I prefer Chanel, though."

"I can't afford Chanel, Mama."

She didn't respond to that. "Well, I'll make do. The doctors have said that my ankle surgery will occur by the week's end. Daddy is hiring a nurse to take care of me at home. Isn't that nice of him?"

It would've been better if he hadn't beaten the crap out of you, which is why you need a nurse.

Bitterness coated my insides. How could she sit here and not see what had happened to me? Had she never cared for me?

"He's coming in an hour. I think you shouldn't be here when he comes." My mother used the makeup mirror I had bought to put on her mascara. "He's still angry with you."

I got away from the bed because my mother disgusted me.

"Why? What did I do?"

My mother set the mascara wand down and looked at me, her eyes fierce. "Well, Esme, you seemed to have gotten *very* comfortable with your sister's husband. We're all quite upset about that. You knew this was temporary, and he's kissing you, and you're holding hands in all those pictures. *Disgusting.*"

I couldn't look away from her. It was like watching a car crash. "Disgusting?"

Mama shrugged. She looked at herself critically in the mirror. "You knew what you were doing was wrong."

"You made me marry him when Viv fucked everyone's life up."

"Don't use language like that, Es. I'm still your mother. Show some respect."

I felt my temper climb. I was tired and beaten. I could still hear how Declan had so quickly said, "Goodbye, Esme," like I was disposable, which I now realized I was. But why shouldn't I be when I allowed my family to treat me that way?

"Respect? Why, Mama? Why should I respect you?" I'd never talked to her this way before. I'd been the loving Esme. The fucking doormat. Declan was right. And it fit that he'd let me walk away because he deserved better. Maybe not Viv but a woman who could stand tall next to him and be a partner. Not someone like me, who was always ready to fall on her knees and get kicked in the solar plexus for the pleasure of others.

"Esme," her voice was tight, "What has gotten into you?"

"I'm trying to understand, Mama, why you think it's disgusting that I kissed *my* husband."

"Because he's Viv's."

"She didn't want him."

"She made a mistake, and now, no thanks to you, that is being corrected. Dec has left you, and you were wrong to think that you could stay with a man like him. Think about it, Es. He was going to leave you, anyway. And you knew that. Isn't this better?"

I noticed she was good at putting on makeup, even with broken fingers. He'd beaten her, and here she was, making herself pretty for him.

"Mama," I pushed my glasses up my nose and looked her in the eye, "don't contact me ever again. Think of me as being dead to you. Tell Daddy and Viv that they should lose my number as well. I'm finished with you. All of you."

"Esme," my mother cried out. "After all we've done for you, is this how you show your gratitude?"

I put my phone in my jeans pocket and walked toward the door. As I opened it, I turned around to see her, this woman who had given birth to me. "Mama, everything I ever did for you was because I loved you, it was never gratitude. But I realize now that you deserve neither my love nor my gratitude."

I walked away, my hands shaking as I quietly closed the door behind me.

We'd never reconcile, I admitted to myself. I wouldn't be able to stand a life where Dec married Viv. I could never forgive my mother, my father, and my sister for taking advantage of me, for not caring about me. And I'd never forgive myself for not being worthy of Dec. I had truly lost him, and it was not because he walked away as I always feared, it was because I'd not had the courage to keep him.

It hurt more than I could admit, but I would move on. I'd never again allow my family to get in the way of my happiness. I'd choose wisely and within my means in the future.

My stride became longer and surer as I walked out of the hospital. I called Mark as he'd asked me to after I talked to my mother.

"I told her we were done," I told him as soon as he answered.

I didn't have to explain to Mark who *she* was and what *being done* meant.

After a long pause, he said, "I'm so proud of you, Esme. And I'm glad you're removing yourself from an extremely toxic situation."

"I don't feel happy, Mark." Tears ran down my cheeks.

"I know, darling. I know. Time will heal."

"Will it?"

"Yes. It'll take time, but it'll get better. Maria and I are there for and with you."

I wiped the tears away, deciding to find a café, some place to sit down and regroup. "I miss him, Mark."

I heard him sigh. "I know."

"He's going to marry Viv, isn't he?"

"I don't know, Esme."

I nodded as if to myself. "How am I ever going to get over him?"

"Come home, Esme. It's my day off. We'll lie in my bed and watch all the breakup hits."

I chuckled. "Yeah. That sounds good."

Lying in bed and watching movies sounded much better than regrouping. I had a whole life to regroup. Today, I had already taken the day off from work because of the New Orleans trip—so I might as well veg out with my best friend. Maybe we'd watch *The Bridges of Madison County*, and I'd ugly cry when Meryl Streep doesn't open the car door at the traffic light when Clint Eastwood waits for her. Maybe we'll watch *Bringing Up Baby* to laugh at the antics of Katharine Hepburn and the woebegone Cary Grant.

I ordered an Uber on my phone.

I saw a familiar car drive up the long driveway of the medical center, and I hid behind a wall. It was my father's car. The driver stopped in front of the entrance, and my father marched out, tall and handsome. His phone rang, and he answered.

"Nina, Viv said he's probably not agreeing to a big wedding. He'd like to keep it small. Just family."

He listened to what she said and nodded. He looked happy. His smile was wide. He'd destroyed my life and built Viv's.

"Viv is with him at the Knight HQ. He's getting past his anger.; she was an idiot to do what she did." He stopped talking and then laughed, "Yeah, yeah. We made the best of it. But she's gone now, and I'll make sure she stays that way. Dec seemed fine with it. He said goodbye to her, and didn't seem too broken about it. He took the annulment papers. I think..."

I walked away as I saw my Uber approach. I didn't need to hear the rest of the conversation. I was done with these awful people. It was time for me to be good to myself.

Chapter 40

DECLAN

My father, who hardly stepped into Knight offices anymore, came into my office. Viv was with me as we went
through some documents for the merger.

"Gerald." Viv walked up to him to hug him. He stepped away
as if she was toxic.

Viv laughed uncomfortably. "Are you okay?"

"Yeah, I'm fine. I want the room, Viv. I need to talk to my son."

"You want me to leave?" Viv looked flustered.

My father's irritation showed. "That's what asking for the room usually means. Do you mind?"

Viv looked at me for direction, and I smiled pleasantly at her. She was driving me up the wall, and I couldn't wait to kick her out on her bony ass.

My father didn't bother to sit. "What the fuck is wrong with you?" he bellowed.

"How much time do you have?" I leaned back on my chair and put my feet on my desk. "What's up, Dad?"

"Your mother tells me you're annulling your marriage with Esme to marry *that* woman?" He said *that* with a sneer. I should've known that my father would have something to say, just like most people in my life did when they heard Esme had left me.

"Sit down, Dad. It's not quite how it looks."

"Ask that Baker fellow to get me a coffee."

Before I could even call my assistant, there was a knock on the door, and it was Baker with coffee service. *Worth his fucking weight in gold.*

"Hello, Mr. Knight; how are you doing?" Baker set the tray on my desk. "Coffee black with one sugar?"

My father nodded.

"You met his wife?" he asked Baker.

"Yes, sir."

"You think he should leave her to marry that skinny snake?" my father asked.

Baker controlled his smile. "I believe Dec is working on...how did he say this, saving his marriage, wife, and company while fucking over Julien and Viv."

"He's a damn good assistant," my dad admired Baker as he closed the door behind him. "So, what the fuck is going on?"

I told him and saw his eyes harden when I described how Julien had been abusing his wife and Esme. I then told him about Project L.

He smiled finally. "It's a good plan...a little too optimistic, but I don't think there's much positive in this situation to do better. How can I help?"

"You can help by getting your wife off my back."

My father frowned. "Viv reminds me of her. Two overly ambitious women...not that ambition is wrong, but you must still be human."

"Dad, why haven't you divorced mom?" I asked bluntly.

"Just never bothered," he confessed. "If I met someone and fell in love and all that jazz, I'd drop her like a hot potato. I'm sorry, son; I know she's your mother, but I can't fucking stand her. I was so happy to meet Esme. She's living a real life. Doing social work and helping...*ah*...fucking hell, now I see why she works with abuse victims."

"Yeah, I felt that realization punch me in the gut as well."

He drank some coffee and set his cup down. "I think we need to add an element to the plan."

"What?"

"That we can take Julien into an alley and beat the crap out of him. Son of a bitch."

There was a knock on my office door, and I asked the person to come in. It was my mother.

"You're here?" She looked shocked to see my father.

"Yeah, still a major shareholder in the company."

My mother wore a lovely pale pink and blue Prada suit. She looked serious and elegant. Viv would look like that if she wore a similar suit. Esme would look like a fucking knockout—total sex on legs.

"Dec, I want this wedding to be the year's media event. I don't know why you're resisting it."

"No." I swung my feet down to the floor. "If that's it, Mom, Dad, and I were in the middle of something."

"Like what?" she couldn't believe we'd have anything to discuss.

"Did you know that your best friend knocks his wife around?" my father asked.

My mother waved a hand in disbelief. "She fell down the stairs. It happens. You've met Monica; she's a ditz. And Julien tells me she's on Valium, Xanax, Ambien, and a plethora of other drugs."

My father shook his head in disgust. "Nina, here is what I'll tell you. Julien is an abuser. You can make excuses for him..." he held up his hand when my mother was going to respond, "but let me clarify. He's not allowed anywhere near my house."

"Your house? Excuse me?"

"Nina, the money is mine. And the house is mine. Sure, you'll get something when I die—but until I do, the shares are *mine*, not *ours*."

I enjoyed watching my parents together for the first time in a long time. Usually, my father walked away, but today he was taking the time and effort to put my mother in her place.

"Excuse me? You think I need your money?" my mother sneered.

"You used to be a judge, Nina. And now you're retired. That outfit you're wearing? You could only afford it with my money. You didn't earn a fortune working the courts. You lived the way we did while you were a judge because I had the money. So, let me be *abso-fuckin-lutely clear*, Julien is not welcome into my house. You bring him in; you can leave with him."

"Your money? You ran the company into the ground. It was Dec who made it what it is."

"Then it's his money. Still not yours," Dad countered.

My mother watched him, stunned. Dad winked at me and stood up. "Time for me to go."

Is this what my marriage with Viv would've been like if we'd stayed together? Probably.

"What's gotten into him?" she sat on the chair my father had vacated.

"Mom, I have a meeting. This is my workplace."

She frowned. "I don't like how Esme is spreading rumors about her father. But what can you expect from people like that?"

"People like that?"

My mother rolled her eyes. "Oh, please. I'm just saying there's something low-class about them. That's all."

"Because they're of Mexican heritage?" I wasn't about to let it go. It was time I put my money where my mouth was. Just as I wanted Esme not to allow her parents to take advantage of her, I needed to confront my mother, who was more interested in status symbols than her only child's happiness.

"What a thing to say," my mother scoffed.

"But that's what you mean when you say people like *that*, right? For all your big D democratic agenda, Mom, you're a racist and a snob."

Her eyes widened. "How dare you speak to me like this?"

"Just telling it as it is, Mom. You know where the exit is if you don't like it." I waved my hand toward the office door. I stood up and walked to the tall windows. I looked out at the vast city before me and wondered where and how Esme was.

"Don't you dare ignore your mother, Declan Knight," my mother reprimanded.

I turned around to face her.

"Do you know why you like Viv? Because she's like you. All show but nothing inside. The pursuit of status and power is what you both are after. And you know what, good for you. But you don't get to look down on those who make other choices. Esme has chosen to help people in the most direct way anyone can. She's not throwing money at some charity ball or putting something out on social media to garner attention for a cause. She's actually on the field, making a difference. Why can't you respect that?" I spoke calmly. I wanted to understand my mother or at least allow her to explain herself.

My mother took a deep breath. "She's not part of a power couple; Dec. Viv is. The Knight family has been at the forefront of politics and business for generations. With Viv, that legacy will continue."

"And what about love?"

"What about it?" she mocked. "Are you telling me you're in love with Esme?"

"What if I am?"

That took her aback. "You've known her for six months. You were in love with Viv for longer. If this is about love, then go back to Viv. Make a life with her. A life I can be proud of."

"*You can be proud of?* Have you ever wondered if I'll be happy? Or will we have a marriage like you and Dad do? You can barely stand each other. You think he's a rich spoiled brat—and he thinks you're a cold-hearted bitch. Why would you want that for me?"

My phone buzzed, and I pulled it out of my pocket. It was a message from Raya: *We have identified the hacker. Come to the boardroom ASAP.*

I responded with a: *On my way in five.*

My mother clutched her bag. All the color in her face had drained. "I don't know what you mean, Dec. Gerald and I have a wonderful partnership."

"I wish I had the time to tell you that you have no such thing with Dad, but I don't." I walked to the door of my office and opened it. "You can see yourself out."

I walked straight to the boardroom, which was on the executive floor, where I had my office.

Four people were already there: Mateo, Raya, my assistant Baker, and a woman whose name I thought was Janice but wasn't sure.

I sat at the head of the table and waited.

"This is Janice Walden; she's been Mateo's temp assistant for the past three weeks while Tim is on paternity leave."

I nodded. "Hello, Miss Walden."

"I'm sorry. They...I didn't know it would be such a big deal."

I looked at Raya for an explanation. She raised her five-foot ten-inch lithe frame and walked to the monitor, and Janice looked nervous as hell. I didn't blame her; Raya looked like a warrior with her cropped blonde hair, well-defined muscles thanks to a strict workout routine, and the tight leather jeans she favored with dress shirts, a leather biker jacket, and biker boots. A complete antithesis to the delicate feminine women Mateo took to his bed. And yet, I'd always felt that they had undeniable chemistry—which Esme had also detected.

Raya nodded at Mateo, who flipped something from his phone onto the large screen in the meeting room. It was a map of the server farm we maintained in Las Vegas.

"The hack was into our server here." A red dot appeared on one of our servers.

Then that dot expanded into a line and came to Los Angeles and Mateo's office.

"God, Mateo, are you telling me you're fucking with our servers?" I joked. "Because you don't need to hack in, you know that, right?"

"Fuck you," Mateo said jovially.

"I'm assuming that Miss Walden here put a Trojan virus into your computer, Mateo, that our security didn't catch, and that's how whoever *influenced* Miss Walden got access to our system?" I surmised.

"Exactly." Raya smiled and sat down next to Mateo.

"I interviewed Janice and hired her," Baker spoke for the first time. His stoic British demeanor was still in place if tinged with some guilt. "We did a background check and found nothing untoward."

I nodded. "Thanks, Baker."

"So, Miss Walden, why did you do it? Money? Love?" I asked.

She cried. "I'm so sorry. This man I met asked me to send Mr. Silva an email and open it on his computer, which I did while he was at lunch one day. That's *all* I did."

"How much were you paid?"

"A hundred thousand dollars." She was still in disbelief that something so simple could be worth so much.

"That's a lot of money. I understand why you were swayed." I tapped my fingers on the polished mahogany table. "And who was this man?"

Raya grinned. "And this is where it gets interesting. The man is a black hat called DemonRum."

"He's a mercenary," Mateo interjected. "Hacker for hire. We already found his signature in the corrupted code. And that helped us track down Janice here."

"Did a competitor hire this black hat?"

"No." Raya was bursting to tell me who had hired this man to sabotage Knight Tech. "Julien Hartley did."

I felt a surge of anger and satisfaction. *Ah, Julien, we now have you by your short and curlies.*

It wasn't uncommon for Knight Tech to host FBI agents now and again, considering our expertise, but never to arrest one of our own.

Per our counsel, Carolina Vega, Janice Walden, who was arrested after that fateful meeting, would be charged with cybercrimes, specifically for unauthorized access, computer fraud, malware distribution, and damage to computer systems.

In the following days, DemonRum was also arrested thanks to information Raya's team had gained regarding his whereabouts. The connection to Julien Hartley was tenuous and would take further investigation.

While we were busy dealing with the fallout of the hacking, my days were getting longer with travel to customer sites. However, I checked in with Mark every day to make sure Esme was alright. Which she wasn't, according to him.

"She doesn't talk to me. She goes to work and then stays in her room. She's lost weight, and I've heard her cry in bed."

It hurt to think of Esme crying alone at night. I wasn't getting much sleep either. I was playing a delicate game with Viv and her father, which required more energy than I had, adding to my stress. It didn't help that I missed my wife all the fucking time. I wanted to hold her and comfort her and be comforted in return.

"She saw pictures of you and Viv at that movie opening," Mark continued. "That was not a good day. She didn't cry and smiled, even cooked dinner. It was torture watching her pretend she didn't care."

"I know what you want me to do, Mark, but I can't," I told him. "She needs to fight for us. I can't keep loving her and have her fold whenever her family gives her a hard time."

"She has PTSD, Dec, give her a break."

"I love her, Mark, and trust me, I know her, and she needs to do this. If I bring her back... she'll never believe in us."

"And in the meantime, I must watch her fall apart."

"Yeah, I'll owe you."

I would have much rather she was falling apart with me, but when she'd signed those annulment papers—she'd chosen her fear over us. She needed to trust me, believe in us, and know that together, we would and could beat the odds. It would take time—and I didn't know how much time, but I knew she'd find her heart. My Esme was strong—and the bond we had built, I knew, connected her to me in a visceral way. It wasn't going anywhere, this love and hunger we had for one another.

But waiting wasn't easy, and I had to talk myself out of going to Mark's place or Safe Harbor to grab her and bring her home, tell her where she was supposed to be almost all the time. That might get her home in the short term, but it wouldn't free her of her parents. Sure, she'd walked away from her mother right now, Mark had told me, but would she be able to fight for me against them? Would she be able to look her sister in the eye and say, "I love him, and he loves me? We're together. So, butt out."

Three weeks after we'd returned from New Orleans and a week before the board meeting, we were supposed to announce my upcoming marriage to Viv when all hell broke loose at Safe Harbor. Maria called me to tell me there had been a fire at the women's shelter. She assured me that Esme was unharmed, but they were scrambling to find a temporary home for the women and children.

I immediately got ready to leave my office and realized that I couldn't *just* go to her. I had to stay away from her until she was ready to come to me. I was frustrated. "What do you need, Maria?"

"Do you have any buildings that are standing empty? Right now, we need space."

I thought about it momentarily and told her I'd get back to her shortly. I called my father. "Dad, you know that building you used to rent to those artist types on Spring street? Is that still available?"

My father, who couldn't remember which day it was, miraculously remembered the building. "The artist's commune. Oh, yes, it's empty. I've been thinking about getting it into shape and seeing if we can bring some writers and painters back there, you know, create an art collective."

"How would you feel if it became a Women's Shelter?"

He was silent for a short moment. "Of course, son."

I sent him to Safe Harbor to deliver the good news to Maria and take care of Esme for me.

Chapter 49

ESME

I wished Declan was with me, I thought as we evacuated everyone from the building. The fire had started in one bedroom, and the fire Marshall suspected it was because of faulty wiring. The building was old, and there were no funds to update the infrastructure.

"Where will we put everyone?" Patricia worried.

"We'll find a way." I didn't know how we would. I knew Maria was working on it. I didn't have a network in LA. If this was Seattle, I could make something happen. However, I knew someone who had a network here. Someone I was dying to talk to.

But he and Viv were back together. The media was all over their renewed relationship. There had been no comment from the Hartley and Knight PR teams. There had been some head-lines that wondered: *Where is Esme Knight?*

Esme Knight was in Skid Row trying to put out a fire. She spends too much time on media websites, which she's never done before.

I took a deep breath and walked away from the noise to the side of the building, where it was slightly quieter. I called Declan. As the phone rang, I wondered if I should've texted him first. But I didn't have to speculate over that for long because he immediately picked up.

"Esme," his voice was a whisper.

"I'm so sorry to bother you, Declan. Are you busy?"

"For you? Never. What can I do for you?"

His words made me feel warm; his cool tone dampened that warmth effectively. "I...do you have some contacts...ah, well, there was a fire at Safe Harbor, and we need a place to move everyone. I... don't know for long, and I wondered if you knew someone with space for us."

He was quiet for so long that I panicked. "I'm sorry. I shouldn't have called. I...this is not your problem. I understand."

"Esme," he tried to interrupt me, but I was on a roll.

"I know I have no rights. And... I'm going to..."

"Esme," he called out again. "My father is on his way. Maria called me earlier, and he has a building on Spring that I think will work well for Safe Harbor. It's in pretty good shape, and he will work with the Knight Foundation to ensure everyone has everything they need to get through the first few days until you can get settled in."

"Oh." He hadn't called me to check up on me even though Maria had told him there had been a fire. I remember when he'd stayed the night with me in the ER with my mother. How he'd carried me when Billy had hurt me. I guess those days were in the past.

"I'm glad you called me, Esme."

"Why?" my voice was hoarse. My heart ached.

"I'm glad I can help you."

"Why?" I asked again.

"Are you well, Esme?" His voice was butter soft, almost a kiss.

"Yes." *No. No, I'm not.* "And you?"

"I'm hanging in there." I heard someone call his name, and he told me he had to go.

It was the first time we had spoken in three weeks. And almost immediately I wanted to call him again and hear his voice. Viv was going to have him as a husband. Couldn't I have him on the phone just once in a while to soothe my aching heart?

Gerald showed up at Happy Mother with sandwiches, water, and cookies for everyone, along with a project manager from the Knight Foundation, a no-nonsense woman who took over the transportation and settlement of everyone from Skid Row to the building on Spring Street.

It took all day and a good part of the evening to make Safe Harbor semi-functional in Gerald's building. It was bigger than Safe Harbor and had more amenities. For example, the Wi-Fi worked like a dream. The kids loved the TV room, which had a massive television and video games. The kitchen had a functioning dishwasher, which made Gina and Betty tremendously happy.

I was grateful for Gerald. He was more like the Declan I had gotten to know during the past six months than the man I thought he was when I watched him from afar as Viv's boyfriend and then-fiancée.

"Esme, I feel like a big steak. And I think you need some food. Have you lost weight?" he thundered.

"I like food too much to lose weight," I countered, but I knew I had stopped eating and drinking wine.

I had also not gotten a decent night's sleep in three weeks. I worked and grieved the end of my marriage. There had been little inclination on my part to eat or even open a bottle of wine.

I wanted to turn Gerald down, but he had spent the day helping, and I didn't want to be ungrateful, though what I wanted to do was go to bed and recount my conversation with Declan this afternoon. Go over it word by word to determine how he still felt about me. Would he still call me *my love* as he used to? Or was that what he called all his bedmates, I thought sadly.

Gerald's driver took us to Chi Spacca in Hollywood. The maître d' seemed to know Gerald, so I deduced he was a regular at the steakhouse.

He ordered a bottle of Bordeaux, one of Declan's favorites. I remembered the evening he'd opened the bottle to serve along with steak with truffled potatoes that he'd cooked. That night, we'd made love on the dining table, high on good food and wine.

"Your pussy takes my cock so well, sweetheart. I've never had this with anyone."

"No one." I gasped as he pounded into me.

"No one, my love, just you. Just us."

I set the wine down before I could start crying. I shifted my glasses to read the menu and didn't feel like ordering anything. But I'd have to, or Gerald would worry. I went for a beetroot salad. Gerald ordered a 36-ounce Costata alla Fiorentina with red wine sauce, truffled potatoes, and seared baby artichokes.

I rubbed my hands on my jeans to warm them. The restaurant was cold, and my cotton t-shirt wasn't much protection. Or maybe I was tired due to lack of sleep, too much grief and my body wanted to slide into a fetal position and stay that way.

"I have a question for you?" Gerald drank some wine as if considering his query.

"Okay."

"Why are you leaving my son?"

I blinked. "Excuse me?"

"Didn't you hear me?"

I nodded. "I... I'm not leaving him. This was always temporary, and... he can now go back to Viv as it should've been from the start."

"He doesn't want to marry her. If he did, he'd have the same fucked up marriage as Nina and I do. Do you know why I travel eleven months of the year?"

I waited for him to tell me.

"Because I can't stand my wife. If he married Viv, he'd also get there. Maybe we could travel together."

"Then why not get divorced," I suggested.

"I don't feel married; I live my life, and she lives hers. I used to show up for celebrations, but now I only come when there's a

Knight Tech board meeting. I don't love my wife, and she doesn't love me. You, however, love my son."

"How do you know?" I squeaked.

He smiled. "I may not be in love, but I know what it is."

"He doesn't want me, Gerald."

"How do you know that? I've known my son his whole life, and he wants you with a desperation that would've unsettled me if you didn't feel the same way."

The waiter came with our food and saved me from responding to him. But I heard every word he said, which echoed in my mind. *He wants you with desperation.*

It was easier to have no expectations because then you never got disappointed. I couldn't, and wouldn't, let myself build castles in the air as my father had warned me not to do. I was going to start fresh. Maybe I'll move back to Seattle. There would be no memories there.

"Is that all you're going to eat?" Gerald was not impressed with my food consumption, and I didn't want to tell him I was in so much pain that there was no room for anything else inside me.

"Thank you for coming to our aid today, Gerald. How long can we stay in your building?" I asked him.

"How long? It's yours. Didn't I tell you?"

I froze. "What?"

"Declan said you needed a bigger place, and I said fine. He said that Vega will ensure the deed is transferred to you."

"Carolina Vega?" The general counsel for Knight Technologies.

"Hmm." Gerald ate steadily, and I was halfway through my salad when he finished his steak. He also consumed three glasses of wine while I was nursing the first.

"But..." I didn't know what to say. Declan gave me a building. He had mentioned that he'd give me money at the end of the contract, but I had not abided by the agreement, demanding an annulment. I signed the document first.

"He can afford it, my girl...actually, it's my building so I can afford it," Gerald said dryly, leaning back on his chair with his glass of wine. "What are you so afraid of?"

"I'm not afraid of anything."

"If we could protect your mother, would you return to Declan?"

I was taken aback. "My mother is in no danger."

Gerald nodded. "Is this what you tell the women you talk to who are being used like punching bags by their husbands? To lie and pretend it doesn't happen?"

"Gerald, this is a family matter and—"

"Stop defending that father of yours." He raised his hand to silence me. "Esme, you're twenty-three years old. If you turned around and said you didn't want to be in a relationship, it's alright. You're young. You have a lifetime ahead of you. So, I want to ask you, do you want Declan?"

I licked my lips and worried my upper lip with my teeth. "Want him?"

"Yes, do you want him to be your friend, lover, companion, champion, husband...all the things they promise us marriage will be but seldom is?"

Declan had been all those things to me. In a short time, Declan had been a friend, a lover, a companion, and when the chips were down, he helped me, like right now, like making sure Safe Harbor was taken care of. Yes, I wanted him, but why would he want me? What did I give him? Nothing. I wasn't as beautiful as the women he usually went with. I didn't have a high-power job. I didn't know how to wear designer clothes. I didn't wear makeup most of the time. I wore glasses, and my ass was the size of Greenland.

"Wanting something doesn't mean you can have it."

"How would you know?"

I looked up at him.

"When was the last time you fought for something?"

"I've had to fight for everything," I responded. "*Everything.*"

Gerald shrugged. "Really? You got this job by talking to Maria and navigating around Nina and Julien. The only reason your father lets you work here is because it's connected to the Caruso family. You didn't demand your inheritance or even support from your family for your education because—"

"I took care of it myself. And how do you know so much about me?" I let my irritation show.

"You think I'd let my son marry someone without knowing everything about them?"

"You weren't even at the wedding," I protested.

The waiter interrupted us to ask if we'd like dessert.

"No," I snapped.

"The chocolate mousse, please, and I'll have a cognac, bartender's choice."

Gerald grinned after the waiter left. "Dessert is the best part of the meal. So, coming back to how you only get *some* of what you want is because you're not ready to fight for the rest."

"You're being unfair. You don't even know me." I felt tears prick my eyes.

"I know enough." Gerald's eyes softened. "Esme, if you don't believe you're worthy of love and respect, why would anyone give it to you? We teach the people around us to treat us like they do. My wife treats me like some trust fund baby, which I am, but I never objected to how she treated me and thought of me—so here we are. The same goes for her. How have you taught your family to treat you?"

My situation was different. I had to protect myself and my mother. My childhood was a dance of being quiet, not making a nuisance of myself, being conciliatory, curbing every desire, and expecting nothing from anyone. I had become accustomed to not trusting anyone, so it genuinely surprised me whenever someone did something kind.

When Mark or Maria remembered my birthday or congratulated me when I got a paper published, I was *grateful* for their attention. But they were my friends, wasn't their support something I should expect?

Having given me food for thought, Gerald smartly changed the topic to his travels in Asia, regaling me with stories about a monkey in Thailand that he'd befriended. When he dropped me off at Mark's place, he hugged me.

"I'm going to tell you something you don't know," he whispered as he held me. "You're kind, beautiful, and good—and worthy of friendship, love, and everything else you want."

Mark had the night shift, so the apartment was empty. I went straight to my bedroom and took a shower. As I lay in bed, I thought about what Gerald said. He was right. I always wondered if I was imposing on someone, taking up too much time, or asking for too much. I'd never *fought* for what I wanted. I'd flown under the radar and been happy with the crumbs.

I picked up my phone on impulse and texted Declan: *Thank you so much for everything today. Gerald is a prince.*

He responded immediately: *It was our pleasure to help. All settled at Safe Harbor?*

Me: *Yes. I had dinner with your father. Did you know he has a pet monkey in Thailand?*

I waited for his response, and when it came, I smiled: *Yes. He has a large photo framed in his home office.*

It took all my courage, but I decided it was time to say what I wanted without worrying about what could go wrong: *I'm sorry about how I left. I should've talked to you first.*

It took nearly ten minutes to get his response, which said. *Thank you.*

He didn't elaborate. He didn't give me hope.

The next day, I saw pictures of him with Viv at a Hollywood party, and I realized he'd been with Viv when he'd responded to my messages. I didn't know how to feel about that.

Chapter 42

DECLAN

L ike a pathetic teenager, I read her texts again and again.

I was being careful with the Hartleys. I kept Viv at an arm's distance and was evasive about the future. The FBI was working diligently with Raya's team to build evidence against Julien. The board meeting was in a few days, and we needed all our ducks in a row before that meeting.

Instead of going to the apartment in the office building where I was staying because the penthouse reminded me too much of Esme, and it was fucking torture to be there, I went on a drive.

The driver didn't comment when I asked him to drive me to Mark's building and park in the dark. Mark was on the eighth floor, so it wasn't like I could genuinely stalk her—but this was creepy I knew, and if the driver knew any better; he'd have told me to get my head out of my ass and go talk to my wife, or go home, drink a bottle of Scotch, and fall unconscious.

I called Mark, and it went straight to voicemail. I got a text from him: *At the hospital. Urgent?*

I responded *no* because he didn't need to tell me how my wife was doing and if she was crying or smiling or missing me as much as I was.

Mark, who had gotten to know me well in the past three weeks because I called him every day, sometimes twice a day to hear about Esme, texted back: *You both need your heads examined.*

No kidding.

I reread her messages and was tempted to text her and tell her to come down and join me in the car. I could make her come again as I had so many times, right here. I could hold her again. Smell that jasmine goodness of hers.

Fuck, Dec, you're an idiot; go home before you lose your mind.

When I got back to the office building, security hailed me. "Your...ah...girlfriend is in your place."

I looked at him blankly. "Who?"

He looked uncomfortable. "Your...I don't know who she is anymore. She's the one you were going to marry, and then you married her sister—so, he first one.

He looked so baffled that I smiled in sympathy. "Imagine how I'm feeling."

"No, thanks. I got one wife and one ex, and that's enough drama for a lifetime."

I took the elevator to the apartment, feeling weary. I didn't have the energy to deal with Viv. One more week, and I could get rid of her. One more week...and the chips will fall as they may. Whether Knight Tech took a massive hit in the stock market or not, there was no situation in which Viv would ever be engaged, married, or, except through Esme, be connected to me.

"Where have you been?" Viv demanded. She was sitting on the couch, her laptop open—a glass of wine on a coaster on the table. She'd made herself at home.

I ignored her and threw my backpack on a bar stool by the kitchen counter, and went to find a drink. Perversely, I opened a bottle of Chablis that Calliope had started to stock because Esme liked it. I couldn't see her, but I could pretend to taste her. Good lord, I was losing my mind. She'd better return home and make me less crazy—and the sooner, the better. But what if she didn't? What if she never came back? Then I'd go get her. Fine, so she won't fight for me, that's okay, I can fight enough for both of us.

I knew that would work for the short term, but not for a lifetime. Esme would only feel like my equal if she learned to put herself and us first.

"Why are you here, Viv?"

"What do you mean? We're together so..." she trailed off.

"Viv, you left. Why do you want to come back so badly?"

She looked away. "I made a mistake. That doesn't mean I don't love you."

Realization struck like a thunderbolt. "Viv, do you hate Esme so much that you want to marry me?"

She looked at me, and I could see the guilt. "This has nothing to do with *her*."

I sat down across from her. How had I missed so much about her? She played the all-powerful woman, but beneath it, she didn't have Esme's strength—she was insecure. She'd just found better ways to hide it. Julien may not have physically abused Viv, but he'd raised her and ensured she'd wrap her worth around making him happy.

"How upset was your father when he found out you married Nick?"

"Daddy has always been supportive of my decisions."

"Viv, did you fall in love with Nick?"

Her eyes clouded for a moment and then cleared. "It was a mistake."

I scoffed. "My god, I thought it was just Esme and Monica he was abusing and controlling. But he's controlling you as well, isn't he?"

"You know nothing about it. Daddy and I are close; he loves me, cares for me, and wants nothing more than my happiness."

She didn't believe it herself. Her father was a narcissist, and they loved no one but themselves. I felt sorry for Viv.

"Do you love Nick?"

Her lips trembled, and her eyes filled. "No. I've always loved you."

I nodded, finally understanding Viv and her motivations. She was just as much of a victim as Esme and Monica were. Julien had been manipulating her just like everyone else in his orbit; he'd just found another way to control Viv.

"Did you ever love me?"

"I've always loved you."

I put my glass of wine down on the table between us and not on a coaster. "Here is what I think happened. You and I were having some fun—and your father insisted you make the relationship more permanent. The merger was a way for him to profit, but to also wed his daughter to someone higher in the socio-economic structure than the Hartleys. Am I right so far?"

She didn't reply; just stared at me.

"You never loved me, Viv. You know that, and now I know that. Do you know how I know that?"

Her eyes filled. She hardly ever showed emotion, not like Esme, whose face was a mirror of what was happening within.

"What did your father do when he found out you married Nick? Did he beat you like he did Monica?"

"No, of course not."

"If you love Nick, go be with him, Viv. Don't let your father manipulate you."

"Are you drunk?" her voice shook a little. "My father isn't manipulating me. I do as I please, and he supports me."

I crouched down to face her. I took her hands in mine. They were cold.

"Your father is a narcissistic bully. While we were together, it wasn't too bad, but we both knew it wasn't love. You figured it out before I did. And now that you have, can you settle for less?"

Tears rolled down her cheeks. I wiped them and felt nothing but compassion for Viv. At least Esme could wear her scars on the outside; Viv had had to keep them within.

"If you love Nick. Be with him. I'm assuming with the way your phone keeps blowing up with messages from him, and that you haven't blocked him, means that it's not over."

"It's over," Viv said unhappily. "I'm with you now."

"No, Viv. We're not together. We've never been."

She sobbed, and I took her in my arms. I stroked her back and crooned softly, telling her it would all work out.

She cried for a long while and it took two shots of whiskey to loosen her up enough, so she'd confide in me.

"He never hit me," she admitted. "But...it was always there, wasn't it, the threat. I was his favorite. I liked that. I had no one. Esme had her mother. I only had Daddy."

I held her hand as she spoke.

"I love Nick, and he...still wants me back, Dec. *But* I don't know if I can do this."

"Sure, you can."

"But what about the merger?"

"The hell with the merger. When did business and money become more important than people?"

She looked at me in disbelief. "Since always, Dec. Since the dawn of time, power has been important. You can lose a lot of money."

"Then so be it. We'll rebuild. It's not the end of the world, you know."

"You fell in love with Esme, didn't you?" There was no accusation in her tone, just understanding.

"I did."

"And she fell in love with you. I could see that. I wanted to hurt her. Since she came into our lives, I've always felt she was the enemy who could take my life away from me." She looked at our hands and then into my eyes. "I will not change overnight."

"No one is asking you to. I'm only asking you to do the right thing. Can you?"

She thought about it for several long minutes. "I love my father, Dec."

"And if he loves you back, he'll love you no matter who you're with, or what your job is. Love is accepting people for who they are, not asking them to change. Love is making someone more than they can be, not less."

She nodded slowly. "We had some good times, didn't we?"

"Yes, yes, we did. We're better friends than lovers, Viv. You can learn to be friends rather than compete with Esme. Trust me, she doesn't have a mean bone in her body and would not understand how to contend with you and wouldn't want to."

She laughed through her tears. "You will not sign the annulment papers, will you?"

"No."

"And what if my father makes her divorce you?"

"Then I'll be heartbroken and do what I can to win her back."

"And you don't mind that the company will lose money if that happens?"

I shrugged. "It's *just* money. We'll make more or make do with less."

"Is she worth it?"

I smiled, thinking of Esme. "Oh yes, she is."

Chapter 43

ESME

C arolina Vega came to my office around lunchtime. She'd made an appointment via email to walk me through the paperwork on Gerald transferring the building to Safe Harbor. I asked her to ensure that the building not be in my name but be considered a donation so that whether or not I was associated with Safe Harbor, the women's shelter would always have this space to continue to support women in distress.

The Knight General Counsel went by Vega. She was several inches taller than me and several dress sizes smaller. Her dark

hair was tied up in a chignon, and she had that air of sophistication some women, like Viv and Nina Knight, innately had, and
I envied. They were elegant and beautiful—and never seemed
uncomfortable in their skin.

"Maria Caruso has made you the manager of Safe Harbor—so
you'll be the signatory on this document. Please sign where
indicated," she instructed.

I did as she asked. I thought she'd leave when we finished,
but she put the building papers in her large Valentino tote and
pulled out another file.

"Now we can go through the annulment papers."

All the breath left my body. Declan had signed. Of course, he
had. He would have so much to lose if he didn't. I couldn't blame
him.

"As discussed, three million dollars will be transferred to your
account. If you don't have a financial advisor, I suggest you get
one immediately to manage the money." Vega was all business,
sharp, and without emotions. She was ending my marriage, and
I'd expected some show of sympathy or even recognition that
this wasn't just paperwork; this was my life.

"Here is the document I request you to read through and sign.
This says you will not make claims on any of Declan Knight's
holdings."

I looked up at her, grief replaced quickly with anger. "How
dare he? Does he think I give a shit about his money? You can
keep the fucking three million for all I care." I snatched the
document from her and signed it and shoved it back. "Anything
else you want me to sign? I'm happy to do it."

Vega didn't react; she just went through her papers, ignoring my outburst.

The son of a bitch. Did he think so little of me I'd want anything from him? Hadn't *he* offered that money? I hadn't asked for anything.

After signing all the papers and putting them back in her bag, Vega presented me with an ornate envelope.

"This is for you."

I knew what it was as soon as she'd set it down. My hands shook as I opened the envelope and pulled out a wedding invitation. Everything inside me shriveled. Declan Knight was marrying Viviane Hartley this Saturday at St. Vibiana's Cathedral at eleven thirty in the morning.

"He wanted me to have this?" I whispered.

"Yes." Vega picked up her bag and stood up. "He thought you should know."

"That he's getting married."

"Yes."

I felt the world collapse around me. My lungs couldn't capture enough oxygen. I'd lose Declan forever. Our marriage was over—with those papers in Vega's bag, we'd ended our time together.

"I'll file the annulment papers today at the county registrar's office, so he'll be in the clear for Saturday."

I nodded, unable to hear her over the blood roaring in my ears.

"Esme," Vega's use of my name pulled me out of my shock.

"Yes."

"Do you love him?"

My eyes filled with tears at the question from the remarkably stolid lawyer. "Yes. Very much."

"Have you ever told him?"

I shook my head. I'd never said the words, had I?

"Then you should at least let him know you do."

"But he doesn't love me." I felt close to tears. "And you can't convince someone to love you. I tried with my parents and my sister and failed miserably."

"How do you know he doesn't love you?" Vega asked, leaning against the door to my office.

"If he did, he wouldn't marry *her*," I replied viciously.

"If you loved him, you wouldn't have signed those annulment papers," she countered.

I had signed them without even speaking with him. I'd been afraid for my mother. *But...* but if I looked within me and was honest, I'd wanted to leave him before he left me. A chill went through me at the realization.

"Have a good day, Esme." Vega left after dropping a bomb on me.

I didn't have time to dwell on the invitation or my epiphany because there were two new women at Safe Harbor, and since Patricia was out with a sick grandchild, I was doing both her job and mine.

By the time I got to Mark's place that evening, it was late.

It surprised me when I heard voices in the living room and was shocked to find that one of those voices belonged to my mother. She was in a wheelchair; a nurse was with her.

"Esme." My mother held out a hand.

I ignored her hand. I looked at Mark, and he shrugged. "I texted, but you didn't respond."

I took my phone out of my jeans and saw that there were indeed three unread text messages from Mark. *Too late now.*

"Why don't I make us all some tea." Mark approached me and kissed me on my forehead before heading to the kitchen.

My mother sat back in her wheelchair. She looked nervous...which wasn't something new. She always looked nervous and unsure. Did I look like her? Had he made me what he'd made her?

I sat down across from her in an armchair. Mark's apartment was not as big as Declan's, but it was comfortable, with two bedrooms, a large living room, a kitchen, and a dining area. Mark had someone who came once a week to clean the apartment and do our laundry. It was a luxury compared to where I'd been living in Seattle.

"Why are you here?" I was usually not aggressive, but it had been a long day, and I felt testy. The wedding card had both numbed and enraged me.

"I wanted to apologize."

"For what?"

She looked at me. "For...well, what happened at the hospital."

I nodded. "That's all? How about abandoning me when I was a child, though I confess the best thing you could have done was leave me with *abuela* since you would not leave *him*. How about letting him treat me like an outsider and joining him in treating me like a pariah as well? Or for asking me to sacrifice my life to marry someone Viv dumped?"

Monica's head bowed, and a part of me wanted to comfort her, but another part, a new and stronger one that was making itself known, did not.

I continued. "Or for letting him hit me and hurt me? Or for controlling me by threatening to hurt you? Are you not going to apologize for that?"

"Esme, I know you're angry."

"Mama, I'm past my anger. I don't want to see you or talk to you. I kept thinking that you'd love me if I did everything you wanted. But you know what I have found out? You don't love yourself. If you loved yourself, you'd be able to love others."

If you loved yourself, you'd be able to love others.

Did I love myself? And was this preventing me from showing Declan that I loved him and believing his love for me?

Like mother like daughter!

Tears rolled down my mother's cheeks. And for once, I didn't feel compassion. I sympathized with her, but my heart wasn't big enough to make *her* feel better. That wasn't my responsibility. Also, I didn't think anyone could make her feel better.

"I'm sorry, Esme, for everything."

"Are you going to leave him?"

My mother looked at me, her eyes pleading.

"Then we have nothing to say."

She pointed to the coffee table, and I noticed some documents. "Your father wants you to...well, he wants you to look at these and sign them."

"What is this?"

She seemed embarrassed to tell me. "Divorce papers."

"Why?"

"If Dec refuses to marry Viv, your father wants to..."

"Threaten him with the divorce papers?" I laughed without humor. "His lawyer probably filed the fully signed annulment documents. The marriage has ended."

"We didn't know."

"Now you do."

She looked uncomfortable. "Declan told your father he would not sign the annulment papers and...."

"He's marrying Viv, Mama. What are you on about?"

My mother looked even more confused. "What?"

I didn't have the energy for her, I realized. "Mama, please leave and don't come back. We're finished, you and me. I'm finished with all of you. I don't want you in my life, and I don't want to be part of yours. I can't be clearer than this. I won't allow you to enter this building or any other place where I am in the future."

My mother was taken aback. "Esme, I know you're—"

"Mama, I say this as nicely as I'm able to, get the fuck out of here."

With that, I walked away and into my room. I was shaking with anger. I was angry with Mama, Julien, and Viv—but mostly, I was angry with myself.

Mark came into my room with tea. "Want some?"

"Sure."

He sat down next to me on the bed. "Her nurse was in the car downstairs. She came and took her."

I nodded, feeling wrung out.

"So, you threw her out?"

"Yes, I did."

"I would've clapped if it were crass. I did it quietly. High fucking time, Esme."

"Declan signed the annulment papers today. And... he's marrying Viv this weekend. In a fucking church. They printed cards."

Mark seemed to control a smile.

"You're happy about him marrying Viv?"

His face straightened. "Of course not. How do you feel about this?"

"Like crap. Like...you know, I told my mother that she couldn't love others because she didn't love herself. That's true for me as well. I love him, Mark. And now he's marrying my sister. It's like a fucking Jerry Springer show."

"Talk about a blast from the past."

"I feel like a fool. I should never have signed those papers. I should've talked to Declan and told him...I shouldn't have let my father and mother manipulate and emotionally blackmail me."

"If you want him, go fight for him, Es."

"But he doesn't want me. If he did, he'd not be marrying Viv. We were having sex just four weeks ago, and he was calling me his love, and now he's marrying her?"

"Maybe he's waiting for you to tell him you love him."

The thought hadn't occurred to me. "You think?"

"Only one way to find out. Talk to him."

I wanted to, but I was afraid that he'd reject me. He'd laugh at me and tell me I was a fool to think someone like him would love someone like me.

Mark kissed me on my head and stood up. "You can be afraid or live your life to the fullest, not just make the best of an unpleasant situation as you do so well but build a future that is not full of compromises. Regardless of how it'll turn out, do you want to live the rest of your life knowing that you didn't do everything you could to get him back?"

"Why can't he come back? Why do I have to fight for him?"

"Because you left him, Es. You chose your mother's safety over your relationship with Dec."

I had no reasonable response because Mark was right. I had single-handedly fucked up my marriage.

Chapter 44

DECLAN

V iv was in my office when Julien and I signed the last legal document to complete the merger between Hartley Industries and Knight Technologies once the newly formed board with members from both companies approved it.

I was living in a fucking soap opera. Engaged to one sister. Married to another. And now being pressured to marry the first sister. Now someone needed to have an evil twin and amnesia and we were set.

Julien grinned. "I can't wait to announce this at the board meeting on Monday."

"Your last board meeting," I reminded him as I leaned back in my chair. *And if I have it my way, your last of many things.*

"You know, Dec, I was worried you'd be stubborn about this marriage dissolution business. But I'm glad to see that you and Viv have reconciled. She was always the right choice, son."

I wanted to tell him not to call me son. Instead, I said, "It's a work in progress."

He waved that off. "The annulment has been finalized and you have only one path left. Don't destroy two companies because you want to prove me wrong. You and Viv are worth building on. Am I right, Viv?"

For the first time, I noticed how cowered Viv was with her father. When they'd both been on the same side of a battle line, they'd been at ease with each other; she'd been confident with him. But now, she wasn't sure if she could stand up to him, which made her afraid. "You're right, Daddy."

Julien sighed. "What's going on with you? Why are you brooding? This is a fucking great day. Celebrate a little."

"I'm just tired," Viv explained as she packed the papers into her briefcase. She rose and smiled at her father. "Let me process these, and I promise I'll celebrate."

"Good, because I already have a woman who mopes around, and I don't need you to do the same. Monica met with Esme yesterday, and she's been crying her eyes out since she came home. She's in that wheelchair and...it's hell."

Viv's lips tightened, but she quietly left my office.

Mark had told me about Esme's meeting with her mother the previous day. I almost buckled then and went to her. But for us to move forward, I had to be patient and have faith in her and us.

"Your mother is very pleased with how things turned out as well," Julien informed me, letting me know that he and my mother were still close, thick as thieves. "And I know your father has some misgivings, but he said he was going to Peru, so you won't have to deal with him."

I don't know why Julien assumed I felt about my father the way my mother did. My father was not a businessman...but he was a good man. When I asked him to give his building away—worth several million dollars—to Esme, he'd not hesitated. I was informed by Vega that Esme insisted on securing the building as a Safe Harbor asset instead of having it in her name, and I was not surprised.

"I have a meeting," I replied tightly, scrolling through my computer.

"Dec, this is the right way to proceed. St. Vibiana's Cathedral and a quiet ceremony with just family is right."

I rose then, wanting this man out of my sight.

Julien didn't notice my irritation with him; narcissists like him never did.

Raya was waiting outside my office, and as soon as Julien left, came in, a triumphant look on her face.

"It's all falling into place," she told me almost giddily.

I waved a hand at a chair. She sat down, and I did the same.

"Well?"

"We tracked the money source to DemonRum, the hacker, and we are now certain that the money came from Julien Hartley's private bank account. The DA and FBI are certain they can make an arrest soon."

"Why do you think Julien wanted to sabotage our biggest account?"

"That was only going to be a start, Dec." Raya explained. "He was planning to keep the pressure on you so that you'd know that not merging with Hartley would mean the end of Knight Tech. The data shows Julien gave DemonRum a list of twenty customers, our top ones to start with."

"I don't understand why he desperately wants me to marry Viv. I married a Hartley; isn't that enough?"

Raya turned on her iPad, looking pensive. "Julien hates Esme because he can't control her. I went through his email communication with Esme for the past years, and it looks like she doesn't make a lot of noise, but she also doesn't always listen to him. He wanted her to get a business degree; she chose social work. He was going to get her thrown out of university, but Esme's thesis supervisor was the program's dean, so he protected her."

I nodded. Esme was compliant when she knew she wouldn't have to go against her values, but if something threatened her morals, I knew she'd navigate that situation, and anyone could.

"Anything else?"

Raya nodded and pushed her iPad toward me. "This is going to be hard."

I raised an eyebrow at her.

"Medical records for both Monica and Esme. They used false names to go to emergency rooms, and since they are Mexican, the assumption made was that they were undocumented. My detective dug these out. There may be more..." she trailed off as I picked up her iPad and scrolled through the files.

As I read the documents, my heart broke for Esme.

Esme had a broken right arm at age two. Monica had two broken fingers at the same time. When Esme was three, her shoulder was dislocated. Monica had several of those happen throughout the years. Esme had a concussion when she was five because she'd fallen down some stairs and hit her head. When she was eight, right before she went to live with her grandmother, Esme had a broken leg, two broken ribs, and a broken jaw. After Esme left, the reports on Monica were fewer and fewer.

I felt tears prick my eyes, and I didn't stop them from flowing down my cheeks. "It's a horror show, Raya."

"I know." She put her hand on mine.

"You know, I called her a doormat once?"

"You didn't know."

"And I'm hurting her now. She should never be in pain after that childhood, yet I seem to keep bruising her, no matter what I do."

I dropped my head in my hands and wept.

Raya came to my side of the table and held me as I cried.

That evening, I met my father for a drink at his favorite wine bar in West Hollywood. A small place called Tabula Rasa.

"I hear you're off to Peru."

My father nodded. "Yeah. But I wanted to talk to you before I left. I'm going to file papers to divorce Nina. I think...I think it's time."

"Congratulations."

He smiled as he poured more of the natural orange wine we were drinking into his glass and mine. "Who knows, maybe I'll find a woman I can fall in love with."

"I hope you do," I agreed.

"I'll be at the church tomorrow."

I drank some wine and felt fear race up my spine. Tomorrow, it could all end the way I wanted it to or it would destroy many lives. Either way, Julien was toast; I could take comfort in that.

"Are you sure you want to do this, Dec?" My father wasn't a big fan of what was happening tomorrow afternoon at St. Vibiana's Cathedral.

"I don't have a choice, Dad."

"There is always a choice, son."

I shook my head. "Trust me."

"I trust you, but you expect a lot from people."

"I know."

My father raised his glass, "To love and foolish plans."

I clinked my glass with his. "To love that forces foolish plans."

Chapter 45

ESME

It was the morning of the wedding, and I hadn't slept a wink. I felt confused, angry, and desperate. For someone who enjoyed my company, today, I *needed* someone to talk to before I went completely crazy.

Mark had been out all night with a *friend* he'd just made, and Maria's phone went straight to voicemail. I tried Raya and then Mateo and Daisy. They didn't answer their phone. I caved in and tried Forest, who I didn't know very well. In a very sultry voice, a woman picked up his phone and told me he was taking a bath.

In another four hours, Declan would marry Viv.

I paced Mark's apartment. I had not bothered to find one for myself. I should have. Why hadn't I? Because I was waiting to move back to the penthouse—the home we had built and lived in for six months.

I had hoped for us to get back together, even though I knew the odds were slim. I had let Declan go, he hadn't been the one to back away. The day I signed the papers, he'd been with me, having spent the night in my mother's hospital room. I could've walked away from my mother and gone to him, talked to him, and asked him what we could do as a team, as a couple. But I hadn't.

I burst into tears and cried for a good hour straight.

Oh, Declan, I wish I could call you and talk to you.

I wondered if I could text him and say something like *congratulations. I hear you're getting married.* Oh, fuck that. I didn't want to congratulate him.

I could say: *Please don't marry my sister. Stay married to me.* How would he respond? Would he respond?

I picked up the wedding invitation and glared at it. I tore it up and threw it on the floor. Then because I felt like it, I stomped on the torn pieces of paper. That felt good.

I took a shower and cleared my mind.

It didn't help.

I changed and put on a white summer dress that Declan always found irresistible on me. Did he see me as attractive? Of course, he did. Hadn't he told me often enough how beautiful he thought I was? Well, he was full of shit if he said that.

I remembered the last time I'd worn the dress. We'd gone out for dinner and made love in the elevator. The entire dinner had been foreplay. I was orgasmic when he entered me, holding me against the elevator wall. His face was buried in the crook of my neck as he pounded into me.

"How did I live without this?" he moaned as I climaxed.

"The same way I did. Poorly."

He laughed then and kissed me.

We'd made a mess in the elevator and sheepishly cleaned up with tissues I'd had in the pocket of my dress. I put my hand in the same pocket now and found the empty crinkle of the plastic wrap that had held the tissue. I discarded it and put my phone and Mark's key fob in my pocket. I couldn't stay here. He'd marry Viv in another two hours. How would I live my life after that?

Well, he annulled our marriage. He could do the same with Viv. But why would he?

Don't worry so much, my love. I promise it'll all work out. He'd said to me often. Where was he now, and why wasn't he saying it?

I should've fought my father and said, "Hell no, I'm not giving my husband up. I'm in love with him." I should've pushed my mother out of my life long ago when I'd realized that she was more interested in being Mrs. Hartley than she was in being my mother—regardless of the many bones he broke.

What did I tell my clients who were friends and family of an abuse victim? You can't save them if they don't want to help themselves. How foolish I was to think I could protect Mama. I couldn't; only she could by walking away. He'd keep hitting her, no matter what I did. He'd find something to be angry about.

He'd say she drank too much at a party. She didn't drink enough. She laughed too loud. Why hadn't she laughed at all? She was putting on too much weight. God, she was skinny and needed some meat on the bones.

He'd done the same with me.

That last time he'd beaten me—it had been because I'd eaten ice cream without permission. Viv had told on me. My mother had driven me to the ER, yelling at me for making my father lose his temper. She'd done what she always did, taken me to a far-away ER. I'd passed out twice in the car before we got to the emergency room, where she checked me in on a fake name.

I'd never even questioned her because this was how we'd always been doing it.

I knew he didn't beat Viv. Oh, no, she was the golden child. She enjoyed that and spent her days making my life miserable. Why did she do that? I was a sad, pathetic child who wore glasses and barely did well in school. Did she know he beat us? How could she not know? But then even the housekeeper who was always there didn't know. Most of the time, Daddy hit us when no one was around, and he was clever enough to hide it. When he was furious and broke something or needed stitches, we had to go to the emergency room or urgent care to get it fixed.

Early on, I learned that broken ribs did not require a doctor's attention. Just grin and bear it; it will heal in a few weeks. It'd hurt to breathe, but that was just pain. I'd seen my mother take painkillers, and it had tempted me more than once. But painkillers made the pain go away, but they also took my mother away to a place where she lay in bed all day. Her pain always came first. She cared for herself and left me alone if he hit both of us. If he hurt me and she was alright, she ignored me, pretending I'd eaten something I shouldn't have. She was his enabler, and by allowing him to take my husband away, I had become like her, an enabler.

I walked around downtown as I tried to unravel my thoughts.

I saw families going out, bicyclists, and people laughing together, bringing home many things. I had, all my life, avoided genuine relationships. I loved Mark, and it would hurt if he betrayed me, but I'd move on. It was a safe relationship.

This was why I refused to go away with Declan.

We'll lie under the sky in Mojave and see the milky way.

This winter, we'll see the Northern Lights. I promise you that.

I didn't want to get any more attached than I was. Well, wasn't that just bullshit? How could I get any more connected to the man I was in love with?

I looked at my watch—thirty minutes before he married again.

Well, hell. He'd marry Viv if he wanted to, but he'd marry her knowing I loved and wanted him.

I called an Uber and impatiently waited to reach the cathedral.

A part of me was calm and knew exactly what I had to do. Another part was scared that I was walking into a humiliating experience that would break whatever was left of my heart.

I stepped out of the Uber and walked up the stairs to the door of the cathedral.

I took a deep breath and opened the door.

I walked in, and all the heads turned to me. They were waiting for the bride...the other bride, not this one. Everyone was there. Gerald and Nina. Calliope, Raya, Daisy, and Forest. Mateo was standing by Declan as best man. I was the most casually dressed, in a cotton summer dress.

I narrowed my eyes when I saw Mark and Maria. What were they doing here? And how dare they? They were my friends. Not his. Sure, they'd gotten to know each other, but...I shook my head to stop myself from getting distracted.

He stood in a beautiful suit, waiting for his bride. He had white jasmine flowers on his lapel. It was my favorite scent. There were shuffles and whispered discussions as I walked up to him.

I saw Nina Knight with her head bent. Her husband whispered in her ear, and she nodded as he spoke.

"Esme," Declan acknowledged, his voice deep and calm. His eyes, though, were bright with something akin to victory. Had I made a mistake? Did he feel like he won because he got me here?

"Declan," I whispered, my voice hoarse because I'd cried so much the past few days.

I licked my lips and smiled uneasily. Here goes nothing, Esme. You love him, and if he doesn't love you, then that's that, but you're going to tell him you love him and tell him he will believe you.

The priest was looking at me and Declan with absolutely no expression. Nothing saying, *is this the bride?*

I turned to face the pews of people first.

"I know you're all here to celebrate...to...well, you all know why you're here. I apologize for the interruption."

Declan waited patiently, not much showing on his face.

I swallowed hard. During the Uber ride, I had planned how to do this. I was going to give it my all, and if it didn't work, well, at least I'd know I tried my best to win my man back.

I went down on my knees, and a gasp went through the room.

Chapter 46

DECLAN

I hoped she wasn't hurting her knees. Maybe I should find a pillow or something....

"Declan, I love you. I know our marriage has been annulled. And that was...is a mistake. I love you. And I know you love me." It was hard for her to admit that I loved her. "We are meant to be together. So, here it is, heart and soul. I want you to be my life partner. I promise I'll never hold back again. I'll let no one, no matter who, come between us. I'll make time to go to the Mojave with you, see the Northern Lights, and do everything you ever wanted to do with me. I'll love you and cherish you. I'll be your best friend. I'll be your lover. And your partner...in everything."

My heart was hammering. I wanted to grab Esme and kiss her and then yell at her for making me wait so fucking long.

"Declan Knight, will you marry me?" Her eyes were full of tears, and I smiled at her. Christ, she was adorable.

I went to my knees in front of her and hugged her.

I barely heard our friends and family clap as I devoured her mouth. It had been four long weeks since I'd touched her, and I'd be lucky not to embarrass the priest by having sex with my wife on the cathedral floor.

When I pulled away, she looked stunned. "I love you, Esme. And I'll love you and cherish you. Be your husband, friend, and lover. I'll be the best person I can be for and with you. Yes, Esme, I'll marry you."

I stood up and took her with me. I looked at the priest and grinned.

The wedding march played from somewhere, and she looked behind me at the door, scared that her father would walk down the aisle with Viv.

"It's for you, Esme," I told her and kissed her again, feather light. "We're getting married today."

"But..." she turned to look at Vega, who was beaming. It had been her idea to make the fake wedding card. Everyone in the room had received a card with my bride's name as Esme Knight, except Esme.

"First things first, we're getting married." I took her hand in mine.

"Where's Viv?" she asked.

"San Francisco, I think."

"What?"

"Where's my father? My mother?"

I sighed. "We need to discuss that later because it's a longer story. Esme, the priest here needs to perform a baptism in forty-five minutes, so let's get married and then do the debrief."

The priest spoke, and Esme's eyes widened. "You were never marrying her. This was all...what? Something to get me here?" She turned and glared at Vega, who gave her a thumbs up sign.

"Focus, sweetheart. The priest has a hard stop."

She looked at the priest, who was smiling, his eyes dancing with laughter.

"Do you, Declan Knight, take Esme Hartley Knight as your..."

"Hartley Knight? Are we even divorced?" she demanded.

"No. We did not file the annulment. I never signed the fucking papers."

The priest continued, "...wedded wife, to love and to—"

"What would you have done if I hadn't shown up?" she asked bewildered.

"Then I'd have to go to the Knight Tech and Hartley Industries board on Monday morning and tell them the merger was going to have to be reversed and that we'd have to take the loss that came with it."

She nodded weakly as if finally understanding what this was. "I'm sorry, Father; please continue."

And he did.

Before he could say you can kiss the bride, I did, and she clung to me.

"I'm so sorry, Declan."

"I know you are, and you'll be punished, don't worry."

She smiled then. "Punished?"

"Hmm..." The few times I had smacked her on the ass while we had sex had ended up with her having an orgasm for the history books.

"I love you, Esme." I picked her up in a hug and gave out a whoop of laughter as I swung her around. She held onto me.

"I love you, Declan."

"I want forever this time."

"Forever," I agreed.

I took her to the penthouse, ignoring the catcalls from my friends and family about making sure we made the reception that was being held at my parent's home later in the evening. We were finally celebrating the marriage that had taken place six months ago with family and friends, as well as key members of the media. It was a good way to put all the rumors about Viv and me to rest.

"I've missed you," I groaned into her mouth as I pulled her on my lap in the car. "You can't do this again, Esme."

She touched my face, her eyes filled with tears.

"Hey, no crying today." I kissed her eyes shut.

"I fucked up, Declan."

"I know, sweetheart."

"What if I fuck up again?"

I brushed my lips against hers. I slid my hand under her white dress to feel, touch, and be inside her.

She was wet and soft; warm and wanting. She moaned when I slid a finger inside her.

"I'll bring you back to me then," I vowed. "And what if I fuck up?"

"Then I'll bring you back...oh god, Declan. *Please.*"

I found her clit; it was swollen, and I couldn't help myself. I pushed her down on the seat and raised her dress. I ripped her panties off her and licked her almost reverently before I devoured her taste, her flesh, and her soul.

"Declan." She had her hands in my hair, gripping as she lifted her thighs to hold my face between her legs.

"This pussy has missed me." I swiped my tongue through her slit and let her flavor burst into me.

"Yes."

"Sweetheart, I can't wait, I need to be inside you." I pulled away and unbuckled my belt. I pulled my erection out and brought her up to straddle me. "This first time will have to be fast, my love. It's been too long."

Chapter 47

ESME

I understood because it was the same for me.

I rode him, and when we came, we came together.

I felt his wetness cream me, flowing down my thighs. I should have gotten up and cleaned myself, but I couldn't. I stayed there, his hands gripping my hips as he continued to pulse inside me, soft jerks as he felt the aftermath. I rested my head against his shoulder.

"Declan, I love you."

He moved his shoulder so I could look into his eyes. "Say it again."

"I love you."

"Good," he muttered, sliding his hand down to smack my bottom hard.

"Ouch, that hurt."

"Good," he said again and kissed me. "You'll let no one take you from me; never separate us. Understood."

He spanked me, and I felt it between my legs. I moaned.

"Say it; I'm sorry, Declan, for signing those fucking papers and breaking your heart."

"I'm so sorry." He smacked me again, and I moved up and then down. His cock was getting hard again like he'd not just come.

"Say, I'll never leave you, Declan." He moved up as I drove down.

"I'll never leave you again."

He pulled the bodice of my dress, taking my bra down with it, and took my nipple in his mouth. "And that you'll have our babies."

My body stilled.

He smacked my ass again, hard this time.

"I'll have our babies."

He looked into my eyes, and I saw his eyes were wet.

"Declan," I whispered.

"You hurt me."

"I know."

"Don't fucking do it again."

"Yes."

"Now, ride me," he ordered.

I rose above him, and as I rode him, I repeatedly promised him I was his and that I'd never leave again.

He carried me home.

And because we'd made such a mess, we took a shower and made a mess again. I went down on my knees in front of Declan like I did at church, but this time, I took him in my mouth.

"Suck deeper, love," he begged because I was sucking only the tip of his erection.

I did as he asked, and he groaned, holding my head. His fingers were tangled in my wet hair.

"Love, I need this." He held my head and fucked my mouth. "Tap my thigh if it's too much," he told me when he saw the tears in my eyes.

He pushed inside my mouth, and I gagged, more tears falling down my cheeks. He didn't let up because I didn't let him, my fingers digging into his tight ass. I knew I was leaving marks, but I needed this as much as he did.

"Esme, make yourself cum," he ordered. "Now."

I held his ass in my left hand and brought my ring hand to my pussy. I didn't think I could come anymore. I was wrong because watching Declan use my mouth led me to find my release. I sat down on the shower floor, too tired to move.

Declan picked me up. "You okay, sweetheart? Did I hurt you?"

I leaned into him. "No. I'm just too...lazy."

"I relaxed you."

"Yes, you did."

We were hungry, this time for food, so Declan made sand-wiches and we ate them with a vintage Veuve Clicquot.

Declan looked at his watch and sighed. "We must get to my parent's place in an hour."

"Why a wedding reception?"

"I want it to be clear that we're married and together. There is a lot of speculation about us because Viv and I used to be engaged—"

"Speaking of Viv, what happened?"

"You know, she's afraid of your father as you are...maybe even more."

I scoffed.

Declan pulled me off my bar stool and lifted me to sit on the kitchen counter in front of his stool. He held me, his hands at my hips, his thighs holding me in place.

"He didn't beat her as he did you, but he controlled her."

"What do you mean?"

"She didn't love me, Esme. She never loved me. He made her be with me. He made her leave Nick. She didn't want to. So, now, she's in San Francisco, begging for his forgiveness and hoping he'll take her back. She loves him."

I felt a pang of compassion. "And what about my father?"

He shrugged.

"Declan?" I warned.

"Yeah, yeah. But it's going to piss you off."

I raised my eyebrows, and he sighed.

"Your father was arrested this morning."

I gasped.

"Let me explain. Do you remember why I had to go to New Orleans?"

"Yeah. Something to do with a customer's system that got compromised."

"Your father hired a hacker to do that."

"He did what?"

Declan tightened his hold on me. "The District Attorney has been investigating, which led to your father. He'll probably do five to eight for cybercrimes and then some for some financial crimes as he used some shady accounts to pay the hacker."

We both were silent for a while.

"He deserves it," I drawled. "And if he's in jail, he can't hurt my mother."

"Your mother has been scrambling to find money for a bond. She's not giving up on him, Esme."

I shrugged. "We can only help those who want help. My mother is, and I have had to realize this in the past weeks, not able to imagine a life without my father. She's made her choice clear again and again. As the cliché goes, she's made her bed, and she has to lie in it."

"Are you sure you're not upset about this?"

"Yes."

He put his head on my lap, and I stroked his hair. "I thought you'd hate me."

"Never."

He raised his head and looked at me. "We're going to make a life together."

I smiled at him. "We already have one. Now, tell me, did you buy me a dress for this wedding reception of yours?"

He grinned. "You can wear the dress you wore to Church..."

"Except it needs to be washed now."

"Multiple orgasms can make a mess."

"And the media will be there, and you don't want them to report that I wasn't dressed appropriately."

"Esme, I love you no matter what you—"

I put a finger to his lips. "Thank you. I want to wear something that makes me feel good."

"In that case, Vera Wang may have made something for you."

"*The* Vera Wang?" I couldn't keep the excitement out of my voice.

He laughed. A rich and deep laugh that came from his soul.

Chapter 48

DECLAN

She looked like a combination of slutty sex goddess and a delicate doll in the white Vera Wang lace dress. It had a tight bodice and a flared skirt, coming slightly above her ankles. Her nude pumps had a small heel, making her tiny feet appear daintier.

"The dress has pockets," she said with delight.

"I made sure." I had because she didn't like to carry a purse.

"Where are your glasses?"

She looked sheepish. She pulled them out of her pocket. "I don't want to wear them because...you know, four eyes and all that."

"You wore them at Church this afternoon."

"No one was taking pictures."

"Sweetheart, wear them, don't wear them. You look beautiful no matter what."

Her glasses were so much a part of her I didn't notice them anymore. But I knew she was conscious about them.

"Am I a fraud if I don't want them on because of the photos?"

"Not at all."

We walked to the elevator, and once the doors closed, she turned to me.

"I know I'm not as good-looking as—"

I stopped the elevator and took her face in my hands. "You're the most beautiful woman I have ever been with."

She rolled her eyes.

"I know no one told you this, but you are. I think you're beautiful and not just because of how you look; but how you are."

"And how am I?"

"Amazing. Do you think I'm good looking?"

She grinned. "Fishing, Declan?"

"Am I?" I persisted.

"You're the most handsome man I know."

I kissed her. "That's exactly how I feel about you. I love you. I want to find good wine with you, go to restaurants with you, help you at Safe Harbor, travel with you, and have babies with you. I want to have you with me, telling me I'll be alright and not fail at managing Knight Tech."

"Thank you, Declan." She kissed me. "Thank you for always knowing what I need."

I restarted the elevator. "Speaking of needs, we have a twenty-minute drive."

"Your Escalade needs to be sanitized, considering what we always seem to do there."

"It's protocol whenever we're in the car," I teased, ridiculously happy.

My mother had gone above and beyond to make the reception a success. My father had talked to her and explained why we were having a church wedding and a proper reception. I needed Esme to come to me on her own. To know that she'd be making several people unhappy. I was scared shitless that she'd not show, and I'd have to start all over again with her because I would not give up no matter what.

As a man who'd spent most of his life fucking everything that moved, I thought I was ready to settle down when I met Viv. But my heart had never been involved. She was successful. We had this merger with Hartley Industries in our plans. My mother approved of her.

Until I met Esme, I didn't even know what it meant to be in love. The violence with which I needed Esme was new—unmatched and coveted by me. And I felt that same need and desire for me in her.

My mother had apologized in her way—but Nina Knight was who she was and wouldn't suddenly become a whole new person. It was galling her that Dad was asking for a divorce when she'd always thought it'd be her who'd demand it first. I wish they'd done this years ago, but better late than never.

Esme was talking to Raya and Mateo when I came to the bar to find Forest nursing a whiskey as he stared at Daisy on the dance floor with her date.

"He's a director. Some big shot. Won an Oscar once for some shit movie." Forest wasn't drunk, but he was working on it. "I asked her to come with me for this shindig. She said no."

"Because you have a girlfriend—"

"Lily is not a girlfriend. She's a fuck buddy. Christ, does no one understand the difference."

"Maybe the big shot director is Daisy's fuck buddy." I knew that would not go down well with Forest, and as proof, he downed his glass of Scotch. He set it on the bar with a loud thud. "If she wants someone to fuck, she fucks me."

He stormed toward Daisy, and I waited for the fireworks. Instead, they surprised me by dancing together, the big shot director finding himself a drink.

Esme came up to me and put her arms around my neck. "Dance with me."

I led her to the dance floor as the band played *At Last* by Etta James. She put her head on my shoulder, and I held her close. We swayed like that for a long while.

She looked up at me, "One question."

"Hmm."

"When do you want to have these babies, you discussed?"

"As soon as you want them."

She smiled at me. "I don't know if I'm ready."

"That's okay, love; we'll practice until you are."

The music changed to something faster, and Esme went on tiptoe and whispered in my ear, "Can we go home now to practice?"

・▼・▼・♥・▼・▼・

Continue the story with the bonus chapter: **Declan & Esme, See the Northern Lights** on my website at www.MayaAlden .com.

Thank you for reading *The Wrong Wife*. If you enjoyed this story, you'll *love* the next book in the **Golden Knights Series**..

Bad Bossis a dark standalone office romance that tells Mateo and Raya's poignant story.

About the Author

MAYA ALDEN HAS A PASSION FOR WEAVING TALES OF LOVE AND DESIRE.

With a background in literature and a heart filled with hope, Maya pours her emotions onto the pages of her novels, capturing the essence of true love and the power it holds to transform lives. Combining unforgettable characters, sizzling chemistry, and heartfelt emotions, Maya's stories will whisk you into a world of passion and enchantment.

Maya invites you to join her on a journey of love, laughter, and happily-ever-afters that will leave you with a sigh and a smile.

Contact Maya

Website/Newsletter: www.MayaAlden.com

Facebook: @authormayaalden

Instagram: @mayaalden_romance

TikTok: @maya.alden

Printed in Great Britain
by Amazon

38726497R00185